BIG ★ TOWN

Doug J. Swanson

 HarperCollins*Publishers*

HarperCollins books may be purchased for educational, business, or sales promotional use. For information, please write: Special Markets Department, HarperCollins Publishers, Inc., 10 East 53rd Street, New York, NY 10022.

FIRST EDITION

Designed by George J. McKeon

Library of Congress Cataloging-in-Publication Data

Swanson, Doug J., 1953–
   Big town / Doug J. Swanson. — 1st ed.
     p.   cm.
   ISBN 0-06-017749-7 (hard)
   1. Private investigators—Texas—Dallas—Fiction. 2. Dallas (Texas)—Fiction. I. Title.
PS3569.W2682B54 1993
813'.54—dc20   93-29503

94 95 96 97 98 ❖/RRD 10 9 8 7 6 5 4 3 2 1

To Susan and Sam

*Special thanks to Tim Jarrell for the encouragement
and to David Swanson for the advice.
Grateful bows also to agent Dona Chernoff
and editor Eamon Dolan.*

Dallas is a rich man with a death wish in his eye.
—JIMMIE DALE GILMORE

V

★

Hal Roper said, "I know just the right guy." He waited for the woman across the desk to ask him who. She didn't, so he said it once more. "Name of Jack Flippo. Just the right guy." The woman scanned the bright red of her nails and then looked at Hal, staring at him until he began to talk again. "He does quality work," Hal said. "Best keyhole man in Dallas, if I might engage in the vernacular, Mrs. George."

This Mrs. George was not bad if you liked them tall, which Hal did not. Right off she had asked him—told him—not to smoke. Her red hair looked to Hal like something out of a flamethrower. And he wasn't wild about the dress—black and plain, but expensive enough. Suitable for a high-end wake. Hal couldn't understand it, she wears a dress like that and puts on four rings.

Now she was gazing at the law books on his shelves, *Texas Revised Civil Statutes* and *South Western Reporters*, which Hal liked to think of as boxes of ammunition. "Is he a lawyer, too?" She asked it as if that were some sort of crime.

Hal sipped from his oversized coffee mug that said SUIT FIRST AND ASK QUESTIONS LATER. "Jack Flippo a lawyer?" He shook his head and thought, lady, if you only knew. "He used to be, but he reformed."

After another sip he sent her a grin, a small gift that she mailed back unopened. Hal broke the silence with a couple of rattling coughs. "Seriously, Jack's been doing investigations for me for some time. We need something knockdown solid"—he rapped the desktop twice with two knuckles—"we call Jack Flippo."

The woman beamed in on her nails again. All right, Hal thought, she just wants to sit there, the meter's running. You practice law for thirty-three years, you see a little bit of everything. Hal once had a client who walked around with a pet mouse in his shorts. The client wanted to sue the restaurant that fired him. Hal got him four weeks' severance after a threat to take the case to the papers. Who eats in a place, he asked the management, where the help's got rats in their pants?

"Then you will call this person?" the woman finally said, lifting her stare to him.

"Absolutely." Hal moved his yellow legal pad into a small circle of light under his desk lamp and pretended to study it. He had written *Marilyn George 2840 Terrace Green wife of Buddy George Jr!! no kids married 10 yr Thinks husb at play we watch.*

"What I should do," he said, "I should put you and Mr. Flippo together very shortly. I'll have him contact you. Did you give me the number? He'll call and collect the information he needs to effect the surveillance of your husband."

"When?"

"Very shortly. Certainly within the next two days or so. That will be satisfactory, I trust?"

"Evidently you weren't listening to me."

Here it comes, Hal thought, every time the curve-balls. He saw dollars down the drain.

"So I'll repeat myself," she said. "Tonight is when my husband will conduct his weekly piece of business. I told you that. Every Friday night."

"Yes, you did. And what I would suggest—"

"Tonight," she said, leaning forward and raising her chin, "he will spend another night with someone other than his wife, and you want to go about this at your leisure."

"Now I didn't say that. With all due respect, what I said—"

"And this crap about collecting information from me. I gave you the information. I told you who, when, and where. What else, exactly, do you need?"

Hal could feel a glaze of sweat forming on his scalp, beneath his hairpiece. Thinking, Give me the old days when the women didn't come on like pro wrestlers. "You're absolutely right," he told her. "Absolutely."

"If you can't help me now, Mr. Roper, I'll find a firm that moves a little faster." Hal felt pinned to the chair by her eyes.

"Please." Hal raised a hand. "No need to do that, Mrs. George. Let's handle this today." He opened his lap drawer, rooted through some papers, and withdrew a calendar book. "No time like the present." Hal let her see the cover only. He studied the space for the day's date, August 19, where he had written *Dentist 3:45.*

Hal made a clucking sound with his tongue. "Well, I have Mr. Flippo stacked very deep here, very deep. But I'll be frank with you, Mrs. George. None of it is of the magnitude of your case."

He snapped the book shut and checked his watch. "It's nine-thirty now. I'll call you around two, how's that, two o'clock, and let you know everything's in place. Give you a ring."

"I'll call you."

"Certainly. Fine. You call me. Whatever's best."

"This is very important for me." She uncoiled slightly. "I can't stress that enough."

"Absolutely," Hal said. "I hear you one hundred percent. I mean, when someone violates the sacred vows . . . "

"You have what you need, then."

Hal rocked back in his padded big shot's chair, checking the legal tablet now in his lap, reading the rest of what he had written. "Don't worry about a thing. Not a thing. Like I said, Jack Flippo's a pro." Two knuckles hit the armrest twice. "Best in the business for my money."

"Good." She clutched the black purse in her lap and uncrossed her legs, ready to stand.

"Ah, speaking of money." Hal straightened and cleared his throat. "I would ask for an initial payment of five hundred dollars today, with a balance of five hundred due at the conclusion of this matter." He folded his hands in front of him. "Of course, should this ultimately become a divorce filing—and let me say, I truly hope you and your husband can work things out, truly. But should it become necessary, we stand ready to assist you."

Her face showed him nothing.

"And in case of that," Hal said, "if it comes to a divorce action, you need not worry about full payment right away. Because a lot of women, and I'm talking about very intelligent women like yourself, a lot of them come in here without ready access to cash. Because the mate controls it, you see."

He paused to let her get a word in if she wanted, but she didn't. "What I've seen, Mrs. George, it breaks your heart. Ladies with fine homes and big cars but—here's the catch—they can't put their hands on their money. Not a dollar, not a dime. These guys, their husbands, they hide it like squirrels with nuts."

Another swallow of coffee and he went on. "Now, I'm not saying it's that way with you, Mrs. George." She didn't move. "But if it is, I'll tell you what I tell everyone else. I tell them, allow Hal Roper to shake the tree. I'll say it again. Allow Hal Roper to shake the tree."

When he finished she opened her purse, picked five hundred-dollar bills from it, and placed them on his desk in a neat stack. "I'll call you at two o'clock," she said. She stood and was out the door by the time Hal had hauled himself from his chair.

The first thing Hal did was pick up the money, count it, fold it once, and slip it into his pocket. The second thing, he fired up a smoke. A couple of deep drags and he had the strength to bellow, "Rose, wake up Jack Flippo." No answer from the outer office, but Hal saw the phone light blink on. He sat for a moment and watched the smoke curl toward the ceiling. Thinking, Nothing like large cash in your pocket to start the day off right.

Rose came in within a minute or two, carrying a waxed-paper bag full of doughnuts, which she added to the clutter in front of Hal. "All I get is an answering machine," she said. "I left a message."

"What answering machine?"

"You asked me to call Jack Flippo," she said.

"Jack's not answering. Beautiful, terrific. These assholes, I swear." He pitched forward in the big chair and punched three digits on the phone. He could hear the muffled rings in the next office. After nine there was an answer.

"About time, Teddy," Hal said. "Glad you could—don't start. Don't start with me this morning. Now listen. I want you to go dig up Jack Flippo, get him back here in an hour." To Rose Hal said, "Reschedule my two o'clock." Then to the phone, "I know. I know and don't care, Teddy. In an hour. And don't let him look like he spent the night in a urinal."

Hal put the phone down and rubbed his temples, two fingers on each. "Teddy says it's too hot to go out, he might get sweaty. Says he hates to go to Jack's apartment because it doesn't smell fresh."

"Reschedule Mr. Schwille?" Rose said. "That's your two o'clock."

"He the guy got hit by the beer truck? See if he can come in later. I got bigger fish to fry."

"At three?"

"Whatever, Rose, work it out. And cancel my dentist. I don't feel like needles in my mouth today."

"You're scheduling Mrs. George at two?"

"That is correct. Mrs. George at two. For a phone call, not an office visit. Are we straight now?" Hal poked through the bag on his desk. "Mrs. George, who is too insistent for my taste, I have to tell you. I will say this, the lady knows what she's after, she's got that look in her eyes. Reminds me of—you get any glazed? I don't see any glazed here. Reminds me of that client we had last year. Remember her? What was her name, Mrs. Wally or something?"

Hal found what he wanted from the bag. "Remember her? Mrs. Wally. Hey, who could forget a woman tries to cut off her husband's private member?"

He took a big bite of glazed doughnut. "Christ, Mrs. Wally hated Mr. Wally, didn't she? Huh? Not that he didn't deserve it."

2

★

The things I do, Jack Flippo was thinking, to pay the rent. Like being a part-time wedding photographer, emphasis on part-time. Or like this, taking a ride downtown with a man who wears two gold neck chains.

Teddy Deuce, as he liked to call himself, slashed through traffic on Gaston Avenue in his leased Mark VII, doing fifty-five in a thirty zone and busting red lights. He used his left fist to pound the horn. The fingers of his right hand he wrapped around the steering wheel like thick worms.

"Is Hal onna rag today," Teddy said. "The phone, I'm not sittinere widdit to my ear like some tumor, waiting for him to call, he goes nuts. He's screaming, 'I need Jack, get me Jack.' I'm like, 'Hal, chill, don't have a stroke.' But I got to tell you, Jackie, your place is not my favorite location inna world to visit."

If you were not up on Teddy's history, it occurred to Jack, you might think Hal Roper had dialed the warehouse one day and said, Send me an overgrown tough but not one of the smart ones. Teddy was twenty or twenty-one, from New York, the unemployable son of a dentist. His real name was Theodore N. Tunstra II, and he would still be living with his parents in Queens, watching cable TV all day, but for the night he punched his girlfriend so hard he ruptured her spleen.

There had been talk of filing charges, so strings were pulled and markers collected. A friend of a friend of the family made some calls, and Teddy caught a flight to Dallas, destined for Hal's payroll. Hal in return got a nice monthly check from New York.

"I told them I'd keep him for a year, or until he did something really stupid. Whichever comes first," Hal said to Jack once. "My money's on stupid."

Jack did not know much more about Teddy and doubted there was much more worth knowing. Teddy stood a few inches over six feet, with the build of someone who had plenty of spare time for dumbbells. He liked imported shoes and silk blazers, and smelled of musk cologne and breath mints. The sight of himself in a mirror stopped him cold.

His ambition was to have his own television talk show. As far as Jack could tell, Teddy was afraid of nothing but work and germs.

"I mean everytime I go to your place, Jack, I'm going, holy shit, what's living inna carpet? You know?" Teddy dropped to forty-five as a police car passed in the other direction. "Hal tells me to go get Jack and I'm like, whoa, how about I send a telegram instead, I ain't had my shots this month. Hey, man, when you plan to get your Chevy fixed? I'm sick of this car service gig."

"When I get the money," Jack answered, slumping in his seat and putting on sunglasses. Even through the tinted windows the glare was like knives. The radio said it was not yet noon and already 99 degrees, headed for a high of 110. "Three-thirty in the morning and my air conditioner dies," Jack said, talking mostly to himself.

"And, hey, your front door looks primo," Teddy said. "The rusty sheet metal nailed to it, that's a touch a class. You do that yourself or hire a decorator?" Teddy acted as if this were the funniest joke he had heard today.

"Someone kicked in the low panel and broke in."

"No shit. When?"

"Last week."

"Just whammed the door in? These punks today, they'll do anything." Teddy braked hard, whipped around the right side of a laundry truck, and powered open the moonroof just enough to stick out his middle finger. "What they get? They take much? I mean, what's to take, right?"

Jack's eyes felt loaded with sand. "I think it was some kids. I was riding my bike at the time, so they didn't get that. I guess they didn't want the answering machine, and my old black-and-white TV wasn't even worth the trouble."

"You see Arsenio last night? Guy's wearing some kinda green jumpsuit wit purple stripes. Purple stripes, man."

"And my cameras weren't there," Jack said. "So they just messed things up and took some change from the dresser. That and a stuffed fish I had on the wall."

"They took a fish? Get outta here."

It's true, Jack thought, I'm thirty-three years old and all I have worth stealing is a varnished bass. "That was it."

"You believe that, man? You go to the trouble to bust into a place, and the only thing you can find to boost is a fish. It was me, I'd be one pissed-off hombre, man. I'd burna place down, get even."

"Life has its disappointments," Jack said.

"Hey, tell me about it. Last week I pick up this bitch, you know? We do a little dancing, then she comes to my apartment. Blonde, big tits, hands all over me, man, like she can't wait to take a bite a Teddy Deuce. I get her clothes off and I'm thinking what a piece of snatch. I'm just about to slip on my Trojan when I see she hant shaved under her arms lately. I was completely turned off."

"Take a right here," Jack said.

"It was so disgusting."

"Right here. This diner."

"This place? For what?" Teddy swerved into the parking lot of the Egg 'N' Waffle Hut. The sign in the plate-glass window said "GOOD" EATING. Jack got out of the car and stepped into the sunblast of the day. He walked across the hot soft asphalt, digging in his pocket for a quarter, and bought a *Morning News*. There was a front-page story about the heat wave for people who needed a newspaper to tell them it was hot.

The inside of the diner was like a salve, though, cold enough to make the flies sluggish. Teddy leaned over the jukebox, dropping in coins and punching buttons. Jack settled into a red booth at a Formica table that needed a wipedown. "Coffee," he told the waitress, and she brought it before he could finish pulling out the sports section. Teddy slammed both hands onto the table as he sat down, and the saucer under Jack's cup filled. "Madonna, man," Teddy said. "The bitch can sing, you know it?"

"Aretha Franklin, that's singing," Jack said.

The waitress took Jack's order, two eggs over easy with hash browns. "What about you, hon?" she asked Teddy. He answered, "What are you, nuts?"

Jack turned to the baseball standings. The Texas Rangers were in their usual August slump, preparing for their usual September collapse. Teddy studied the celebrity news. "Hey, man," he said. "Say somebody like *Hustler* gives you a million dollars to screw Roseanne while they take pictures. You do it?" It was a rhetorical question, Jack figured.

Another record played. It sounded like the same woman to Jack. Teddy sang along and drummed hard on the table, spilling Jack's coffee again. Jack said, "Teddy, give me a break."

Teddy banged on the red upholstery of the booth back instead. That drew an annoyed half-turn of the head from the man behind him. Jack caught a glance: Deep lines around bloodshot eyes. A khaki work shirt. Wavy hair going gray, carefully lubed and combed, and long sideburns trimmed with precision. You had to guess, you'd say a plumber who liked to hit on housewives. The man turned back to his table and Jack went back to his scores.

The waitress brought Jack's order on a battered white platter. "Holy God," Teddy said. "You call that food?"

Jack salted his eggs and shook a bottle of ketchup over his glistening hash browns. Nothing came out, so he slapped the bottom of the bottle with his palm.

"You'd think they'd make these things with a wider mouth," he said.

"Check this shit out," Teddy said. He had discovered something smeared on the inside of the plate-glass window next to him. "Unbelievable, the filt innis place."

Jack said, "So?" and kept slapping at the bottle.

Teddy rolled up a section of the newspaper and reached to wipe the window. As he did, his elbow hit the back of the head of the man behind him. Here we go, Jack thought.

The man brought his cup down on his table hard enough to make some noise. When the man stood Jack could see he was bowlegged, not short or tall, on the skinny side but with arms that could do a day's work. A name, Roy, was embroidered in red over one shirt pocket. Roy stared at Teddy's back.

Jack checked the room to see if Roy had friends. Besides the waitress there was a sad-looking frycook and one other customer, an old man in a greasy jumpsuit. He was hunched on a stool at the counter, blowing on his soup.

Teddy dropped the paper he had used on the smear under the table. He was singing with the juke-box again as he picked up another section and turned to the comics. Roy shook his head in disgust. He said, "You're excused, boy."

Teddy kept singing and looking at the comics. After about fifteen seconds Roy finally took his eyes off Teddy, found his check, and turned to the cash register. Jack went back to his breakfast with relief.

Then Teddy said, "Fuck you, Gomer."

Jack groaned. "Teddy, it's too early for bleeding."

Teddy rose slowly, took off his jacket, folded it,

and put it where he had been sitting. "Guy's being an asshole, Jack."

"That makes you twins, Teddy. Sit down and shut up."

"Too late for that," Teddy said. He reached into a side pocket of his folded jacket, got two clear thin latex gloves, and began carefully pulling them on.

Jack said, "What are you doing, Teddy, surgery?"

Roy held his hands low and made little hooking motions with his fingers. He said, "Come on, faggot."

Teddy said, "I'm gonna have to kill you for that. Hey, Jack. I'm gonna have to kill this fuck."

Jack made one last try. "You two masters of wit have a fight, you'll both go to jail. Jails aren't clean, Teddy."

"Screw it," Roy said. Jack was not sure if that meant Roy was fighting or quitting. Teddy turned up his sleeves three times each.

Jack watched Roy move his hand across the counter and clutch a salt shaker. He picked it up and threw it at Teddy's head. Roy was a lefthander. The salt sailed high and outside, past Teddy, and clattered on the floor back by the men's room. Reminded Jack of Mitch Williams, used to pitch relief for the Rangers.

Teddy charged and Roy swung, missing again. Teddy spun him halfway around and wrapped his left arm around Roy's neck, with his elbow under Roy's jaw. If Teddy did it right, Jack figured, Roy would pass out in about ten seconds. Keep the choke hold much longer and he could be dead.

Jack stood. "You win," he told Teddy. "Let's go."

"When I'm finished," Teddy said. Roy's face went from red to purple as he tried to pry Teddy's arm away. Teddy dragged him behind the counter, grabbed a fistful of the man's hair, and plunged his face into a sink full of dishwater. "Nyuk, nyuk," Teddy said, doing Curly in *The Stooges Commit Manslaughter.*

"You're going to kill him," Jack said.

"Good idea." Teddy smiled.

Jack could hear Roy's bubbles and could see his arms flailing as he tried to reach Teddy. If Roy had any sense, Jack thought, he would reach down and pull out the stopper.

The waitress screamed, "Stop it! Stop it!" and then stood there with her hands over her mouth. The cook had gone, leaving an open back door. The old man at the counter sipped his coffee and watched, just another day at the hash house.

Jack still held the bottle of ketchup. He took Teddy's jacket from its place on the booth, laid it over his forearm, and positioned the bottle above it, mouth down. "Let him go," Jack told Teddy, "or your coat dies."

Teddy's smile vanished. "That ain't funny."

Jack shook the bottle but nothing came out. He couldn't hear any more bubbles from Roy and the flailing had stopped. He shook the bottle again.

"That ain't funny at all, Jack." Worry was building in Teddy's eyes, but he kept both hands on the back of Roy's head. "That's a four-hundred-dollar jacket. That's what you owe me, man, you mess it up. Pure fucking silk, man."

Jack gave the bottle three hard shakes. Nothing. The old man at the counter laughed out loud, with a wide-open mouth and no teeth. "That damn Heinz'll take ten minutes," he said.

But as he spoke a long tongue of ketchup oozed from the bottle, falling thickly toward Teddy's coat.

Teddy yelled, "Shit!" and jerked Roy's head up and out of the sink. Jack pulled the jacket aside like a matador. The ketchup hit the floor and splattered on one of his tennis shoes. "Great," he said.

Teddy dropped Roy, bulled from behind the counter, and snatched his coat from Jack's arm. "You're crazy, man. Four hundred bucks you woulda been out," Teddy said. "Think about that."

Roy lay on the floor, heaving and blowing dishwater. "Let's go," Jack said as he pushed Teddy toward the door.

In the car Jack said, "I have no time for assholes like you, you hear me?" He was surprised to find himself shouting.

Teddy fishtailed out of the parking lot and turned up the radio. It was one of those songs that sounded like someone shouting while slamming a drawer full of silverware over and over. Nobody played Wilson Pickett anymore. Jack reached down and turned it off. "Let me tell you something, Teddy. You want to go psycho like that, do it when I'm not around. You understand? You have to be a lunatic, do it alone."

"Jackie, what do you think, I was gonna kill that guy? No way, man. Not a chance. I was just showing a few moves. Dancing the Teddy Deuce."

"I mean it, Teddy. The only reason I cut in back there is so I wouldn't have to talk to cops. That's all. I don't like talking to cops."

"Like I could give a shit, Jack."

"You think I stepped in just to help you out? I don't do that."

Teddy peeled off the gloves, lowered his window, and threw them into the street. Then he took a small rectangular foil packet from his shirt pocket. With his

elbows on the steering wheel he tore open the envelope, withdrew a folded, wet paper towel, and wiped
his hands and face. The smell of rubbing alcohol and
peppermint filled the car.

"Jack, you really think I was gonna do that guy?
For what? Huh? I was just playing wittim, just having
fun."

Teddy winked and turned the radio back on. Jack
had seen better mornings.

Buddy George, Jr. telephoned his office from the front passenger seat of his three-year-old Sedan De Ville with the license plates that said WAYUP. He had just finished counting the cash and checks from a canvas bag—$3,930 and change, a decent take for two hours' work.

He cradled the car phone on his left shoulder, zipped the bag of money shut, and nestled it between his thighs. After three rings a young man's voice came on the phone and chirped, "It's a great morning at Motivational Enterprises. How may I help you?"

Buddy said only, "She there yet?" Thinking, she had better be, the money he paid her. When she picked up her extension Buddy said, "I been calling all morning, Paula. Where the hell you been?"

The Cadillac, driven by a pimply part-time Pentecostal seminarian named DeWayne, blew past the shopping strips and car lots on Airport Freeway. A few more minutes and they would be in Dallas. "Well, all right, I called you once," Buddy said. "You weren't there. Were you. That's what I thought."

He let her talk for a while. Something about she had time off coming, the hours she put in, and what right did he have to question it. Buddy noticed he would have to tell DeWayne his shoes needed polishing. Better yet, show it to him in the book, *Selling Anything and Everything, Anytime and Everytime* by Buddy George, Jr. From Chapter Three, he could quote it by memory: "A good shoeshine is like a smile for your feet."

Buddy checked his own footwear, baby-blue hand-tooled cowboy boots. Shining, it seemed to Buddy, like a picture of the Western sky in a laminated place mat.

She was asking questions on the phone. "Look, I don't know how many people we had," Buddy said. "I was too busy to count. A couple hundred, I'd guess."

"One hundred seventy-nine," DeWayne said.

Buddy ignored him and took a pair of half-moon reading glasses from the breast pocket of his baby-blue blazer. He studied a program with his picture on the front. "It was," he said to the phone, "the semi-monthly luncheon of the Greater Dallas–Fort Worth Airport Area Chamber of Commerce. At that Holiday Inn by the Esters Road exit. I gave them Lesson Six, 'Yes You Can,' but Part One only."

Now she was talking about money. "Hold on, Paula, listen to this," Buddy said, still checking the program, wondering if he should have his publicity photograph reshot. "I flat put it on the people. I said, 'Friends, you've filled your bellies with this fine food. Now let me fill your heads with big plans.' Hey, the stars come out to hear old Buddy talk. We had the mayor of Euless. We had the manager of the dress shop for large ladies at Irving Mall. We had a boy owns six Denny's."

Buddy took off his glasses and flipped down the sun visor to check his hair in the mirror. Forty-five years old and hardly any gray.

The questions she kept asking began to ruin his mood. "Hey, Paula, stop yapping for a minute and I'll tell you: I don't know what the gross was, okay? Are you my banker? I thought you were my executive assistant. Did old Buddy miss something? Somebody make you my accountant while I wasn't looking?"

He listened for a few seconds and sighed. "It takes time to put these numbers together, okay? That's the trouble today, everybody's in a hurry. They got their instant coffee, they got their microwave ovens. Some things just take—hang on a second."

Buddy stuffed the phone under the bag between his legs. "DeWayne, how many of those new videos we sell this morning?"

DeWayne cleared his throat and swallowed. "Eleven."

"Eleven." Buddy watched the scenery pass. Muffler King. David McDavid Pontiac. The Kroger warehouse. Texas Stadium, which reminded him how much he hated the Dallas Cowboys. His video, *How to Win Like the Cowboys,* had been one of his biggest sellers. Then in 1986 the team turned to crap, costing him $10,000 a year. So Buddy takes the video out of production, drops it from the catalog. Then the SOBs all of a sudden start winning again, and Buddy's got nothing to show for it. That was the problem with the world today. Nobody ever did a damn thing to help the businessman along.

"DeWayne," Buddy said, "I'm up there telling the good people what they need to know. You're supposed to be at the display table selling books and tapes."

"Yessir."

"You display them like I told you?"

"Just like you—"

"I don't think you did." Buddy turned from the window to face him. The boy needed a haircut, too. "Son, we discussed this. The people want to buy these products, they just don't know it yet. Your job is to let them know. You do it right, they'll be giving you money like it hurts their hands to hold it."

The car passed over a narrow, almost dry fork of the Trinity River. The skyline of Dallas heat-shimmered in the hazy distance. To Buddy the big mirrored buildings looked like cathedrals.

"Gaze on that, my friend, that's a beautiful sight. Greatest city in the world, Big D. Think about that. *Big* D. You think anybody'd move to a city called Little D?"

"No, sir."

"Well, they wouldn't. They'd pass right through."

Buddy pulled a hair off his tongue and dropped it in the ashtray. "Let me ask you something, DeWayne. You ever sell cookware door to door? 'Course you haven't. The children of today, they don't want to work. They want it all handed to them while they watch television. I was sixteen years old, still in high school, I sold Kingcooker cookware. I sold it in every town within smelling distance of Odessa."

He smiled at the memory. "Let me tell you what. Great men have written volumes on closing the sale. Let's just say that when Buddy George Junior was selling Kingcooker cookware he *always* got the cash down payment of twenty-five dollars. You think that's easy?"

"No, sir."

"Well, it's not. Not unless you know how." Buddy laughed a little and wagged his head. "My friend, I've seen men dig it up in jars from the backyard. I've seen 'em pull it out of the family Bible. Ladies'd pluck bills from their bras to buy my cookware. You ask, How can that be? Well, you make 'em want what you have more than they want their money, and this"—he held up the bag of cash and checks—"*this* is what you get."

Buddy set the bag on the floor and took the telephone from between his legs. "Got so wrapped up in my story I forgot about the phone." He put it to his ear and said, "Listen, I got about two dozen things I need before the show tonight . . . Hello? Paula? You there? . . . Well, I'll be goddamned."

4

★

Hal Roper was the only man Jack knew who still called women broads. It fit him, an accessory to the shiny suits and cheap toupee. Hal talked too fast and sweated year-round. He ate and smoked like someone begging for a coronary. When he wore shoes with thick heels, he probably cleared five-three.

He still did criminal trial work now and then, but Hal's specialty was divorce, blue-collar division, with some small-time torts and debt collection thrown in. It was a living.

"Plus," Hal told Jack once, "it's a good way to meet broads. They're in here crying, all broken up because their old man's run off, I might take them for a ride on the couch. It's therapy, really, making them feel wanted again."

Hal had come to Dallas when it was still a burg, in 1957, down from Chicago. He had rented an office downtown, where he had been ever since. It was in a building on Main Street, flanked by vacant storefronts, that no one noticed anymore. Now here was

Jack, going to the eighth floor in an elevator that rose slower than a diving bell. Teddy, fresh from his wipedown with his moist towelette, was parking his car.

When the elevator finally lurched to a stop and the doors scraped open, Jack walked past Dalworth Vending Sales & Service and an empty chiropodist's office to get to Hal's suite, 803. The waiting room had three chairs and some old copies of *Reader's Digest*. Rose was typing at her desk. "Go on in," she said without looking up, moving her head toward Hal's office.

Hal, behind his desk and on the phone, motioned for Jack to sit on the couch. He took a chair instead.

"Who cares if she don't like to fish?" Hal said to the phone. He had a voice like a dull hacksaw through a rusty tin can. "She wants half the boat. Half." He lit a Camel and rocked back in his chair. "Hey, listen. I say we cut the boat shortways across the middle. You think I'm bluffing? Watch me. I'll have that boat in two pieces."

The desk was buried under stacks of files and a scattering of paper scraps and pink phone messages that looked to have snowed from the ceiling. In one corner of the room a potted palm was dying on top of a brown stain in the carpet. "I'm thinking your man keeps the boat," Hal said, "and my lady takes the car. That's what I'm thinking."

Jack put his head back and closed his eyes. Hal cranked up the sound. "Don't give me the sad routine! Spare me! Hey, he should of thought about that before he followed his dick around."

It went on for a few more minutes with Hal slowly winding down. Finally he said, "Yeah, okay, send the papers over and I'll take a look."

Hal hung up and shook his head like a man who had seen it all. " 'Ciao,' the guy says. You believe that? 'Ciao.' Attorney calls me, crying about his client will lose everything. Six weeks he's been doing this dance. I told him, hey, your man follows his dick around, he's got to pay. You hear me tell him that?"

Jack nodded. "That's what I told him," Hal said.

"I heard you."

"Of course, who would know that particular lesson better than you?"

"Thank you, Hal."

"It's a good case and I'll make a couple of bills off it. But it's nothing like the one I got for you, Jackie. This one I got for you"—Hal clapped his hands once and rubbed his palms together—"this one's got my juices flowing. You know this guy Buddy George Junior?"

Jack didn't know him.

"Sure you do," Hal said. "He has those commercials late at night when they're showing reruns of *The Rifleman*."

"So you can't sleep either."

"See, you know him. Big bucktoothed joker. Looks like he should be selling Buicks in Wichita Falls."

Jack rubbed his forehead. "Never heard of him."

"This guy's a jewel. You buy his videotape, you can be the greatest salesman ever lived, only twenty-nine-ninety-five plus shipping and handling. I know you've seen this clown, Jack. Talks like L'il Abner."

"You ever have one of those headaches, Hal, that feels like you've been hit with an ax?"

"Like a drill, you mean. Right between the eyes. All morning I had one. Murder."

"I think it's the heat. Last night at three-thirty, I'm just getting to sleep and my AC dies. I have to pull all the Reynolds Wrap off the windows so I can open them up. When the sun comes up I find out it's nothing but a fuse."

Hal picked up the phone and punched three numbers. "Rose, bring Mr. Flippo an aspirin. She'll bring you an aspirin, Jackie. I'm feeling so good about this case, I won't even deduct it from your fee, I'm feeling that good."

Jack said, "Yeah?"

"'Cause this guy Buddy George Junior has a problem with his pants." Hal leaned forward. "Yeah, he's got a problem with his pants. They keep coming off in motel rooms!" Hal shot off a couple of rockets of laughter and showed Jack all his bridgework.

Rose came in without knocking, gave Jack two pills, and gently guided a paper cup of water toward his shaky hand as if he were some old man with Parkinson's.

Hal lit another cigarette and began to search through the files on his desk. "His wife was in here this morning with the whole tragic tale. Jackie, the broad wants this guy's stones medium-well over a slow flame. I told her, hey, roasting husbands is my specialty. You hear me tell her that, Rose?"

Rose had already left the room. Jack washed down the aspirin. The water was warm. "You know this Mrs. George?" he asked.

Hal kept looking through the stacks of files. "Never saw her before in my life. She called yesterday afternoon, said she'd been referred. Said she needed an appointment in a hurry."

"Yeah?"

"Yeah. So after she leaves this morning I get on the phone and run a few traps. Deed records, tax records, plus I do a TRW. We're not talking tar-paper shack here."

"Yeah?"

"What did I just say? Yeah. And how come you keep saying 'yeah' with this look on your face like you got piles?"

Jack said, "What do you need from me?"

"What do you think, Jack? I need a peep. I need you to nail the husband. Where's my notes?" He ransacked the paper on his desk. "I got the skinny right here. Keep your shirt on, it's all right here."

Hal moved a file labeled Wilk v. Brandi's House of Hair Weave and found a legal pad beneath it. "Right here, all the facts. You got a pencil?" Jack shook his head.

"Jesus, Jack." Hal rolled his milky eyes. "You come in here wearing a shirt with flowers on it and some pants I wouldn't go bowling in, and you don't even have a pencil."

Jack could hear Teddy laughing in the next office. The ketchup stain on his shoe had picked up some dirt and turned brown. Hal tossed a pen at him and shoved a piece of paper in his direction. "Write this down. Nine o'clock tonight, give or take, Buddy George Junior and his girlie meet at the American Executive Inn. It's on Stemmons near Parkland. You know the place?"

Jack didn't know it.

"Were you listening? I said it's near Parkland. That's a big hospital, maybe you heard. Every Friday night our man does a show, a speech, whatever, at this motel. After which he meets his friend in the bar. Then it's off to his room."

Jack stopped writing. "How do we know all this?"

"Does it make a difference, Jack? His wife told me, all right? All I want from you is some shots of them together at the bar, let's hope they're grabbing ass, and a tap on the room."

"You want a tap on the room, just like that."

"Let me finish, Jack. Then we'll set aside a special time just for you to complain."

"Fine," Jack said.

"He has room three-thirty-three, okay? Three, three, three—write it down. Now, I've made a reservation for you in the room next door. Get this, I call the motel, I tell them I need room three-thirty-four for a second honeymoon, it's a sentimental attachment, so I have to have that room exactly. The girl says, 'Oh, that's sweet.' You believe that? 'Oh, that's sweet.' "

"You sure three-thirty-four is next door? It could be across the hall."

"It's next door, Jack. Right next door. So all you have to do is cone the wall and you got your tape. Okay? All right? Any more questions?"

"How much?"

"I'll pay you three and a half, plus the room."

Jack capped the ballpoint and started to put it in his pocket, not thinking about it until Hal snapped his fingers and held out a palm. "You're offering three-fifty," Jack said, giving him the pen. "That means you're charging the client at least seven hundred. At least. I'll take five-fifty."

"Then you won't get the job." Hal dragged on his cigarette and blew out the smoke as if he were trying to reach the far wall behind Jack. "End of discussion."

"And I'll need to rent a car. Mine's in the shop."

"I'll pay you four-twenty-five. That's it, no more. Four-hundred, twenty-five dollars. You're busting my balls."

Jack worked some kinks out of his neck. He said, "This woman, the client, she just walks in here this morning? Does that strike you as strange?"

"I told you, I checked the broad out. You didn't hear me, I'll say it again. I. Checked. Her. Out."

"Yeah?"

"Look, the job pays four-fifty. You want it or not? I know plenty others'll take it, you don't want it."

Jack stood and stretched. "I'll think about it at breakfast. Want to come?"

"Sure, Jack. It's only one-fifteen. Top of the goddamn morning. Why not breakfast? Some coffee, some OJ, get a fresh start on the day. Jesus Christ."

Jack folded his notes and put the paper in his shirt pocket. Hal said, "You kill me, Jack, you really do."

This was Hal's standard introduction to his lecture on the failings of Jack Flippo. Jack would have left the room right then but he had a problem. His landlord wanted $300. The mechanic was holding his car for $145. He had about $50 in his pocket and not much more in the bank, and he had shot only two weddings in three weeks. Hal might as well have had him chained to the chair. He sat down.

"How long we known each other, Jackie?"

"Too long."

"Very funny. Hilarious. You should be a comedian, except you'd probably screw that up, too." Another Camel butt went to the overflowing ashtray. Hal leaned back, put his hands behind his head, and looked toward the ceiling. "First time I saw you, Jack, you remember? First time, we're in the courtroom. What was it, four or five years ago? All my life I've been see-ing assistant DAs across the courtroom and damn few of them are worth a second look. But I noticed you. Tell me why."

Jack said nothing. To answer would only prolong it.

"I mean, you looked like all the rest of them with your wing tips and your pinstripes. But I'm watching you—sort of tall, a little too skinny, with that big schnozz of yours and blond hair sticking every which way—and I'm thinking, here's a kid with a little extra to show. Someone maybe to watch, that's what I thought. Someone with a future. And for a while I was right, wasn't I? Huh?"

Jack rested his head on his hand and waited for Hal to recite the rest. Kicked out of the district attor-ney's office. Promising career down the dumper. Practically disbarred. "Wait a minute," Jack said. "It never went to the state bar. It never left the DA's office."

Hal did not even slow down. The aimlessness, Hal said, the self-imposed limitations. Thirty-what years old and nothing but wasted talent. Could have been a star and now he was taking pictures of wed-dings, for God's sake. Pictures of people getting married and people training for a divorce, Hal said, what a combination. Jack listened to the words rolling by like landmarks on a bad road you drive every day.

Finally Hal wound it up. "You know, Jackie, you'll be an old man someday. An old broke geezer with hair growing out of your ears. I see you living in a rented room somewhere, all alone, just a beaten-down old man in baggy pants. Making macaroni and cheese from a box, cooking it on your hot plate."

When Hal was through, Jack looked up. "Make it five hundred dollars and a rental car," Jack said. "Five and a car, you've got yourself a deal."

5

★

Fridays at the Salon d'Elaine were always busy. It was worse today because the regular nail girl was out sick again. So Sharronda Simms got to take a break from shampoos and fill in.

By lunchtime she had done four manicures and two pedicures, collecting nearly $50 in tips. Before she went home she would hide the money under the front seat of her car, slipping the bills into a folded newspaper and stuffing the package between the springs. If her boyfriend, Delbert, couldn't find it, he couldn't steal it.

Sharronda had a few minutes before the next appointment and was about to go to the bathroom when she heard her name from the front of the shop. The cashier was looking at her and wagging the phone.

She picked up an extension. Thinking, Delbert again. He would be calling for the fourth time today to tell her how bad he was hurting.

Three nights before Delbert had been drinking

with his friend Royse, who lived in a trailer park in East Dallas, down against the train tracks. Delbert passed out there a lot.

"I crashed," Delbert told Sharronda later, "and when I wake up I hear voices and some noises outside like somebody using tools. I'm like, shit, they're stealing Royse's pickup. So I go charging out the front door, I'm gonna catch the mothers."

Delbert had been right about thieves. But they had not taken the truck. They had stolen the stairs to the trailer. He was supposed to wear the cast on his right wrist for a month.

The doctor had prescribed a week's worth of Percodan, but Delbert took them all in a day and a half. He had been calling Sharronda all morning, demanding more pills. "What I'm supposed to be," she told him the last time. "Sharronda's drugstore?"

Now she held the pink phone to her left ear, with a finger over the other ear to block the hair dryer noise. If she had Delbert on the other end, calling from home, there would be something like Anthrax or Twisted Sister in the background. She couldn't hear music.

"Hello?" Sharronda said.

"How do you look right now?"

It was a woman's voice. Sharronda said, "How do I *what*?"

"You have to look gorgeous."

Sharronda turned toward a mirror. She had her father's thin nose and her mother's full lips. She was eighteen but her makeup made her look twenty-one. Her eyes were a muddy green and her hair was long, dark, and tightly curled.

People had told her she was beautiful, but she

wasn't sure if she believed them. Her skin was what you get when a white Bekins driver marries, not for long, a black waitress. When he used to come around her father would tell her, "You're the color of a cup of coffee, heavy on the cream."

The woman on the phone said, "Are you listening, Sharronda? You have to look wonderful, because tonight's the night we make our money."

When she heard that, the voice had a face. "It's you," Sharronda said. She thought of the woman's red hair, her long pale hands and the way she had once said, We could make a lot of money, you and I. Sharronda could make five hundred dollars, just for one night's work. That's what the woman had told her.

The voice on the phone said, "Do you remember everything we talked about?"

It was like asking her if she remembered her name. "All of it."

"Good. I'm glad to hear that. Because we're all set for tonight. Everything is in place. Now, are you paying attention?"

Sharronda was paying attention. The woman gave her the name of a hotel, the American Executive Inn, and an address. "Be there at six forty-five tonight," she said. "Be on time, and wait at the lobby entrance. I'll meet you."

Sharronda wrote it down. "Six forty-five," she repeated. "The lobby entrance. You meet me."

"Very good, Sharronda. Wonderful. I think this will be good for both of us, don't you? I have nothing but good feelings about this. How do you feel?"

Sharronda felt as if she had sprouted wings.

6

★

Jack still had one credit card that had not been cancelled. He used it to rent an eight-year-old Buick Le Sabre from a place on Ross Avenue. The car was an oxidized yellow, too long in the sun. It had a compass on the dashboard, four good tires, and a brown vinyl top gone leprous.

The rental office was in a trailer occupied by a sweaty man who introduced himself as Hoss. He drew up a contract and told Jack the rental fee could be applied toward a purchase. "You can have it for thirteen-fifty," Hoss said. "Be a damn fool not to."

The Buick pinged a little, but it had started quickly, idled smoothly, and blew good AC. Jack turned on the radio and caught the news: 109 degrees at 3:30, no rain for the last six weeks. In some parts of the city dead birds were dropping from the trees. Old people without air conditioners, the ones who had nailed their windows shut to keep the burglars out, were being carried from their houses with heatstroke. Boats rested on the hard mud of dry lake bottoms. The whole place seemed ready to crack like cheap brick.

Jack took Ross Avenue all the way through downtown. At Elm he turned right, cruising past Dealey Plaza and the grassy knoll, and through the triple underpass. Even in this heat a few tourists were standing on the sidewalk, gazing up at the sixth floor of the old school book depository and pointing. You could see them there every day of the year.

He turned right again on Industrial Boulevard. The air above the street hung in a greasy haze. Jack rolled past machine shops, plumbing wholesalers, and skin-video stores.

DRW Photo Supply and Processing was on a side street off Industrial, up against the Trinity levee. Jack had met Don Ray Wagner while prosecuting a break-in of his shop. The offender was on his third trip through felony court, and Jack got him sent away for life as a habitual. Don Ray, happy as he could be about the sentence, found out Jack liked to take pictures. Said come on by, we'll cut you a deal on supplies, use the lab if you want.

Jack took him up on it, and worked harder on his photography. He started roaming the city on weekends, everywhere but the north side, looking for the right people. Jack liked to shoot portraits of hookers, bikers, barflies, street preachers, and skinheads. He made himself a regular around tattoo shops, leather bars, and massage parlors. He got to know an interesting group of people.

His wife, Kathy, didn't quite understand it. Kathy didn't react well when Tiffanie from the Oriental X-tasy Massage on Harry Hines called Jack at 4 A.M., trying to cadge some glossies for her portfolio because what she really wanted to do was model. Kathy didn't know what to think when four fat hairy dudes on Harleys came roaring into her suburban front yard on a Sunday morning, there to ask Jack if he'd seen somebody named Grunt last night.

These kinds of people, she said to Jack, don't you see enough of them in court? All day long you're in a room with killers and rapists and drug dealers, and you want to hang out with them on weekends?

Jack answered with something smart. Saying with a laugh, It's like the showroom salesman visiting the factory floor. He gets to see how they put the product together. Kathy looked away, then asked again, Why are you doing this, Jack? He didn't answer. The truth was, he didn't really know.

When his marriage finally went in the tank—far more than pictures put it there—and when Jack scraped bottom, Don Ray Wagner was one of those who gave him a hand up. Don Ray told Jack he'd been there himself. Don Ray, who these days had a kind of barrel-chested, pinkie-ring prosperity about him and smoked good cigars, said he remembered what the skids were like. He had given Jack a key to the place, said come and go as you please.

Now Jack parked the rented Buick in front of DRW Photo Supply and Processing, next to Don Ray's new pickup truck, and entered the shop through the front door. Don Ray, from behind the counter, said, "He lives."

"Maybe," Jack said and shook his hand.

Don Ray had once been a boxer, though not much of one. He never got beyond club fights in Fort Worth, but it left him with a big pounded-on nose mashed against his face. He had a couple of gold teeth in front and his knuckles hurt when the humidity was up. When he was with old pals and the phone rang, he'd yell out, "What round is it?" to get a laugh.

"Left you a note, Jackie." Don Ray motioned with his head toward the back.

"Let me guess."

"Not a bill," Don Ray said. "More like a statement."

Jack smiled. "Don Ray, you don't have to apologize for wanting the money that's owed to you."

"I'm sure you're good for it."

"I'm doing a job," Jack said. "That's why I'm here."

"See what I mean?" Don Ray smiled, flashing the two gold teeth. "I got a hunch, Jackie. I think you're turning the corner."

Jack couldn't take any more sympathy. He told Don Ray thanks and walked to the back of the shop, past the lab and the stock shelves to a locker. A typewritten note had been taped to the front: *JF, your amt due for rental and chemicals now $147. DRW.*

He dialed the combination and opened the locker. A white lab coat hung from a hook. Below it were two canvas bags. One contained a couple of cameras, a battery pack, and a flash. Jack took that one to weddings.

The other bag had an assortment of equipment, most of it belonging to Hal: a tape recorder, various microphones, and some small tools. Hal liked to call it his cheater-beater kit. Jack used that one on stakeouts. He pulled one of the cameras and the flash from the first bag and put it inside the second, and took that one with him.

On the way out he said, "Later, Don Ray."

"Jump on it, champ."

Once Industrial reached a slightly better neighborhood its name changed to Market Center Boulevard. Jack stayed on it until Stemmons Freeway, where he took a left and kept to the access road for a half mile. The American Executive Inn and Conference Center sprawled between a boot warehouse and a nearly new, completely empty office building. The marquee below the American's sign said BUDDY GEORGE JR 7:30 THE WAY UP in red letters. The man had his name up in lights.

Jack checked in and got the key for Room 334. It was a decent enough place, the American. Maybe twenty-five years old, but not long past a face-lift. Jack's room had a color TV bolted to its stand, a painting of coastal sand dunes screwed to the wall, and a closet full of hangers that couldn't be removed from the rod. Your traveling businessperson of today, Jack figured, must be a light-fingered one.

On his pillow was a coupon good for a free order of fried cheese sticks at Olde Ben Franklin's Pub, off the lobby. Jack sat on the edge of the bed and dialed Room 333. When he got no answer he went outside, walked next door, and knocked. No one came to the door.

Back in his room Jack opened his bag and found a small electric drill. As he had hoped, a double doorway connected the two rooms. This would be easy. He unbolted and opened the first door. Then he knelt and began to drill through the second door.

As he drilled Jack counted up the offenses he was committing or about to commit: Criminal mischief. Operating as a private investigator without a license. Unlawful interception of oral communications.

About three quarters of the way through he stopped to blow the shavings out of the hole. No use leaving a telltale pile of them on his neighbor's carpet. A few more seconds of drilling and the bit pushed clear.

Next Jack unpacked the tape recorder from the bag. He unwrapped the cellophane from a blank tape and put the cartridge in the recorder. A microphone smaller than a cigarette was already attached. "August nineteenth," he said and checked his watch. "Four twenty-five P.M. Tape survey of room three-three-three at the American Executive Inn, Dallas, Texas." The tape moved when he talked and a red light on the recorder flashed.

Jack dropped to his knees, about to slip the microphone through the hole, and was glad no one could see him doing it. It made him think of two cops he had known when he was with the DA.

Cameron and Welch were young investigators assigned to Vice. Cameron was a good-time type who enjoyed himself. Welch talked a lot about Jesus and the end of the world. Their job was to patrol the porno moviehouses and dirty bookstores, busting the lewd and lascivious, which meant men with their pants down.

When Jack was still working misdemeanor court he had done a couple of ride-alongs with Cameron and Welch, getting the feel for the police end of things. He remembered crouching in a film booth the size of a hall closet with Welch. The place smelled of disinfectant. He and Welch were peering through holes in the wall.

"Here he goes," Welch had whispered. "Watch him." Jack looked through the hole into the next booth, and saw a man put a quarter into a slot. When naked people appeared on his little screen, the man dropped his pants and began to massage himself. "Got him," said Welch, who went next door and made his arrest.

Working the lewd and lascivious beat had always seemed to Jack like a sorry way to make a living. And now here he was, peeping into motel rooms, waiting for people to take their clothes off and moan so he could get paid.

The way things had gone lately, it wasn't as if he had fallen from the penthouse to the pavement. It was more like slithering from the basement to the sewer.

7

★

Sharronda Simms stood before a dresser so old its mirror had gone dull. This is what it must be like when the years get you, she thought as she rolled on lipstick. You have the cataracts and everything goes fuzzy. Next thing you know they put you in a home. That's where Delbert's grandmother was, the Rest-Easy Manor on Military Parkway. And that's why Delbert had her house and all her furniture. We should go visit her, Sharronda said once, make sure your grandma's doing okay. Delbert answered, My ass.

Now Delbert yelled over the music from the other room, "You get them pills I tole you?"

Sharronda finished with the lipstick and thought about the lady she was meeting tonight—thought about how Sharronda was doing the lady's nails at the Salon d'Elaine one day and began to talk about herself.

The lady was pretty old, way past thirty, and with her long pale face and her red hair nothing like Sharronda. But she asked Sharronda soft questions and watched her with nice eyes, so Sharronda told her the whole story: About how she's been in Dallas for four months and everything is messed up. About how Delbert said he'd marry her but all he does is get high and steal her money. About how all she wants, all she really wants, is enough money to get free.

Sharronda said she'd do anything for it and she was trying not to cry when the lady put two fingers gently to Sharronda's cheek and said, You're so beautiful, I'm sure it will work out. She came back the next day and told Sharronda, I have an idea for us to make some money together. You and me, that's what she said. Told Sharronda she had been looking for someone like her. Then the lady asked: Five hundred dollars will get you free, won't it?

Now Delbert said, "Where in hell you goin'? All dressed up and shit." Sharronda walked past him toward the front door, telling herself she would pack her stuff tonight after he passed out, and then she'd be gone. Wouldn't have to mess with Delbert anymore because she'd be out of town.

"Hey," Delbert said. "I ast you a question." He lay on the couch with an almost empty pint of Early Times. He rested his arm with the dirty cast across his bare stomach. His hair had not been washed in a week.

Delbert was so skinny he barely dented the couch cushions. The color of his skin reminded Sharronda of spoiled milk. You made the same mistake I did, her mother told her once. You took up with a white man.

"Where's my cigarettes?" Delbert said.

Sharronda checked her purse for her keys. "I'm working tonight. You don't wait up, I'll be back late."

"For that butthole Germy?" Delbert couldn't keep his eyes open. His words came out stretched and rubbery. "Workin' for that fag Germy?"

"It's not for Jeremy," Sharronda said. Jeremy was the manager at Salon d'Elaine. "I got a private job."

Delbert managed to sit up halfway. "Go get me a six-pack first. Six-pack a Bud. Where's my cigarettes?"

Sharronda watched him search his pockets in slow motion, his eyes still closed. "I'm leaving," she said.

"You get my pills?" he said as she opened the front door. "Oh, man, my arm," he said as she walked out.

Sharronda started her old Toyota. A worn belt under the hood gave off loud yelps for the first ten seconds or so. She drove out of the neighborhood, for the next-to-last time, she hoped. Then she headed up Buckner Boulevard, past the car lots and the Sonic Drive-In that had been converted into a church. Billy Wayne's Kountry Kookin' Restaurant was behind her, Kmart ahead. In the distance to her right were the red-brick buildings of the Buckner Children's Home. She imagined little girls' faces in the windows. If the light at the corner had been red she would have run it, just to keep going.

She took I-30 west, toward downtown, as the lady had told her on the phone. Sharronda was afraid that if she drove too slow she would be late, but if she drove too fast she might have a wreck and never make it. She settled on sixty-three mph and gripped the wheel so tightly that after a few miles her hands ached.

At 6:15 by her watch she pulled into the parking lot of the American Executive Inn and Conference Center.

She wasn't supposed to be at the lobby entrance for another half-hour. It was too hot just to sit in the parking lot, so Sharronda drove around the building maybe twenty times, hoping the car wouldn't boil over. She had never seen a clock creep like that. Nothing could go that slow, she thought, and still be moving.

Finally Sharronda parked and walked to the front door of the hotel. Cars came and went, dropping people off and picking them up. A hotel van pulled up and men in suits spilled from it with their bags.

A large silver-blue car rolled past her and stopped. The license plate said UPTOO. The driver's door opened and the lady she had been waiting for motioned Sharronda to get in.

This was the first time Sharronda had sat in a car with leather seats. The lady had on a black dress that Sharronda could imagine wearing to a great party. All her jewelry—the gold rings and necklace and earrings—looked great on her. Sharronda couldn't believe how lucky she was to have met her. It was the best thing that had happened since she had come to Dallas. "You really look nice tonight," Sharronda said.

"Close the door." The voice was hard, giving orders, with no more gentle fingers to the cheek. "Hurry up."

They passed through rows of parked cars with nobody speaking. Finally Sharronda said, "Is everything okay?" The lady didn't answer. At the far end of the lot she stopped the car. They sat without talking, just them and the blowing of the air conditioner.

Sharronda tried to think of what she had done to make the lady mad. She looked for a run in her hose. Maybe her dress wasn't right.

The lady turned to her and said, "Sharronda."

Anytime anybody said your name like that, Sharronda thought, just said it and nothing else, they were about to tell you something you didn't want to hear. "Is something wrong?" she said. "Is it I don't look right? 'Cause I'll fix it."

"Nothing is wrong, Sharronda. Nothing at all. If you're ready to do your job, nothing is wrong."

"I'm ready. You say five hundred dollars, I'm ready like you wouldn't believe." She looked at the plastic box at her feet. "I have all my stuff I brought."

"You have your what?"

"My nail stuff. Polish, files. Glitter and designs, in case the people want to get fancy."

The lady closed her eyes and shook her head. "This is not going to work. I should have known. You're not right for this." She sighed. "You should probably just go on home."

"It'll work. I'll make it work. You tell me what you need, I'll make it work." Sharronda suddenly felt as if she were at the bottom of a hole with dirt pouring in. "Because I have to have that money, miss. I'll make it work."

"Sharronda, did you think I was going to pay you five hundred dollars just to do nails for an evening?"

Sharronda tried to remember what she had thought. "I don't know."

"You don't know." The lady shook her head again. "Well, I'll tell you. You say you've got to have that money. Then you need to spend a few minutes tonight with a man."

Sharronda took a deep breath. "You're not saying everything."

"His name is Buddy. He has a performance here tonight, and afterwards you will go to his room with him."

"A singer or something?" Sharronda had known a girl in high school who said she'd made it with every metal band that came through town. Carla Weber, and she ended up marrying a preacher.

"He's a speaker. He gives speeches." The lady checked her watch. "I've reserved a front-row seat for you. What you do is you sit there and you listen to Buddy give his speech. And while he gives his speech, you never take your eyes off him."

Sharronda watched the lady's mouth and waited for the rest.

"When his speech is finished, stay close to me. I'll introduce you to Buddy. I'll tell him you would like to have a drink with him. Are you following me?"

Something inside Sharronda nodded her head for her.

"That's where I'll leave you," the lady said. "When you get to the bar tell him how much you liked his speech. Don't let on that you know me, don't even mention it. Just tell him how much hearing him meant to you. Let him talk. He likes to talk. After he finishes his drink, say he looks tense. Ask him if he wants to relax in his room."

Sharronda had been in a motel room with one man before—Delbert. He had dropped a burning cigarette into a trash can and scorched one wall.

"That's your job, Sharronda. Go with him to his room and do what he wants to do."

"What does he want to do?"

"For twenty minutes or so, what difference does it

make?" The lady turned the rearview mirror toward herself and brushed her hair with her fingers. "Look, Sharronda, if you're having trouble making a choice . . . "

Sharronda loved the way white people like this were always talking about making choices. Like you could go to the store and order the life you wanted.

"If you're having trouble, maybe you don't really need that money." The lady checked her watch again. "You've got about thirty seconds. Yes or no, Sharronda? Five hundred dollars or nothing."

The lady opened her purse and took out some bills. "Here's a hundred dollars. You get the rest when you finish your job. Yes or no, Sharronda?"

Sharronda could not look at the lady. She took three breaths. "Yes," she said.

At just after seven o'clock Jack Flippo walked to the Founding Fathers Room at the American Executive Inn and laid down twenty-five cash—Hal had advanced him $100—for a ticket to see Buddy George, Jr. He bought it from a skinny kid who was sitting at a table full of books and tapes.

Another ten dollars and change got Jack a copy of Buddy's paperback, *Birth of a Salesman!* Buddy's color photograph was on the front cover, a picture of him holding two bags with black dollar signs on them. The man had a pompadour, it looked to Jack, the size of a canned ham.

The show didn't start for another twenty minutes or so. Jack decided to kill the time at Olde Ben Franklin's Pub, see if he could stand the excitement.

He ordered bourbon. A large, soft man who had put on some weight since he bought his dark suit settled onto the stool to Jack's left. The man asked for a beer and sang along with Olivia Newton-John on the jukebox. The beer came and Jack heard the man say, "You're here for Buddy, am I right?"

Jack turned to see a fellow in his late thirties, with a round face and dark hair beginning to go. "I noticed you have his book, so you must be here to see Buddy." The man offered an overstuffed hand. "I'm Bo Harrison, commercial real estate."

"Jack Flippo. Nothing in particular."

"I got you. This damn economy, hey, a lot a people's swinging loose." He pulled a business card from the monogrammed pocket of his white shirt and gave it to Jack. The card said, BO HARRISON, THE ACE OF PLACES.

"Lots of people swinging loose," Bo Harrison said. "That's why I'm here. Buddy George, there's a man can show you how it's done. Tell me I'm wrong, but I believe Buddy can make money for you."

Jack thought, he's making five hundred for me. "You're not wrong."

"Amen. Amen and case closed." Bo Harrison drank his beer. "That's why I've come to see him fifteen times."

Jack looked at the Ace of Places.

"Fifteen, count 'em up. The man's a genius, what can I tell you."

"You think so?"

"I know so. But don't just take my word for it, ask anybody that's been here. If Buddy can't motivate you, my friend, you don't have a pulse."

Jack nodded and sipped his bourbon. "Let me ask you something."

"Fire away," Bo Harrison said.

"You ever hang around after these dog and pony shows—"

"Buddy calls 'em way-uppers."

"—and talk to Mr. George? You know, touch the hem of his garment."

"Sure I do. Hell, we're old pals at this point. I shake his hand, tell him he's done it again, by God. Buddy says come back. I always do. 'Course it's a business expense, so I don't have to pay the freight. Fifteen times at twenty-five a pop, that comes out of the operating account. Some jobs have excellent, excellent benefits."

Jack rattled the ice in his glass, drunk chimes.

"At the end of these evenings . . ." He wondered about offending the faithful but plunged ahead. "When he's leaving after his show, does he have a woman with him?"

Bo Harrison rolled his head back and laughed. "Who, Buddy? Shit, I imagine."

"A dark-haired woman? Dark-skinned?" Jack asked. That was what Hal had told him. "Maybe Hispanic?"

"Dark-headed, blonde-headed, Mexican, French, Martian, East Texan, what can I tell you. The man is no monk. Now I'm not gonna say they could all be Miss America. That would be a lie, and I won't lie to you except it's to sell commercial real estate." He gave Jack a smile full of tiny teeth. "Some have a few miles on 'em but, hey, who doesn't? They like Buddy, though. And why not? He's probably got a million dollars."

Hal hadn't told Jack anything about lots of women. The way Hal had explained it, Buddy was a monogamous cheater. Jack started to ask another question, but his nose shut him up. There was a smell, a fragrance, that stopped him. His thought disappeared like a jet into a cloud.

His wife—his ex-wife—had worn the same perfume. When you're with a woman, it seemed to Jack, her perfume caressed you, all fingertips and air. When she was gone and you smelled it again, it got you by the throat.

Jack looked to his right, as if he would find the former Mrs. Flippo standing there with a second chance for him, all wrapped up like a Christmas present.

The woman he saw was not anyone he had ever been married to. But if she asked him on the spot he'd think about it.

When he chewed it over later, Jack tried to explain to himself what had drawn him to the woman in an instant. She was attractive enough—tall, trim, pretty face, nice hair, good clothes—but that wasn't it. Her eyes were what really got him. Even in the dim bar light they seemed to burn up everything around him.

She asked the bartender to change a twenty. Jack tried to break from his stare and say something to her, and wondered if he could do it without sounding like a barstool reptile.

The bartender counted out her bills. When the last one was in her palm Jack said to her, "That's great perfume you're wearing."

She flicked a glance on him and off him, turned, and walked quickly from Olde Ben Franklin's Pub. Jack watched her go.

"Hell of a deal," Bo Harrison said when she was out the door. "Hey, maybe Buddy can give you a few tips on handling the ladies."

9

★

"Jesus was a salesman," Buddy George, Jr. said. Jack listened from the back row of the Founding Fathers Room. "Sure he was. People say, 'He has millions of followers.' I like to think of 'em as customers."

Buddy stood on a low stage, with a microphone but no lectern, anchoring the white beams of two spotlights. Behind him stretched a banner that proclaimed, THE WAY UP!

"And just think," Buddy said, "how many more customers he would of had if he could of put his message out on television!"

The crowd applauded. There were maybe two hundred people in the place, sitting in straight rows of padded banquet chairs, almost filling up the room. "Don't you know he would of done 'Good Morning America'?" Buddy bellowed into the mike. "Can't you just see him on a 'Barbara Walters Special'?" There was more clapping and some laughter.

"It's called maximizing your presentation," Buddy said, his voice rising. "My friends, it's called bang for the buck. They can't want your product if they can't see it. You got to show it to 'em. It's called *sales!*"

From what Jack had seen before the house lights went down, the crowd was made up of people he sometimes found when he tried to buy a shirt or a couch. The kind the state liked to fill up a jury box with. They had fresh uncomplicated faces and clothes from the mall. Enthusiasm seemed to radiate off them. Jack felt like a heathen in the temple.

"Now," Buddy said, and picked up a glass of water from a wooden stool on the stage. "You ask, 'Buddy, why do you keep saying that word *sales?*' You say, 'Buddy, don't you have a fancier word?' You say, 'What about *merchandising?*' Let me tell you a story."

Buddy paused to sip from the glass. Something about his face and the way he flipped his hands when he talked reminded Jack of a man he once prosecuted. Orwell Thulen, who got five years for selling phony insurance policies, they could have been twins.

"Not long ago I was on a cross-country flight," Buddy said. "I began to talk to the gentleman next to me, a friendly man with an easy smile and a firm handshake. You ever meet one them sour fellas that gives you the dead fish?"

Buddy made a face and held out a limp hand. This got a lot of laughs. He pumped his hand up and down to wring out a few more. "Well, this old boy did none of that. His name was Stanley and when he shook hands your knuckles cracked. As soon as I recovered the feeling in my fingers"—Buddy paused for a few late-arriving guffaws and Jack saw a man who licked the plate clean—"I said to him, 'Stanley, tell me what you do.' He said, 'Oh, I'm a manufacturer's rep,' and named a big company, a fine company."

Buddy brought the microphone closer to his mouth and dropped his voice. "I said, 'Stanley, you mean you're a *salesman*. Say it loud and say it proud. A *salesman*!'" He boomed the last word.

"Well, me and old Stanley must of talked from Atlanta to Albuquerque. We talked across the mountains, the valleys, the rivers, the streams. I kid my beautiful young bride, my angel, about gabbing with her girlfriends, but you should of heard these two old salesmen talking shop."

The crowd applauded again, though Jack wasn't sure why. "Now friends," Buddy said, "there's three words that's the secret to your success, my success, anybody's success. Those three words are 'close the sale.' I'll say it again. Close the sale, close the sale, close the sale! And listen to what old Stanley told me about that . . ."

Jack got up, walked out of the room, and strolled down the carpeted hallway to the men's toilet. He did his business, splashed water on his face, combed his hair, took his time. At least ten minutes had passed when he opened the door to the Founding Fathers Room again, but Buddy was still on the airplane. ". . . And my friend Stanley looked me straight in the eye and said, 'Buddy, I want to tell you something about winning over your customers. You triumph when you combine *try* with *umph*!'"

Jack closed the door and walked away. It wasn't that he felt superior to the people listening to Buddy George, Jr., but he lived somewhere else. They were tuned to frequencies he didn't pick up.

Back in Room 334 he checked the tracking meter on the tape recorder. The tape had not moved. Then Jack called his apartment, trying to remember as he dialed if he had turned on his answering machine. There were three messages from three different people representing three separate business concerns, all saying pretty much the same thing. Which was: Where the fuck, please, is the money you owe us?

10

★

Around nine Jack was back in Olde Ben Franklin's Pub, waiting. He had put away half a beer when Buddy and the girl walked in. The stool at the end of the bar gave Jack a view of the whole place, which wasn't something you would pay extra for. But it let him watch Buddy and friend make their way to a table in the rear.

The girl had long, curly darkish hair and skin tawny enough to keep her out of the city's finer country clubs unless she wanted to clean tables. Her eyes were big, her lips full, her nose small. She was younger and far better looking than Jack had expected, given the Ace of Places' rundown of Buddy's companions.

Either Buddy had changed subjects or this girl wanted to learn the secrets of selling. As far as Jack could tell, her gaze almost never left Buddy's face. Jack let them order drinks and then it was time to go to work.

He took his camera from his lap and went straight to Buddy's table. "Wow, Buddy George

Junior!" Jack popped the flash the instant Buddy looked up. "You're my hero. Let me get one more for my scrapbook." He shot a frame of Buddy and the girl, and when Buddy moved his hand in front of his face Jack fired again.

It was an old trick. The guy was only trying to shield himself from the flash, but in the photo he'd look like a subpoenaed Teamster leaving the court-house.

"Wait'll I tell my wife I seen you," Jack said.

"That is some piece of bright light." Buddy rubbed his eyes with a thumb and forefinger and shook his head like somebody who had just taken a punch.

"I'm Earl Teems," Jack said. "Just possibly your biggest fan."

"Well, good for you." Buddy, still blinking hard, took his arm from around the girl and lifted his glass an inch. "Appreciate the good words, appreciate the heck out of it. And we'll be seeing you."

"God Almighty, I'd like to stay and have a beer with you," Jack said, watching Buddy's face lock up. "But I got to get to work. Security guard over to the convention center."

"Well, good seeing you." Buddy grinned.

"'Course, it's just something I'm doing till I get my real deal working. And lemme tell you, Mr. George, or can I call you Buddy? Buddy, I feel like I know you. You been one big-time inspiration to me. I mean, you tell it like it is, no bullcorn."

"Thanks a bunch. So long now."

"I mean they's none better." Jack shot another frame.

"I wish you wouldn't do that," Buddy said.

"Just had to get one last pitcher." Jack backed away, keeping the grin on, giving Buddy a thumbs-up. Buddy turned to the girl and began to rub her arm. Jack raised the camera and shot again.

Jack sat on the bed and unloaded the film from his camera. In about ten minutes he heard the key in the lock of Room 333. The red light on the recorder was flashing. Jack knelt beside it and slipped on some headphones.

"And people think this is easy," he could hear Buddy saying. "They think it's a snap to get up there, to make people listen. To teach 'em, and that's the key. Come on in, honey, and relax. What I'm saying is, they think Buddy George Junior has an easy job. Well, I'm here to tell you it ain't so."

With Jack thinking, the man says his name for the tape—what more could you ask?

"It's damn tough work," Buddy said. "Every day a push to greatness, day in and day out. Makes a man tense, gets him so he needs to blow a little steam now and then . . . You know something, you're a pretty sweet-looking piece a milk chocolate."

Jack took the headphones off. This was a made payday. Any minute now the bedsprings would begin to speak. Buddy didn't look like a marathon lover, so Jack figured he could be packed up and gone inside the half hour.

He made another trip to the bathroom and washed his face again. After peeling the shrink-wrap from a plastic cup, he drank some tap water. In the dry Dallas summer it took on the taste of chlorinated mud.

The light on the recorder was still flashing. Jack

packed his camera in the canvas bag and put the roll of film in his pocket. With nothing else to do, he sat in an orange chair and paged through Buddy's book. He stopped at Chapter 8, "First Impressions Are Important!" Buddy started out by telling how to bang on a customer's door: "Give it a good, hard, knuckle-bustin' knock! Don't peck like a bird! Let 'em know you're there!"

Jack went on to the next chapter, "You Can't Catch Fish Without Good Worms!" He was about to scan the Top Twenty Ways to Land a Customer when he heard something break.

It came from Buddy's room, but it didn't sound like glass, exactly. The sound was more throaty, like crockery shattering. He guessed that one of the lovely bedside lamps with the glazed ceramic base had been killed off.

Jack put on the recorder's headphones. The girl's voice was saying, "Get away from me." Something else broke. Buddy said, "Colored slut. You whore." The girl said, loud, "No, don't." Then Jack heard grunts and the sound of a struggle and what could have been a slap.

For a moment he caught himself thinking he should stay out of it, stay put, just listen and record, and collect his fee later. He had no reason to keep Buddy George, Jr. from making trouble for himself. Then a better idea: Call the police, say somebody's slapping their date around in Room 333, and get the whole arrest on tape.

He heard Buddy say, "Why, you goddamn slut." After that came some choking sounds. While he was weighing his options, a woman was being strangled in the next room.

Jack could have made the argument that he was

forced to do something out of his own self-interest. If Buddy killed the girl and the police found out he had listened to the whole thing as part of a money-making deal, he might be facing charges. He could see a grand jury buying it.

All of that occurred to him later. Something else, he wasn't sure what, pushed Jack out the door of his room. Twice in one day, Jack was thinking, he had to stop one person from killing another. Like he was some kind of PI with his own TV show, a handsome guy with a sports car and theme music, zipping around town to halt crimes in progress.

Jack ran outside and banged hard on Buddy's door. *Don't peck like a bird!* "Hotel security," he shouted and banged some more. There was no answer.

He said again that he was hotel security and knocked hard three more times. "We got a complaint. Open up." He turned and saw, seven or eight rooms down, a hotel maid watching from behind her house-keeping cart.

Buddy cracked the door a few inches. Jack could see the girl next to the bed, getting up from the floor. He moved closer and wedged his foot against the door. Buddy had a red scratch running down his left cheek. His pants were unbuckled and unzipped. He was grinning like the town drunk.

"Hey, partner, about that noise. We was just—" Buddy's eyes flashed recognition and the goofy grin dropped like a stone. "You again. Hotel security, my butt."

Jack managed to push the door open a little far-ther while Buddy zipped his pants and buckled his belt. "Big joke, I guess," Buddy said. "I'm just laughing my tail off. Do yourself a favor and move on down the line."

The girl was still behind him, standing now. She was wearing just underwear and clutching some clothing and a purse. Buddy said to Jack, "The hell you want, anyhow?"

For an instant Jack wondered if he had misread everything. Maybe Buddy and his lady friend used strangling as foreplay. He'd heard of stranger stuff. Jack said, "What I want is . . . " and didn't know how to finish the sentence.

Just then the girl pushed by Buddy and burst from the room, flying past Jack in a blur of pink underwear and dark skin. "Her," Jack said. "I want her."

She darted through the open door into Jack's room.

"Hell, you can have her," Buddy said. "She's nothing but a whore. A whore!" He aimed the last word over Jack's shoulder, a shot fired at a getaway car. Then he looked at Jack. "What're you, her pimp?" Jack moved his foot and Buddy slammed the door. In his own room Jack found the girl, wearing nothing but bra and panties and making little hurt noises as she stood in front of the dresser mirror. She was breathing hard. The fear had not burned out of her eyes yet. She pushed her fingers gently against her neck, as if she were inspecting flowers for damage.

Jack shut the door and turned off the tape recorder, then couldn't keep himself from staring at her, rolling his gaze up and down her skin. Thinking, every middle-aged man, when the old lady's shape starts to go, dreams about young meat like this. When she turned and saw him doing it, caught him lapping her up, he felt shame wash over him.

"I'm sorry," he said. "Are you all right?"

She began to pull on her dress. "Man's crazy. I mean a sicko." She looked at Jack as if she weren't too sure about him, either. He could imagine what she was worried about: She escapes from one whack job and finds another behind door number two.

Jack backed off to the chair in the corner of the room, keeping his distance from her as she buttoned her dress. "Does he always do that?"

"How I'm supposed to know? Once with me, that's enough."

Jack said, "You've only been with him once?"

She looked at him. "Who are *you*?"

"I'm Jack."

"Why you asking me questions?"

"You need a ride?"

"I got a car." She stepped toward the door.

"Wait just a second." Jack wasn't sure why, but he took a hotel message pad from the nightstand and wrote his name and phone number. He tore off the sheet and held it toward her.

She took it with a hand still trembling. "What's this for?"

"You might need a friend, someone to help you or something."

"Nothing against you, Dad, but people keep saying they do stuff for me and they don't do shit."

With Jack thinking, *Dad?*

"He out there?" She peered through the peephole in Jack's door. "He might be, man's crazy enough."

"What's your name?" Jack said.

She stayed at the peephole. "Sharronda."

"Sharronda, you don't have any shoes."

"You running from a crazy man, you don't stop for shoes. I'm lucky I got my purse."

Jack picked up the phone and dialed. When there was an answer he said, "Buddy, Sharronda left her shoes in your room. Kindly place them outside the door."

They waited until they heard Buddy's door open and shut.

"Thank you," she said to Jack. "Now I'm outta here."

W

★

Hal Roper put Jack's photographs from the motel bar in a clearing on his desk. He spread them out as if he were laying down a royal flush. "Hey, she's not bad, this punch of his. She's what, Mexican? She's a hot tamale, you think?"

"I don't know," Jack said.

"One of the swarthy hordes, I love it. I can't wait to hear the tape. She climax in Spanish?"

It was past midnight. Jack stretched and looked out the window. Across the street the lights were burning at Countywide Bail Bonds. "Where's the client?"

Hal studied the photos and then slipped them into a manila envelope. "Teddy's waiting in the lobby for her. He'll bring her up. I think that adds a touch of class, don't you? An escort."

"You got any aspirin?"

"She called me right after I heard from you. I'm her lawyer, she doesn't even want to give me her home phone, you believe that? She has to call me."

"You think Rose has some in her desk?"

"It's locked, Jackie. Rose locks that desk like she's got Pentagon secrets. So I tell the client, 'Mrs. George, I just heard from Jack Flippo, he's got the goods.' She says she'll be right down. I was about to say first thing in the morning, but she's got to have it tonight. Her old man's been jumping strange for years but she's gotta talk right now this minute. I'm sitting home in my robe, she can't wait for sunrise."

"As long as we're doing things right now, I'll take my check."

"Love to, Jackie, but Rose locks that up, too. I tell you, that dear woman ever croaks, this office grinds to a halt."

Jack sat in a chair and studied the brown water-marks on the ceiling tile. Hal said, "So I tell her downtown Dallas is no place for a woman after dark. I tell her I'll have my assistant, Mr. Tunstra, pick her up. She goes nuts about how her neighbors might see, how her husband might come home when Teddy's there." He shrugged. "So we wait."

"Where does she live?"

Hal opened a file folder and ran his finger down a page.

"Twenty-eight forty Terrace Green. That's Park Cities, can't be more than fifteen minutes away." He leaned back in his big black leather chair and put his tiny feet on his desk. Hal was wearing wing tips with a blue and white jogging suit. Jack tried to imagine Hal actually jogging. Hal couldn't have run to the door if the room were on fire.

"I tried to suggest to her," Hal said, "let's do this in the a.m. when we're fresh. She practically accuses me of being in favor of adultery. Actually, I am in favor of adultery. You think I'm sorry people say their wedding vows like they're ordering fries? Ask my wallet."

Jack had placed two cassettes, the original and a copy, on Hal's desk. Hal tapped them with a finger. "Jackie, since we got a few minutes, give me a quick fill here. That way I can let this Mrs. George know what she's in for. Just tell me the highlights, the greatest hits."

"I didn't listen to it."

"No, seriously, I need to know."

"I didn't listen."

"What do you mean, you didn't listen?" Hal pulled his feet from his desk and sat up straight.

"What do you mean what do I mean? It's very simple. I don't know what's on the tape."

Hal's voice got louder. "You call me at my home, I'm watching Clarice Tinsley on the news, you tell me, 'Hal, I got the tape.'"

"That's right."

"And now you're saying—what? That we're all in for a surprise here? That this is some mystery package and we all get to guess what's inside?" Hal lit a cigarette in a hurry even though he already had one going in the ashtray. "Is that what you're telling me? If that's what you're telling me, I don't wanna hear it."

"I'm telling you whatever happened in that room is on the tape. I wasn't in there with them, so I can't control what they did. I taped it, which is what you're paying for."

"Unbelievable. Jesus Christ." Hal put his hands to the side of his head.

"Look, after I left the hotel I took the tape and the film to the lab I use. While I was processing the film I duped the tape high-speed, volume down. That's all there is to it. You want to know what's on the tape, play it."

"You kill me, Jack. I mean what happens if my client—*my client*—walks in here and we put this tape on and the guy and his girlie are singing show tunes? You think that'll be a pretty scene? You think I can bill her for that?"

The office doorbell rang. Teddy's voice from outside said, "Yo, Hal!"

"Just beautiful," Hal said. "I won't forget this, Jack." The bell rang twice more. "I'm coming!" Hal yelled. He shuffled past Jack, stopped, and returned to stub out his cigarettes. The bell rang again. "All right, all right!" Hal called.

Jack waited in the chair. He heard Hal struggle with the front door lock, saying, "Hold on, don't worry, I'll get it," and, "Stop ringing the goddamn bell, Teddy." Finally he heard a click and the door swinging open and Hal saying, "Mrs. George, please come in."

A woman's stone-cold voice said, "Thank you." Teddy said, "Hal, something die in that elevator? Man, it stinks."

The footsteps and the voices came up behind him and into the office. Jack stood up, turned around, and then almost fell over.

He didn't know what he had thought Mrs. Buddy George, Jr. would be. A frumpy, teary housewife, maybe, or a mall queen with a face-lift. But he had not expected this: the woman from the bar, the one wearing his ex-wife's perfume and giving him the brush.

There were introductions. The woman shook his hand but didn't hold the grip, barely looking at him. She sat in the next chair.

Hal said, "I know this is hard for you, Mrs. George."

The long black dress was gone, replaced by acid-washed jeans and a white silk blouse. The gold jewelry had come off. Now she wore silver and turquoise, with no wedding ring.

She had long, thick red hair and pale skin with tiny smudges of freckles. For someone not too far from forty, she was carrying it well. Her forehead was high, her face longish but not horsey. The eyes that had stopped Jack dead in the bar were gray.

Jack could imagine having a drink with her, floating in soft music and dim lights, looking into those eyes and telling her his life story. Which would be, I have a history of doing really stupid things for women like you.

Hal said, "Actually, we need not listen to this tape now. In fact, there may be a great deal of what we call dead air in it, perhaps some inconsequential action, which I could edit out overnight. Then in the morning—"

"I want to hear it now," she said. The woman didn't seem to Jack to be wracked with grief. If early on she had thrown a few plates or cried herself to sleep, that was behind her now. Now she looked like someone working on payback.

Hal handed her the manila envelope with the photographs. She opened it, examined the pictures one by one without expression, and put the envelope on her lap. "Good," she said.

"Again, Mrs. George . . . " Hal rattled through a desk drawer and came out with a tape player. "Again, any time you need to stop this tape, take a break, let me know."

She looked at him and said nothing. Finally Hal cleared his throat and said, "Well, let's proceed."

Jack half-listened to the part he had already heard, with Buddy whining about how tough his job was. Hal leaned back, eyes closed, and massaged the bridge of his nose with his thumb. Teddy stood to the side, flicking lint from his shirt and smoothing his hair. The woman stared at the tape player.

Buddy's voice said the girl was a pretty sweet-looking piece of chocolate. She filled up a dress, Buddy said. Take it off, he told her. Slowly, he said. That's it, that's it. Yes, ma'am, Buddy said.

The next thirty or forty seconds of the tape were full of the sound of rustling fabric and Buddy saying, Widdle Buddy yikes it, widdle Buddy yikes it.

"Holy shit," Teddy said. "What's this clown's problem?"

Jack watched the woman keep her stare on the tape recorder. She didn't move. Hal had opened his eyes and was nodding rapidly, a worried man getting what he wanted.

Now lie down on the bed, Buddy said. That's it, right there.

"Love-stick time," Teddy said.

Hal said, "Shut up, Teddy."

Pull your little underpanties down, Buddy said. A little more. A little more. Oooh, that's what I like.

There was the light tinkle of a belt buckle being unhooked and more rustling of clothes. Then Buddy said, Look here in my hand. Look what I got. Looks good, don't he? I call him the Woolly Mammoth.

"Fuckin-A!" Teddy shouted. Jack thought he saw the woman flinch. Hal turned off the tape, glared at Teddy, and said, "Out."

"What'd I do?"

"Stay in your office," Hal said. "I'll call you when we need you."

"I dint do nothing."

"Right now," Hal said.

Teddy walked out muttering, "Guy names his cock and I get jumped."

Hal waited until Teddy had gone. "My sincerest apologies, Mrs. George. I am truly sorry. He's a young man and—"

"Play it," she said.

"You're the boss." Hal pressed the button.

Just lie there, Buddy said. I ain't gonna touch you. Just lie there. Keep your little underpanties down just like that. Show it to me. That's right. Show it, oh my, oh yes.

He went on like that for at least a minute, maybe two, nothing but oh my and oh yes and oh boy and heavy breathing. What a sight that must be, Jack thought—Buddy George with his pants around his knees.

Then on the tape the girl laughed. Buddy said, What're you, what're you laughing at? Next there was the sound of a slap. The girl cried out. Buddy said, Don't you laugh at me, whore. Another slap. Get away from me, the girl said. Then came the sound of the lamp breaking.

The woman sitting in Hal's office never moved. But Jack saw her eyes change, saw the gaze turn inward. She's got the carcass strapped to the fender, Jack told himself, and she's wondering do I stuff him or make him into a rug?

Jack listened to his own banging on Buddy's door and shouting that he was security. When Buddy said,

"You again," Hal leaned forward and cocked his ear toward the recorder. The last thing on the tape was Buddy screaming that the girl was a whore, and asking Jack if he was her pimp, and then slamming the door.

"What'd she do?" Hal said. "She run out of the room?"

Jack nodded. "Sounds like it."

"Interesting," Hal said, and Jack could see him filing something away in his head. "Well, Mrs. George, there you have it." Hal hit the rewind button. "In a way it's unfortunate hotel security showed up. Not to be overly harsh, not to be insensitive, but if he'd seriously injured that female, this would be to our advantage, litigation-wise."

She didn't answer. Hal said, "However, I think we have plenty here to work with, should you wish to pursue legal action." Jack watched him fold his hands on the desk in his wise counselor's pose. "Why don't we set up a conference," Hal said, "and we can decide on our next step in the matter."

The woman extended an upright palm. "I would like the tape, please."

"Certainly," Hal said. "Of course. I'm rewinding it now, won't be a minute. Now, Mrs. George, I'm sure a great many things are running through your mind. The initial reaction in such matters often is an immediate thirst for revenge." He paused and they all listened to the whirring of the tape machine.

"Now, I'm not saying that's you," Hal said. "But it would be perfectly natural. And I must say I sense in you a certain desire for a balancing of the scales. The important thing is to have a plan of action."

The tape stopped. She sent her palm Hal's way

again. He gave her the tape and she slipped it into the envelope with the pictures.

"A plan of action," Hal said. "A map, if you will." He put on a big smile. Jack watched it shrivel as the woman stood up. "But, hey, it's late," Hal said, raising himself from his chair. "We can talk tomorrow. Early afternoon, maybe. Should we say one o'clock, two?"

The woman took some bills from her purse, Jack couldn't tell exactly how much, and placed them on Hal's desk. "You have what I owe you," she said.

"Thank you," Hal said. "Now as to the fee for the divorce filing, as I said, don't worry if you don't have that right now. We'll shake money loose. The dollars will fall like coconuts in Samoa, believe me."

She turned and headed toward the door. Hal struggled from behind his desk and tried to head her off. "I'll have Mr. Tunstra escort you to your car," he said.

"That's not necessary." She kept walking, with Hal being pulled along as if on a short leash. Jack followed behind.

"I insist," Hal said. "This part of town, if I might be so blunt, crawls with scum after dark. One second, let me get Mr. Tunstra."

"I'll do it," Jack said. "I'll walk you down."

"I need you here, Jack. We gotta talk." Hal turned to the woman. "One second, please, Mrs. George. Just wait right here."

She looked irritated, but she stayed. Hal vanished behind the door to Teddy's office. Jack and the woman stood in the silence of the waiting room.

After a moment Jack said, "That is a great perfume. As I said earlier this evening." She snapped her eyes to him, going over his face.

"Excuse me?"

"What's it called? The perfume, what kind is it?"

For the first time there seemed to be a crack in the wall. She seemed almost embarrassed. "It's called Poison."

With Jack thinking, Imagine that. "Really?" he asked with a smile.

"No," she answered.

12

★

"So what do you want?" Jack said when Teddy and the woman had gone.

"What?" Hal cleaned his glasses on his jogging jacket.

"You said to stay. Here I am."

"No, I didn't."

"You said hang around, we have business."

Hal dropped into his chair. "I said that? I must of been punchy from the late hour. Go home, Jack, go to bed." He looked at his watch. "Christ, it's midnight. Come back Monday morning, we'll cut you a check. You did good, Jackie."

"That woman," Jack said, "she really has a charge to her, doesn't she? But it's all beneath the surface."

"What woman?"

"The one that was just in here, Hal."

"What about her?"

"It's all hidden," Jack said, remembering her face, "but there's a lot of electricity there."

"Yeah," Hal said. "And she uses it just like an electric eel. To kill her food."

Jack rode the clanking elevator down from Hal's office and walked to the Buick. An odor like rotten meat rose from the mud of the Trinity River bottoms, the fragrance of summer nights downtown.

Ten minutes later, all it took to get to East Dallas, the Buick's lights swept across his weedy yard as Jack turned into his driveway. He lived in an old garage apartment that had been widowed after the larger house in front was torn down. It leaned a little and needed some paint, but it was cheap. He had landed there after his wife kicked him out.

The apartment was dark, making Jack wonder if he had turned off all the lights before he left or if the electric company had cut the power. He unlocked the front door, which still had the metal sheet over the burglar's hole, and flipped on the light switch for the stairwell. Nothing happened. Jack sagged but then revived when he remembered that the bulb there had burned out two days before.

At the top of the stairs he was welcomed by the sound of the laboring refrigerator compressor. He crossed through the closed, stale heat of the apartment and into the bedroom, where he turned on the window-unit air conditioner. Then he stripped and dropped his clothes to the floor, standing in the Sears version of a zephyr.

When the room had cooled some, Jack lay on the bed in the dark. He thought about this Mrs. George he had seen in Hal's office and played what's wrong with this picture: The woman hires someone to spy on her husband at a motel but shows up herself. Then the woman comes to get the incriminating tape and photos, and she bags them like someone making a purchase from Neiman's.

When he didn't come up with any answers Jack gave sleep a try, but not much of one. More and more lately, when he closed his eyes at night, there was something like a little electric motor whirring beneath his solar plexus. He would lie in bed feeling as if his eyelids were spring-loaded.

It had been this way last year, about the time he was bringing everything down in a slow-motion crash around himself. He was still Assistant District Attorney Jackson Flippo then, one of the DA's pets, eight years on the job. Word had it he was on track for first assistant someday.

What had kept him awake then was not just that he was seeing another woman. He had done that a couple of times before and skated easily enough around guilt and complications.

But the other flings had been just that—sex three or four afternoons, followed by his calling it all off. Jack told himself he did it to keep life interesting.

Then came Marla Kendrick. She was a twenty-two-year-old clerk in the tax office who stopped traffic when she walked the halls. He had tried to talk to her a few times in the courthouse cafeteria and got no response. But one day, out of nowhere, she was interested in him. She was separated from her husband, she said, and she had been noticing him for some time. It wasn't long before he was stopping by her apartment nearly every day after work, and finding it harder each time to leave there to go home.

Marla was beautiful and she was built, but she was more than that. Jack had never been with anyone who seemed so desperate for him. Kathy loved him, but he knew she could survive without him. Marla made him think that if he walked away from her he took the air from the room.

Before long he began to feel the same about Marla. The workday became something to endure so he could go to her for an hour. His wife was more and more just a person he lived with and lied to.

Jack would find himself before dawn, flat on his back in the master bedroom of his nice home, staring at the blackness of the ceiling. Kathy would be asleep beside him, drawing deep breaths. Jack would lie there thinking of Marla, with the little electric motor whirring in his chest.

A month into it the district attorney, Johnny Hector, called Jack into his office. Johnny Hector had thin silver hair parted in the middle, bright blue eyes too close together, and a bulldog underbite. He chewed unlit cigars and addressed every man who worked for him as Son.

"Son," he said when Jack sat down, "you got a felony case on a coke dealer name of Barron Lamont?"

"Set for trial in three weeks," Jack told him. "A major dealer." Johnny Hector's coatholder, Emory Gilpin, sat on the district attorney's couch. Jack glanced at him. Emory Gilpin looked quickly away to study the tops of his shoes.

"I got a call," Johhny Hector said. He picked a shred of tobacco off his lower lip. "I got a call yesterday from someone said you got a girlfriend name of"—he checked a piece of paper on his desk—"Marla Kendrick."

Jack tried to speak, tried to move. "Yes or no, son," Johnny Hector said. "Yes," Jack finally answered.

Johnny Hector set his wet cigar on his desk blotter.

"This person on the telephone, they suggested we back off Barron Lamont. I'm thinking we may have to."

Jack shook his head, confused. "I don't get it. I'm missing something."

"You telling me," Johnny Hector said, "that you get a piece on the side and don't know who it belongs to? That's Barron Lamont's old lady, son. That's his goddamn wife. I got a copy of the marriage certificate right here."

Jack could do nothing but stare. "How you think," Johnny Hector asked him, "that'll look on the front page of the goddamn newspaper?"

Barron Lamont quietly got probation. Jack lost his marriage, his house, and his job. There was only one benefit to it: He could finally sleep. In fact, he could do little else. Fourteen, fifteen hours at a time, swimming out of bed after noon, back in the sack around sundown, up at midnight for a few hours, then back to sleep till noon.

This went on for weeks, for months. His white sheets turned gray. Dirty clothes, old newspapers, and unwashed dishes piled up around the garage apartment like roach highrises. His bank account drained close to empty.

On an early May morning he woke up with $153 to his name. That wouldn't go far, even for a man who slept for a living, so he had to find something. He wasn't ready to go back to being a lawyer and didn't know when he would be. His only other skill was photography. Jack emerged from his apartment-cave with camera in hand and began shooting the weddings of friends, acquaintances, and anyone who answered the one-line want ad he placed.

It was at a wedding that he ran into Hal Roper, camped at the buffet table. I hear you hit a rough patch, Hal said with a mouth full of finger sandwiches, what's your deal now? Taking pictures, Jack told him. Hal handed him a business card and said to give him a call. One night Jack's shooting the bride and groom at the wedding cake, and a week later he's training the long lens on a couple of adulterers banging away in the back seat of a Ford.

The work wasn't really steady, but it gave him something to do some of the time. When things got extra tight, when there had been no weddings or nooners for a week or two, Hal would pay Jack $30 to drive out to his house in the country and cut the grass.

It was penance and rehab. Jack counted as a good sign the revulsion he would sometimes feel when he was on a peep for Hal. He looked on his conscience as something that had crashed in the jungle but was still sending out weak maydays.

Knowing wasn't doing, but at least now Jack was thinking that he would rejoin the world someday soon. Which was what had once more fired up the little engine that kept him awake nights.

But there was a difference. Before, he had been watching himself drive his life off a cliff. This time he was wondering if he would screw it all up again.

Around 2:00 A.M. Jack got up from the bed, put his clothes back on, found the keys to the rented Buick, and walked downstairs and out of his garage apartment. His first stop was a twenty-four-hour Taco Viva for a burrito and a Dr Pepper to go. After that he headed south on North Central.

The radio played the WBAP truckers' show, full of

liquored-up songs and ads for headache powder. Jack drove the freeways, orbiting Dallas three times on LBJ, dodging drunks and reading billboards that advertised evangelists and vasectomy reversals. He tried to put his thoughts of this Mrs. George aside by dreaming up country–western songs he could write. Call one "You Can't Buy Love but You Can Borrow Mine Tonight." Make another one "Since You Left, I Ain't Right."

Four hours after he started, Jack watched the sun rise from the window of a diner along an eyesore stretch of the interstate east of Dallas. He'd had too much coffee and night driving and not enough rest. His hands shook and he smelled bad, and his eyes were so bloodshot even the waitress stared. His head felt as if it were full of cold grease.

He wanted to ask himself, Where in the world am I? Across the freeway, next to a beat-up shopping center, he got his answer from a fat blue water tower catching the dawn light. The faded black letters on the tank said Big Town.

No kind of place, Jack thought, to make small plans. Halfway through his Lumberjack Platter, as he smeared mixed-fruit jelly on limp toast, he knew what he had to do: He had to go find the woman.

By eight he was showered and shaved with fresh clothes on and ready to go to the address Hal had told him the night before. It took him about twenty minutes to drive there.

The George house was on the edge of Highland Park, in a neighborhood of farm-team rich. Not the wealth of kings here—more like the affluence of high-end middlemen. The housekeepers didn't live in and the pools tended toward the small.

Jack parked in front of a red-brick Tudor, enough house that he could imagine three bedrooms and a den. The sidewalk, also brick, made an S-curve from the curb to the door. Jack cut straight across the yard. If Buddy George, Jr. answers the door, he thought, I just smile and leave.

And if the woman answered—what? Tell her there was something strange about this case of hers, and could they discuss it? Tell her he wasn't sure why he'd come, except he couldn't put her out of his mind? Maybe just let it roll the way it rolled, sail without charts, just Jack and the woman talking, see what developed.

Jack rang the doorbell and got eight cheerful chimes to announce the caller. You didn't hear doorbells like that in households that got a lot of visits from the repo man or the parole officer. He was starting to feel like a welcome guest.

Something was about to happen, Jack knew it. He had this sense coming on that he was the right man at the right time, that the fates had just handed him a check to cash. He couldn't say why, he just had the feeling.

A dog yapped and scratched behind the door. Before Jack could ring the bell again, he heard the deadbolt click. The door opened.

He found himself facing a gray-haired woman in her fifties. She wore a pink housedress and some fuzzy white slippers that the dog hid behind. She was a pleasant-looking woman with tired eyes.

"May I help you?" she said. The door was open about a foot. The dog, a chihuahua, danced and yapped.

Jack made himself smile. "Is this the Buddy George residence?"

"Yes," she said, and Jack started to feel like someone who reaches for his wallet and finds nothing but pocket.

He asked the question anyway. "Is Mrs. George in?"

"Yes," she said. "I'm Mrs. George."

★

Hal played his copy of Jack's motel-room tape for the sixth time. Then he sat thinking, alone in his office, the Camel smoke curling around his head. He said aloud, "That son of a bitch." For the next two hours Hal sat and smoked and worked possible combinations, as if he were trying to break a code.

A few minutes after nine in the morning, Teddy rang the office bell. "I told you to be here at eight," Hal said when he opened the door. "That's what I said, eight o'clock. What time is it now, do you think?"

Teddy said, "You look like the dog's leftovers. I looked like you I wouldn't go outta the house. Your dry cleaners burn down?"

Hal turned and walked back to his desk. "You do what I told you last night, Teddy? Talk to me."

"Piece a cake." Teddy relaxed in a chair, crossed his legs, and brushed some dust off his slacks.

"I'm listening."

Teddy shrugged. "I walked her to her car, like you

said. But what a bitch. Alla way down the elevator, I'm tryna make conversation, just be polite, you know? I'm saying, hey, that tape was something else. Or like, can you believe that guy names his cock? She dint say nothing back. Not a fucking word. Like I'm not a person, too, you know?"

Hal made a cranking motion with his hand.

"That's all there is to it," Teddy said. "She gets in her car, I get in my car and follow her. She goes straight home."

"Did you hang back? I told you to hang back. You didn't stay on her ass, did you?"

"Hey, we're talking Teddy Deuce here."

"'Cause she don't need to know we're on her tail."

"She dunt know a thing."

"'Cause I don't want to set off the alarm yet till I know what I'm dealing with."

"Hey, Hal. You listening to me? I was loose, all right? I stayed back. If youda said stay tight, it woulda been like I had my hand inna pantyhose. You said hang back, that's what I did."

"So where does she go?"

"She goes straight home."

"To where, Highland Park? To a house on Terrace Green?"

"This place was on Fishburn Street."

"You're telling me she went home to a place on Fishburn Street?"

"What, is the hearing aid turned off?"

Hal opened a desk drawer, shoved his hand under some papers, and came back with a map of Dallas. He unfolded it and said, "What's the number?"

"The number?"

"The house number. The address, Teddy."

"You dint say nothing about getting the address, Hal. You just said tail her, see where she goes." The two stared at each other. Finally Teddy said, "Am I right? That's what you said. You told me to tail her. The word 'get her address' was not mentioned."

After a moment Hal said, "Try this again. You remember where on Fishburn her house was?"

"Sure, I remember. It was a couple blocks off that street wit the queer bars."

"Cedar Springs."

"Faggots all over the sidewalk, man. I'm turning right and a couple of 'em walk in fronna the car. I shoulda juiced it."

"Turn right off Cedar Springs," Hal said, "and then two blocks?"

Teddy unwrapped a roll of Certs. "Yeah."

"And then what?"

"And then she's home. What else is there?"

"How do you know it was her home?"

"Hey, she pulls inna driveway, she goes inside, she turns onna lights, ten minutes later she turns off the lights. Else you want?"

"Big house? Rich man's house?"

"Next door there's two spades sitting onna porch drinking beer. That tell you something?"

"Then you weren't in Highland Park," Hal said. "No colored people allowed in Highland Park after dark."

Teddy shook his head. "Man, she was such a bitch in the elevator."

"This is getting good," Hal said.

"No smile or nothing."

"Listen to this. Tell me who this is." Hal pushed a button and put the motel-room tape on fast forward.

"Alvin and the Chipmunks," Teddy said.

Hal, watching the location meter on the recorder, punched the play button and said, "Who's this?"

A man's muffled voice said, We got a complaint. Hal turned the machine off. "That security guard," he said, "who is it?"

"I give up," Teddy said.

"Now listen to this." Hal played some more, stopping after the voice on the tape said, I want her. "Now tell me who it is," Hal said.

"Some guy wants to be a hero. Who cares?"

"It's Jack," Hal said.

"Jack."

"Jack Flippo."

"Jack? No shit."

Hal rocked back in his chair and smoked. "The broad gets in trouble, who's there to help her out? It ain't the caped crusader. And what does the other goof say? He says, 'You again?' "

He took the tape from the machine and locked it in his desk. "And then, get this, last night Jack waltzes in here and claims he don't know a thing about what happened on the tape. What does that tell you?"

Teddy chewed another Cert.

Hal said, "It tells you that there's a turd in the soup. The redheaded broad says she's Mrs. Buddy George and she lives in Highland Park. You say she lives in some colored neighborhood in Oak Lawn. Jack says he knows nothing. The tape says he knows something."

Teddy leaned forward and pointed two fingers at Hal. "Let me tell you what I think. What you got here—"

"Somebody's working a deal," Hal said. "The red-head's got something going and I think Jack's got something going. Wouldn't be any big shock they're working together, would it?"

"The two of 'em," Teddy said.

Hal stood and hitched up his jogging pants. "Can you believe that piece a crap Jack? I give him a job and he tries to play both ends."

"Unbelievable," Teddy said.

"The son of a bitch."

"He's an asshole."

Hal dropped back into his chair. "There's money about to change hands here, Teddy. I can smell it. Somehow, some way, no question about it. It don't take a genius to figure it, either."

"They dint fool me, no way."

"Big money changing hands here, Teddy, and how much are you and me raking off? We're not raking manure, you'll pardon my bluntness."

Teddy pounded a fist onto his thigh. "Man, that pisses me off."

"Me too," Hal said. "But I got an idea."

14

★

DeWayne sat at the desk outside Buddy George, Jr.'s office. He told Paula Fontaine, "Buddy said don't let anybody bother him." She walked in anyway.

There were twenty or thirty framed photographs on Buddy's wall. In the year Paula had worked for Buddy she had never taken the time to count. Most of them showed him shaking hands with a celebrity. You saw Buddy with Art Linkletter. With Lorne Greene. Dick Van Patten. General Westmoreland. With Jimmy Dean, who was holding a sausage in the other hand.

Paula had some photographs she didn't think Buddy would want to frame. These were the shots she had purchased at Hal Roper's office the night before.

"We have some trouble," she said as she sat down. She crossed her legs and placed the envelope she was carrying in her lap.

"What's new," Buddy said. He was at his desk, worrying over a sheet of figures. "You want trouble, look at what these TV pirates charge me for air time.

I oughtta buy my own damn station. What do you think, call it KBUD."

Paula took a deep breath. "They claim you beat up a girl last night."

Buddy looked up from his numbers. "Who the hell is *they*?"

"Some man, he didn't say who he was. He called this morning and said you beat up a girl at the American Executive last night and it's going to cost you."

"Bull. That dog won't hunt. That dog can't even bark."

And now the cornpone, Paula thought. She played ahead. "Can we be candid here, Buddy? Because I think we need to be. With all due respect, this is not the first time something like this has happened."

"Hey," Buddy said, throwing up his hands, "what's done is done. It's past history, Paula. I might of made some mistakes with a woman or two. Show me a man that hasn't. Tell me I'm wrong, Paula, but I think we paid one gal's dental bill and we bought the other a plane ticket home. What'd it cost us, eight hundred bucks?"

"Buddy, this person who called this morning, he wants ten thousand dollars."

"Do what now?" Buddy looked as if he had been hit in the stomach with a rubber mallet.

"He said he wants ten thousand in cash by tomorrow. To keep this quiet."

"Somebody's out of their cotton-pickin' mind."

"He said he'll go to the police and the media if you don't pay. That's what this man told me."

"Who said this?" Buddy's voice grew louder. "Cut the mystery crap and lay this on the table, Paula. Who called you and what did they say? Let's hear it."

"I'll start from the beginning."

"Fine. Go."

"A man called the office about seven this morning. I'm the only one here early on Saturday, you know. I answer the phone. He asked who I was and I told him I'm your executive assistant. He did not identify himself, okay? Then he said you beat up a girl last night and unless you pay ten thousand—"

"This is such bullshit."

"—he will go to the police and the papers and the TV stations."

"Go to them with what? Some whore with a sad story? Rotsa ruck."

Time for the other shoe, she thought. "I was going to ignore it. I thought it was a prank. And then I saw this. It had been pushed through the mail slot."

She handed him the manila envelope. It said BUDDY GEORGE CONFIDENTIAL! in shaky letters that she had written with her left hand. Buddy opened the flap and watched as the pictures of him and the girl fell out on his desk.

"I knew it!" He brought both hands down hard on the desktop, palms down, and launched himself from his chair. "I knew that lying piece a trash with the camera was up to something. I'm minding my own business in the bar, doing nothing but having a high-ball, and this son of a bitch starts taking pictures. I should of laid some hurt on him then and there. I should of had him spitting camera parts."

Paula reached across the desk for the envelope and withdrew the cassette. "There's a tape in here, too. The man on the phone told me there would be. He said what happened in the room is on this tape. Buddy—" She stopped.

"I'm listening." He had turned and was leaning against the window, gazing out across the city. "Go ahead, I'm listening."

"He said you tried to kill this woman and it's all on the tape."

Buddy whirled and glared at Paula. "This woman? You talk like she was some kind of stranger. Take a look." He tossed a picture at her. "You brought her to me, remember?" Buddy made his voice high and mincing. "*Here's your biggest fan, Buddy. She'd like to have a drink with you.* Remember that, Paula?"

Paula, holding the photo, did her best to appear shocked. "This is who you beat up?"

"I didn't beat up nobody, damn it."

"I had no idea. She was just somebody in the audience who asked to meet you. I'd never seen her before."

"Well, I told her to hit the road. Her and her pimp with the camera. Hey, she's a friend of yours? My advice to you is find a new friend."

"She was a complete stranger, okay?"

"Whatever you say." Buddy sat down. His voice had lost its hysteria. His eyes narrowed. He looked like a snake about to strike.

"The man on the phone said small bills," Paula told Buddy. "He said small bills and he would call back with instructions."

"He's been watching too many TV shows."

Paula reached across the desk and touched his hand. "Let me handle this for you. Let me take care of it, okay? That's what I'm here for. You don't need to be involved. Just get the money to me and I'll get it to them. It's not that much for peace of mind."

"I'm too busy to mess with pissant chiselers like

this. All this work . . . " He fanned his hand over the papers on his desk.

"Yes, you are," she said. "Let me handle it."

"Ordinarily I might, Paula. Any other circumstances, I might do that."

Paula pulled her arm back, working on not looking as if she'd been smacked in the face. "What are you saying?"

"Any other time I might say, 'Here's some money, pay the leeches,' and then hope they go away. It's like spraying for roaches. You do it and hope they move next door."

Paula kept trying despite the sick new feeling that it wasn't going to work. "Buddy, I think that's the best strategy here, too. I really do."

"Let me tell you something, Paula. See, the man who asks for big money, you have to respect him. I don't care if we're talking deals or steals here, you follow me? He knows what he wants and he aims to get it. He's a pro. He wants the chicken, not the chicken feed."

"Can we get back to—"

"But it's these cockroach types that get you. They want to infest you. They want to nibble away at you the rest of your life, crap on everything they touch. So what do you do for roaches, Paula?"

"Buddy, I don't think that's the case here. I think if we pay these people and make it clear to them we've reached our limit, they'll go away. I really believe this."

"Sure, you can spray for roaches, like I said. But you know what I like to do? Shine a light on 'em, and when they run across the floor you squash 'em flat. Bring a size-ten Justin boot down on 'em. That's what I like to do for cockroaches."

Paula knew that to keep him from talking now would be like trying to stop a speeding truck by stepping in front of it.

"All these bastards want is to bleed me dry," he said. "They got a tape of me and some gal in a motel room. I didn't do nothing, I barely touched her, but they think 'cause I'm a big name and I got a wife and I got a reputation in Dallas, Texas, that I'll pay 'em cash money to shut up. So they say, 'Hey, Buddy, give us eight or nine thousand bucks.' "

"Ten thousand," Paula said.

"Fine. Ten thousand. I got ten times that just in the office safe."

With Paula thinking, You do?

"They say give us ten thousand. So you do that and next week they're back for more."

"You don't know that, Buddy."

"See, what they don't understand is what it means to work. They think people're supposed to give you money. Hold your hand out, the good fairy drops dollars in it. That's the way they see the world. They don't know what it means to sweat for a living. Makes me maddern hell, Paula."

"Me, too, Buddy. I think, however, that—"

"Well, I got news for them. Things don't always work out the way you plan. You put a machine together with cheap parts, it breaks down on you."

Buddy smiled. It was not something Paula wanted to see. One minute she was running the show and before you knew it she was looking for the exit. "I would urge caution here," was all she could manage to say.

"I'm gonna drop a wrench in their gears," Buddy

said. "I'm gonna take the air outta their tires. See, I got a phone call this morning, too."

Paula was suddenly sure that she had been trapped, that someone had set her up. She had to grip the arms of the chair to keep from jumping up and running from the room. "I don't understand," she said, telling the truth.

"Half an hour ago, the phones are ringing. DeWayne's on another line, you don't pick it up, so I grab a call. Some old boy says he just has to talk to me, it's life-and-death important, on and on. He says he has information to help me out of my predicament. I say what predicament. He says then you don't know about it yet. I tell him I guess I don't."

Paula soothed her panic enough to run down a mental list of faces and names, looking for the lowlife who was trying to get a piece of her action. Could be the weasel lawyer, she thought. Could be the tall guy with the messy hair who took the pictures and made the tape. Could be the girl herself, sharper than Paula had imagined, working with a friend. "Did he say who he was?" she asked Buddy. "Did he tell you anything?"

"Hey, I wasn't paying hardly no attention. I'm sitting here running TV rates, he's talking about my predicament. I told him come on in if he wants. I figured I'd talk to him, see what he's after. I had no idea what the man was talking about. Now I do."

"This makes no sense," Paula said.

"So me and him will have a little chat."

"I don't think you should do that," Paula said. "I really, really don't, Buddy."

"Him and me, we'll talk some binness."

She tried to read his eyes, to see what he knew. Not much, she thought, because he was still talking to her, still letting her sit in his office. Buddy wasn't one to let vengeance simmer. Buddy hit back right away.

"This oughtta be good," Buddy said. He was smiling viciously now.

15

★

Teddy tried to remember everything Hal had told him. A guy getting scammed, Hal had said, will want information. He'll want to know who's nailing him and how. Tell him knowledge is power, Hal said. He'll pay for that.

For once, Teddy had to admit, Hal had been worth listening to. One thing you had to give him credit for, the little prick knew how to work an angle. Three times Hal had said, Show him the bait, set the hook, reel him in. After the last time Hal had said, No telling what we'll catch.

Now Teddy stood in front of the runt at the desk and said, "It don't make no difference what my name is, I got an appointment." Twenty seconds later a door opened and a man was saying, "How's it going, friend, I'm Buddy George."

"How's it hanging?" Teddy said and checked the guy over. This Buddy George had on a blue western shirt with snap buttons, white jeans, and the ugliest blue cowboy boots Teddy had ever seen. "I'm Teddy Deuce."

"Glad to see you, Mr. Deuce. Come on in, neighbor," Buddy said with a big grin.

Teddy thought it so hard he almost said it out loud: I can take this goober to the cleaners like a pair of pants. "You can call me Teddy," he told him.

"Well, Teddy, come on in," Buddy said again, leading him into his office. "I want you to meet my assistant, Miss Paula Fontaine. Paula, this is Teddy, I believe he said."

Teddy turned to face the woman, and it was like rounding a corner top speed and getting a board in the face. He looked at Paula and blurted, "I thought she was your old lady."

Buddy laughed. "Well, Paula is awful good-looking, but I'm afraid I'm spoken for."

"Won't you sit down, Teddy," Paula said, giving him the eye like someone sending out brain waves. Teddy wanted to back out of the room slowly, maybe drive around the block a few times and work this out in his head. One night she's this, the next day she's that. "Man," Teddy said.

When Buddy turned away the woman locked her stare onto Teddy and put a finger to her lips. She motioned to a chair with the other hand and said, "Please have a seat."

Teddy sat and waited for someone else to talk. The woman jumped right in. "I think I've seen you before," she said.

"Hey, no shit," Teddy said.

"No, this is really strange." She was talking to Buddy now. "I was at a coffee shop on North Central early this morning and I could swear I saw someone who looked"—she faced Teddy again—"exactly like you. Could that have been you?"

Teddy shrugged.

"I remember I had just ordered an omelette and I wanted—"

"Excuse me, Paula," Buddy said. "But who the hell cares how they cooked your eggs." He leaned forward and put his elbows on his desk. "This gentleman here," Buddy said, "has something to help me with my predicament, as it was put to me. Right?"

"Maybe," Teddy said. He looked around the room. One thing you had to give the guy—he had met some big stars. Teddy spotted pictures of Sally Struthers, Larry Hagman, and Hugh Downs.

Buddy nodded and smiled. "Frankly, I suspect he wants to sell me something. So let's see your sample case, friend. What have you got?"

After a while Teddy said, "You tell me."

Buddy said, "You're joking, right? Paula, the boy's joking, you think?"

"Perhaps he's just being discreet." Paula showed a thin smile.

"Is that it?" Buddy said. "You're being discreet?"

"Could be," Teddy said, straightening the cuff of his jacket, wishing these people would use words he knew.

Paula cleared her throat. "Buddy, could I speak with you for a moment about another matter?"

"Like what?"

"Well, it's not something I feel comfortable talking about in front of someone else." She turned to Teddy. "You wouldn't mind, would you? Just for a moment."

It gave Teddy an idea. He said to Buddy, "I'd like to talk to you alone, too."

Buddy wagged a finger back and forth. "Eeney, meeney, miney, mo, my mama said you go out." His finger pointed at the woman.

"Adios, Paula."

She said, "Buddy, I only want to talk to you for a brief moment."

Buddy raised a hand and waved good-bye to her. Teddy noticed a fair-sized diamond ring. "So long," Buddy said.

"Buddy, I—"

"Thank you, Paula. We'll talk at you later."

"Please, Buddy."

"Somebody's not listening to me," Buddy said. "Are they, Teddy?"

When the woman had shut the door behind her, Buddy looked at Teddy and said, "I'm all ears, my friend."

That was the truth. They looked to Teddy like wide-open car doors. "I guess the best way to put this," Teddy said, doing some neck stretches while he laid the plan down, "is I hear you might have someone leaning on you."

"Ain't nothing that travels like bad news, is there? Bad news catches the morning train."

"So maybe I can be of assistance." Teddy said it just as Hal had told him. You use the words *be of assistance* the right way, Hal had said, it has much more class than just standing there with your hand out.

"Well," Buddy said, "if I don't die of old age waiting for you to tell me what you got, then maybe we can do a deal."

"You got problems wit a tape recording and some pictures, am I right? You and some chick." Teddy smiled. Show him the bait, reel him in, Christ, it was easy.

"One of these days," Buddy said, "you're gonna offer me a deal. I just know it."

"So for a price," Teddy said, giving his neck a couple more stretches, "my associates and I can provide you wit the identities of the individuals scamming you." That was another Hal touch, *associates*.

Buddy locked his hands behind his head. "You said for a price, but I ain't heard any numbers."

"My associates and I think five thousand dollars is fair." Teddy took out a stick of Doublemint, unwrapped it, put it in his mouth, began to chew, smoothed his collar, and said, "We think knowledge is power. Because if you don't have knowledge"—he flicked his fingers as if he were tossing glitter—"forget about it."

Buddy tugged at an ear and rubbed his eyes. Teddy wanted to say, hey, five K is not worth it, pay up and let's roll. Buddy said, "Teddy, you ever heard of a fellow named Isaac Ferris?"

Teddy couldn't believe it, he wanted to give a quiz. "Maybe. I don't know. I mean, unless he's got five grand to give me, what difference does it make?"

"Ike Ferris, Teddy, was an old boy who worked at the Farmhouse B-B-Q Beans cannery in Fort Worth. He was a laborer on the production line, Teddy. Ike Ferris spent a lot of time watching beans go by, a lot of time. Ike Ferris must of seen a billion beans in his life."

Teddy said, "Is this gonna be a long story?"

"Ike Ferris spent twenty years at the bean cannery, Teddy, twenty years drawing an hourly wage. Had him a house in Grand Prairie, made payments on a Chevrolet. And usually more broke than the Ten Commandments."

"Five thousand dollars, yes or no," Teddy said. "I need an answer in like thirty seconds."

"Now in his spare time, Ike Ferris liked to tinker. He'd go out to his garage and put things together and take them apart. And old Ike Ferris, believe it or not, the same fellow working the factory line, came up with a piece of machinery that revolutionized the canning of B-B-Q beans."

Buddy stood up and leaned over the desk at him. "I'm proud to tell you, Teddy, that Ike Ferris sold that idea of his, that technology, back to the factory. Sold it for more money than he ever dreamed of making his entire life. Bought hisself a lake house, bought hisself a bass boat, drives over to the horse races in Bossier City whenever he pleases. Hey, you don't believe me? Call the good folks at Farmhouse B-B-Q Beans, they'll give you the same story, word for word."

With Teddy thinking, what the fuck are B-B-Q beans?

"My point, Teddy, is that unless you're working for yourself, you're working for the wrong man. You might be growing a ton of corn, but if you're just a sharecropper, what does it get you? Well, it damn sure don't get you out of Muleshoe."

Beans, corn, mules—this act belonged on "Hee Haw." Teddy said, "Hey, I got no time—"

"Me neither, Teddy, me neither. So let's get down to the nitty. I look at you, I tell myself somebody sent this boy here. Somebody sent you here, told you to shake money out of Buddy George's pockets, bring it over to the house and we'll split it up. My guess is your split won't be as big as the boss man's. Tell me I'm wrong, but I'm guessing they'll eat the pie and leave old Teddy the crumbs."

The guy was starting to make some sense. "Maybe," Teddy said.

"So let's talk binness. Here's my offer. I retain you as an independent consultant. You furnish me the information I want, I pay you two thousand dollars, cash money, all yours, you don't have to split nothing."

Teddy liked the sound of that, independent consultant. Who needed Hal? He could go back, tell him Buddy said no deal, Hal would probably forget about the whole thing. "Tree grand," Teddy said.

"My goodness, Teddy. You been reading my books." Buddy was grinning with one side of his mouth. "Twenty-five hundred."

"Tree grand, end of discussion." Teddy cracked his knuckles, getting his hand ready for the bills he'd squeeze as soon as he could tell Buddy it was Jack Flippo and the cunt that was just in here.

"Three thousand, done. But for that kind of money, this is what I want." Buddy sat down. "There was a girl in a motel room with me last night. I want to know who she was. I want to know who her friend was with the camera. I want to know where I can find them. I'll pay you five hundred dollars now. You give me the information, and if what you tell me turns out to be the truth, I'll pay you the rest. And then," Buddy said with a wink, "I might have another job for you."

"You want to know all that?" Teddy said.

Buddy cleaned his reading glasses with a handkerchief. "I'm listening," he said.

"You want it now?" That bit about the girl in the motel room, that could be a problem.

"No time like the present," Buddy said.

"I need to check out a few things first," Teddy

said. "Shunt take long. You know, a couple loose ends here and there. Two, tree days, tops."

Teddy figured he'd spend a day trying to run down the motel girl. If he couldn't find her, Jack's name would probably be worth at least a grand, which was a pretty good one-day haul, you thought about it. Plus he hadn't even begun to put the squeeze on the nervous redhead. "Piece a cake," he said.

"Now we're cooking with gas." Buddy punched the intercom and said, "We need you, Paula."

Teddy watched her walk in with her eyes wide, looking scared to death that he'd dimed her. It was the funniest thing he had seen all day.

"Our laughing friend Teddy, here, is consulting with us," Buddy told her. "He's going to let me know just who is causing us all these problems. Aren't you, Teddy."

"You got that right."

"What do you mean?" she said to Buddy.

"He's going to help us find the cockroaches," Buddy said. "After that, he might even help us squash 'em."

"If the price is right," Teddy said. "Speaking of which . . . " Buddy stood and took a roll of bills from his pants pocket. He counted $500 into Teddy's hand. "See you tomorrow," he said. "Same time, same place, more money. You need anything, talk to Paula."

"I'll do that," Teddy said.

The woman followed Teddy out of the office, into the hallway, and onto the elevator. He didn't have to say a thing. Check it out, Teddy told himself. Guys handing me money, bitches following me around. Life is sweet.

When the doors shut Paula flipped the emergency switch and stopped the car.

"Yo," Teddy said. "Small world."

"What did you tell him?"

"You're inna clear, so far." Teddy smiled at her. "We could work something out, you and me."

The woman moved a step closer. "What's he paying you?"

"He's putting large money on me."

"I'm guessing he's paying you a few thousand dollars. So your plan is to sell my name to him, or maybe you get a little more from me and you keep your mouth shut."

"Sounds like you got it all figured out."

"Or maybe you get something from me but you sell me out anyway, so you get paid twice. Have I got all this straight?"

Teddy hadn't thought about that, but it sounded pretty good. He said, "I hear words from you. How come I don't hear numbers? How come I don't hear a pretty lady saying, 'Teddy, you big hunk, here's five grand to keep me outta this?' "

She put a hand on his arm. "Why are you going down so cheap?"

"The fuck you talking about?"

She moved even closer. "Work this thing with me, not against me. Do a job for me and I'll pay you ten thousand. One little job. Ten thousand dollars."

Teddy had always known that someday it would start happening like this. When you have the talent, he told himself, you end up on top.

16

★

Delbert had just turned on the TV when the phone rang. He let Sharronda get it. "Iffat's Royse," he yelled, "tell him run his ass over here."

Royse had saved his life the night before, bringing him three Percodans after Sharronda had walked out. And he'd promised two more for today. It was clear to Delbert that Sharronda didn't care how much his wrist hurt. He could be dying, she didn't give a shit. But Royse, that was a friend. "Tell Royse right now," Delbert yelled.

Delbert had just taken some speed, another gift from Royse. So he was half mellowed from the Percs and starting to buzz from the speed. He felt in control, on top of things. He called it the Commander Delbert feeling: sharp but not flipped out. Perfect for getting into some Saturday morning cartoons.

Sharronda still hadn't told him who was on the phone, which was just like her lately. The last few weeks she didn't open her mouth she wasn't complaining. Delbert couldn't make sense of it. He takes

Sharronda out of a South Texas shithole and brings her to Dallas, and all she can do is nag him about finding a job. Like somebody's going to hire him when he's in a cast, when he's in the kind of pain that knocked other dudes to their knees.

Delbert rolled off the couch and walked down the hallway to the back of the house. Sharronda was sitting on the bed, her back to him, hunched over with the phone to her ear.

Delbert crept in as close as he thought he could get away with. He had to stay far enough from her that his own personal vibes, his own energy field, would not beam into the back of her head. He was thinking, Good thing I took that speed because it gives me ears like a hound.

"No way I go back to that motel room," Sharronda said into the phone. Delbert wondered, What room? "Some other place," she said. "Not there, no way. I'm not going back in that room again, not where that crazy man tried to kill me."

This is getting good, Delbert thought. But his underarm was itching like a mother. If he scratched it she might hear him and turn around, end of show. Delbert told himself: Ninja warrior discipline, man. Don't move, do the Zen thing.

Or maybe just scratch it a little bit, staying real quiet. He did that. Sharronda talked some more.

"You promise he won't be there?" she said to the phone. "And I get the rest of the five hundred dollars?"

Firecrackers of joy started popping in Delbert's head.

"You promise he's gone?" Sharronda said. "Okay. Uh-huh. You promise . . . You'll be there? Okay . . . I'll come now."

He watched Sharronda hang up the phone. She stood and looped her purse strap over her shoulder. Then she turned, saw Delbert in the doorway, and made a noise like a girl seeing a spider.

"Baby, Delbert could get real pissed at his woman doing something with a man in a motel room. Couldn't he?"

She didn't answer.

"But Delbert thinks five hundred dollars would make him forget all about it."

"I don't know what you're talking about."

"My wrist might be broke but my ears work fine. Let's get in the car, go to that room you were saying, and get the money."

"You're crazy, Delbert. You don't know what you're talking about."

Delbert moved closer. "Keep it up, bitch. I think one arm's about enough to handle you."

Sharronda tried to walk past him. Delbert stepped sideways and blocked her.

"I have to go to the bathroom, Delbert."

"Hold it till we get back."

"I'm having my period."

He let her pass. She hurried into the bathroom and shut the door. Delbert heard the lock click. He pounded twice with his good hand. "Soon as you flush that commode," he told her through the door, "we hit the highway."

Delbert did a little dance, watching himself in the mirror on the closet door at the end of the hallway. He was wearing a pair of cutoff jeans and nothing else. He had a snake tattoo on one bicep and a two-headed dragon on the other. Seeing them gave him an idea: Use some of the money for an iron cross tattoo on his chest with a chain all the way around his neck. He hit the door again. "Let's go!"

It was amazing what taking the speed did for his hearing. He stood in the hallway for a minute or so just checking the sounds. Like he was a big radio antenna, one of those big-ass orange and white towers, pulling in signals. He could hear water running in the bathroom and Sharronda banging around in there. The air conditioner hummed in the front room. A Cap'n Crunch commercial played on TV.

Delbert danced some more and then listened again. The water was still going, and so were the TV and the AC. And then he heard a faint sound from outside the house—a squealing much like that made by a worn belt under the hood of an old Toyota.

Delbert yelled, then bolted to the front of the house and threw open the door. Sharronda was backing the car out of the driveway. He couldn't believe it, she had crawled out the bathroom window.

"Hey! Hey!" He ran through the weeds toward the street. "Come back here!"

She left him in a blue cloud of oily smoke. He screamed, "I'll kill you!" as the car sped away. "I'll cut your throat!"

The car made the corner at the end of the block and pulled out of sight. Delbert stood on the hot asphalt and felt a roaring in his head. There was an empty beer bottle in the gutter. He picked it up and smashed it on the street. "Mess with me, she dies!" he shouted.

Delbert felt as if he were going to blow open. He couldn't kill Sharronda, he'd have to kill something else. Then he saw the old lady who lived next door.

She was standing in the driveway beside her car,

holding two bags of groceries and staring at him. In the months he had lived in his grandmother's house Delbert had never even talked to the woman. All he knew about her was that she sat on her porch at night and listened to radio preachers.

He knew that, and he knew she had a car in the driveway.

Delbert went straight for her. She saw him coming and dropped the groceries and her pink purse. Apples, tomato soup, and a bottle of Diet Shasta rolled down the driveway. She turned to run and fell.

Delbert grabbed the purse and plunged his hand into it. "Where's the keys?" he said. The woman began to crawl away, crying and asking for Jesus.

"The keys, goddamn it. The car keys," he said. "I'll kill you, too, I don't get no keys." Delbert clawed through cigarettes, matches, wadded-up tissues, a pack of Life Savers, pictures, makeup, nail polish, loose change, and hairpins shaped like ducks. He turned the purse upside down and junk rained from it onto the driveway. Still no keys.

The crying woman was struggling to her feet as she tried to get away. Saying, "Oh, God, help me. Please, Jesus." Delbert was about to grab her and give her arm a good twist when he saw the key ring in the grass where she had fallen.

Her car was a green Dodge Dart with hot plastic seat covers. Not much to look at, but it cranked right away. Delbert backed out and gunned it in the direction Sharronda had taken—left at the corner and then three blocks to Buckner Boulevard. Here he had to guess left or right. She had talked about a motel, and Delbert couldn't remember any motels to the left.

He took a right, drove as fast as he could for

about a mile, and spotted her stopped at a red light. This detective shit is a snap, Delbert thought. If he'd known it would be this easy he would have stopped at the kitchen on the way out of the house and grabbed a Bud.

Delbert stayed behind Sharronda as she took I-30 toward downtown. He found some good tunes on the radio, first Anthrax and then Megadeth, and thought about the five hundred dollars. After the tattoos he would get some new speakers. And have a big party to break them in, with fifty people at least getting wasted for three days.

When she reached downtown Sharronda took Stemmons north. Delbert had her in sight as she exited at Market Center and pulled into a motel parking lot. By now he felt completely wired from the speed. He stayed in the car and watched as she parked and walked in a hurry across the lot.

The way she was shaking her ass, wearing her tight shorts and her T-shirt with no bra—Delbert wanted to run her down right there. First she screws around on him and then tries to steal money. What Delbert thought he'd do, after he got the five hundred, was go home, pile all Sharronda's clothes in the front yard, and have a bonfire. "Make her watch," he said out loud, "while I toast marshmellers over it."

Sharronda reached the sidewalk outside the first-floor rooms and headed toward some stairs. Delbert parked the green Dodge at curbside, got out, and followed her, creeping up the stairs after her, his bare feet not making a sound on the carpet. He was about twenty feet behind her, stalking her like a big jungle cat, like a cheetah. Or was a cheetah a monkey?

She left the stairwell at the third floor. Delbert

peeked around the corner and saw her almost running down a hallway. When she stopped in front of a room she still had her back to him. He was right behind her before she even had a chance to knock. Delbert said, "Hey, baby."

Sharronda whirled around, and the look on her face—Delbert wished he had a camera. "This the place?" he said. "This room here?"

She didn't answer. She just shrank down, nothing big about her now but her eyes. Delbert thought she might try to run again. He mashed his hand against her face, slamming her into the door, and pressed himself hard against her. "Party time," Delbert said. "Payday."

The door opened and they tumbled in.

17

★

A skinny guy was sitting next to his three-hundred-pound woman. Teddy thought the skinny guy looked like Barney Fife, and the woman should have been harpooned. It was "Little Men with Big Wives" day on "Geraldo." "This is sickning," Teddy said to the empty room.

Teddy watched from Number 333 at the American Executive Inn and Conference Center. He had pulled down the bedspread so he could sit on the sheets, because they washed the sheets.

The skinny guy started to talk about their sex life. "Oh, man," Teddy said. "Spare me."

That was when something hit the door. Teddy turned down the volume on the TV and could hear a man's voice outside. He peered through the peephole and saw nothing but the back of somebody's head. Teddy opened the door and two bodies fell in.

One of them, the girl, hit hard against the dresser, rattling it when her head slammed into the corner. She went in a heap to the carpet and stayed there.

The man, if you could call him that, stumbled but kept his feet.

Teddy closed the door and sized him up, which didn't take long. He was a scrawny thing with a broken arm, wearing nothing but short pants. He had long, stringy hair and beady eyes, and he twitched all over. "Where's the money, man?" he said.

"The fuck are you?" Teddy asked him.

"Let's have it," he said.

The girl moaned but didn't move.

"You know what I'd like?" Teddy said. "I'd like for you to say good-bye."

"You have the money? The money's mine, man. Anything you was gonna pay her goes to me. Pay up and I'm gone, man. Simple as that. And I ain't leaving till I get it."

Teddy wanted to ask him, what is it with nutcases always jabbering? How come they couldn't be crazy and quiet? This one was shaking just like one of those little dogs about to pee on the rug.

"Come on, man. Right now. All of it."

Teddy looked at the little dogman, who was holding out a hand with dirty nails. I could swat this thing, Teddy thought, and leave nothing but a grease spot.

But then what? The redhead with the big plans hadn't said anything about taking care of some trembly little bastard. All she said when she gave Teddy the key to the motel room was meet this Sharronda and tell her to come with him for the payoff. Take her to his place, that was the plan, then lock her down. After that, the redhead said, you call Buddy and say pay me big, big money or the girl, the one with you in the pictures and on the tape, dies. Dies and gets dumped in a very public place. Like your front yard.

It seemed like a good idea to Teddy until the little dogman came along. Teddy looked at the girl. Blood from her forehead ran onto the carpet. She still hadn't moved. "She a friend of yours?" he asked the dogman.

"Screw her, man. She just takes off, it's like so long, Delbert. All I done for her and then she sniffs some money and it's kiss my ass."

"Delbert. That's you?"

"Yeah, man, what about it?"

The names they have down here, Teddy thought, it was like they made them up hanging around the hog patch. "This is your old lady or what?"

"So?" Delbert began to twitch a little harder. "What're you waitin' for, man? I'm real tired of this delay shit."

So they were husband and wife or something like it, as far as Teddy could tell. There was nothing else to do, Teddy thought, but to do it. "You want money?" he said.

"Five hundred dollars, man. Just like you told her on the phone."

"You want money? I got money. It's inna bathroom."

This threw Delbert off for a few seconds. "Bullshit, man. Nobody keeps money in the bathroom. Who does that? Shit."

"I wipe my ass with the five-spots, all right? You want it or not? I got no time to screw around here. You think this is the only drop I make today?"

"You better have it there, man." Delbert walked toward the bathroom, with Teddy behind him. "I don't see no money," Delbert said when he got there.

"You think I'm gonna keep it in the open?"

"I don't see no five hundred dollars," Delbert said.

"Hey, Delbert. Can I tell you something? You got a lot to learn about doing business."

"Like what."

Teddy took a pair of latex gloves from his pocket and pulled them on. "Like, number one, your bret stinks so bad I'm about to toss my breakfast."

"Say what stinks?"

"Your bret that comes outta your mouth, man. Rinse your mouth out inna sink, then we start counting bills."

"You're shittin' me, man."

"I want you to rinse your mouth out, that's all, Delbert. Give me a break here, a little professional courtesy."

"And then you pay me."

"Every bill." Teddy held up his hands. "See, I even got my counting gloves on."

"I guess I seen it all now," Delbert said. He even popped a quick, stupid smile. Teddy couldn't believe it—the guy was actually missing a tooth.

Delbert turned on the cold water and leaned over the beige oval bowl. He cupped his hand and filled it with water. "Like this?"

"Perfect." Teddy caught himself in the mirror that covered the wall above the sink. There were five light bulbs in a brass fixture along the top, the way it might be in a star's dressing room. He made a fist and held it under his jaw, admiring the roundness of his bicep pressed against his shirt sleeve.

Delbert, hunched over, slurped water from his hand.

Teddy rammed his fist down against the back of

Delbert's head, and Delbert's face seemed to melt into the porcelain. Teddy gave it to him four more quick times the same way, coming in with the punches right at the base of the skull. Thinking, Don't let him up. Put him away and get the girl out of the room.

But on the last blow Teddy's little finger struck the faucet, jamming the knuckle. It sent blue volts of pain up his arm. His finger hurt so bad he almost went to the floor.

Teddy cradled his hand and staggered back against the open door. Delbert raised up, showing a wreck of a face, nothing but two wild eyes and a bloody smear. He made some kind of wounded mutt sound and charged.

Teddy caught Delbert in the face with his good fist and again pain shot from his hand. It wasn't as bad as the first time, but it was real, and when Teddy looked at his hand he saw why. Embedded in the big joint of his middle finger was a yellow tooth.

"Motherfucker!" Teddy screamed. He pulled the tooth out and a red pearl of blood formed at the hole in the glove. The sight of his blood made Teddy scream again. The dogman had germed him.

Delbert was slumped against the sink, one hand over what had been his face, coughing and crying. He reached with the other hand, the fingers sticking from the cast, and got a grip on the doorframe.

Teddy put his shoulder into the metal door. It slammed on Delbert's knuckles. Teddy kept the pressure on until he thought he could hear cracking over Delbert's cries. He opened the door a few inches and Delbert fell to the floor.

Teddy thought for a moment about kicking him in the face but didn't want to get his shoes bloody.

Instead, he pressed his heel onto Delbert's throat, and it was almost like stepping on a paper cup the way it gave under his weight.

Delbert jerked and flopped like a cat run over by a car. Then he went limp.

Teddy used his left hand—the right one was still throbbing—to drag Delbert to the toilet. The guy weighed nothing, just a bag of sticks. After he took the dead man's wallet from his rear pocket, Teddy draped him over the rim and pushed his face into the water. "So long, Delbert," Teddy said. "Now you're sailing with the Ty-D-Bol man."

He peeled off the gloves, dropped them next to Delbert's ears, and flushed. Then he washed his hands with soap and warm water, scrubbing extra hard around the tooth mark. Worrying, Can you get that AIDS shit from a bite? As soon as he finished this piece of business he was going to the doctor and get every kind of penicillin they made, the works. And he was going to charge the redhead an extra five thousand. There had been nothing in their deal about taking care of some jerk-off with bad tattoos.

All he was supposed to do was grab the girl. Which, now that he had washed up, he was ready to do. Scoop her up off the floor, put her in his car, take her to his place. That was the plan. With the dogman on ice, he told himself, it should work fine.

When he walked back into the room the girl was gone.

18

★

Jack took another shower, wishing he could wash off stupidity. He was drying himself with a thin towel when the phone rang.

"Okay, you were right," a woman's voice said when he answered. "I need help. Where do you live? I'll come there."

She talked fast and was hard to make out. The background was full of motors gunning and car doors slamming. Plus Jack's head was fogged in from no sleep. He said, "Who is this?"

"Sharronda." She said it as if this were something he would be expected to know. When he didn't respond she said in the same tone, "From last night."

Now he remembered her standing in his room at the American Executive in her pink underwear, staring at the mirror and touching her neck.

She said, "Listen, are you Jack from last night? Don't tell me yes if it's no."

"I'm Jack from last night. Where are you?"

"You said call you, remember? Call you if I need

help, I might need a friend, that's what you said. You told me that."

Jack thought he heard the sound of life about to get complicated. Unless she was asking for money, which would make this a short, unhappy conversation. "What kind of help do you need?"

"I need someplace to stay for a little bit. I need one right now. Can you hear me?" She had to shout over the roar of a jet. Jack envisioned her at a pay phone outside a 7-Eleven, yelling into the mouthpiece while getting the fish-eye from Slurpee drinkers. "Can you do it or not?" she demanded. "If you can't, just tell me, I'll go somewhere else."

He gave her directions and got dressed. Twenty minutes later he heard her knock ten or twelve quick times. Jack walked downstairs and opened the door. She came in like something blown by a stiff wind. Her forehead was swollen and bloody and her eyes had an on-the-run look. Jack half expected to glance outside and see a pack of dogs trailing her down the street.

"Always a pleasure," he said, motioning toward the top of the stairs. She scrambled up.

Jack had not slept in the last thirty hours or so. His ears seemed full of white noise. He climbed the stairs as if weights were strapped to his ankles. The apartment's feeble air conditioning didn't reach the stairwell, which was on the side that caught the sun until noon. It must have been ninety-five in there. Just out of the shower and he was already breaking a sweat.

He found Sharronda kneeling backward on his couch, peering out the window toward the street. "Hi, there," he said and she jumped.

"Don't do that. Don't sneak up on me. You think that's funny or something?"

She seemed younger than she had the night before. Today she wore no makeup and her long dark hair looked as if it had been combed with a claw hammer. The slinky dress had been replaced by tight shorts and a T-shirt. She was trembling and her eyes darted around the room. Her forehead was a mess.

"What happened to your face?" Jack asked her.

"I don't know."

"Great," Jack said. "More mystery." He went to the kitchen and put four ice cubes in his only dish towel. "Keep this on it," he said as he handed the ice pack to her.

Sharronda lay on the couch, looking like something tossed up in a storm. Jack took the only other seat in the room, an aluminum lawn chair with nylon webbing. "Is somebody after you?" he asked.

"Maybe . . . I don't know. I'm pretty sure, yeah." She took the ice off her head. "This makes it hurt more."

"Let me see that." Jack got up and leaned over her. He put a finger lightly under her chin to lift her face toward him. There was a gash about half an inch wide over her left eye with angry swelling around it. "I think you should see a doctor," he said.

"I'm not going back outside, no way."

"You're going to have a scar if you don't do something. A face like yours, you don't want a scar."

"I'm not going out."

"Ever?" Jack couldn't get over how young she seemed.

"Not till dark. When I can go out without someone seeing me, then I'll go."

"Go where?"

"I don't know." She trembled harder and began to cry.

"Look . . . " Jack sat down again in the lawn chair. "We need to talk, because there are some things about this I don't understand. Like who you are, and how you fit into this whole deal."

That was like turning up the gas. The crying became full, cascading sobs. Jack wondered if he had some Kleenex for her. When he couldn't find any in the bedroom he went to the bathroom and tore off about three feet of toilet paper. By the time he was back to the couch the storm was winding down. "Here you go," he said, handing her the paper.

Sharronda took it and blew her nose. "I'm really tired and my head's hurting bad," she said. "I'd like to rest awhile. Is that okay? For a little while."

"There's the bedroom." He pointed behind him. "I just put the foil back up on the windows, so it's nice and dark."

She picked up her purse and walked past him. Jack turned and watched her slip off her shoes and sink into the unmade bed.

It seemed like a good idea. He slumped to the couch and collapsed on it. Jack couldn't keep his eyes open any longer. The little motor in his chest tried to start, but even it was out of juice.

19

★

"You had to *what*?" Paula said. She was in her bed, phone to her ear, fortunate now that she had taken a Valium an hour earlier.

"Hey, the motherfucker infected me," Teddy said. "I could die from what he gave me. Think about that."

"Oh, God," she said. "Oh, no. I'm not hearing this."

"Then I'll talk louder," Teddy said, and did. "The little prick just shows up, says he's her old man and he wants money. I hadda do it, what do you want?"

Paula felt as if something were swallowing her. "This was not," she said, "this was not supposed to happen."

"Hey, tell me about it. You dint say nothing about somebody else. You said get the girl, that's all. A two-for-one deal we did not have."

"How was I to know—"

"So I'm gonna have to charge you extra."

Paula sat up and finished off the glass of white

wine on her bedside table in two gulps. Three minutes before she had slipped into the cool sheets, naked, the Valium making her feel as if she gave off a soft glow.

She had been telling herself how well she had done with damage control that morning. The way she had turned the situation around, kept it from careening out of her grasp, had been something to watch, if she did say so herself.

Now here was Teddy saying, "Five grand extra. 'Cause you dint say nothing about doing that guy. Plus I'm gonna have doctor bills out the ass for shots and pills. No telling what I got."

Paula watched the white blades of the ceiling fan turn and told herself not to think of the person who had been killed. She was not the one who had done it, and there was nothing she could do for him now. The important thing was to stay on track.

"But you do have Sharronda," Paula said. "She's with you. You have the girl."

"Hey, what do you want from me? I hadda fight for my fucking life inna batroom and you're asking did I do something else, too?"

"What are you saying?" Even with the Valium, Paula was having trouble taking a full breath. "What are you trying to tell me?"

"I'm not trying nothing, okay? I'm doing it. I'm telling you the chick went someplace else. I come out from taking care of her friend and she ain't there."

Paula sat up straight and tried to picture a clear, hard center to herself, like a diamond.

Teddy said, "So I'll come over this afternoon and pick up what you owe me."

"You must be dreaming." Paula didn't know where she had found those words. They just came out and sounded great. "You don't get Sharronda, you don't get a penny from me."

"Hey, lady, people who fuck wit me don't end up happy. You don't believe me, ask the dogman. See what he thinks about Teddy Deuce."

She told herself the old Paula would have folded right there. The Paula of a year ago, the one who didn't know how to find her center, couldn't have handled it. "No Sharronda, no money," she said.

"What I should do," Teddy said, "I should go back and see that country friend of yours right now and let him know you're the one behind all this. He'll pay me for that."

Paula waited a couple of beats before answering. "I thought we covered this ground already. If you want to sell me out, you can do it any time. You don't need to call me and announce it. If you want to cash in your chips with Buddy right now, I'll give you his phone number."

"Listen to the bitch get tough," Teddy said, but Paula could tell he had lost steam.

"You now have to make a choice," she said. "Small change or jackpot? Asleep in the easy chair or celebrating in the winner's circle?" The line came from the video "Dream Big! With Buddy George Jr.," $19.95 plus postage and handling.

Teddy said, "The fuck is the problem wit you people? The way you talk, it's like brain barf."

Paula lowered her voice, put a caress into it. "My point, Teddy, is that by yourself, with what you know, you're worth a couple of thousand dollars to Buddy. At most. But you and I together, when we find Sharronda—well, that ten thousand for you we talked about earlier might be conservative."

He was quiet for a moment. Paula was sure she had him, and waited for Teddy to snap to it. Finally he said, "It's still gonna cost you five grand extra. 'Cause you dint say nothing about doing that guy."

"We'll split the take fifty-fifty after five thousand off the top for you. Will that do?"

"The guy fucking bit my hand. I had no choice. I mean I'd do the same thing it was a dog."

"Of course you would."

"I had a gun I woulda blown his head off. Nobody bites me, man . . . "

"Listen," Paula said. "We need Sharronda. What I want you to do is go to her house."

"I don't know where she lives. How'm I supposed to—"

"I know, okay? I want you to go there. If she's not there, wait for her. Just get inside and wait and get her when she comes home. Sooner or later she'll show up. Can you do that?"

"They got a TV?" Teddy said. "I mean, if I have to sit there waiting a long time, I'm not doing it widdout no TV."

20

★

Maybe someone somewhere awakened like a leaping blue marlin breaking from the ocean, gleaming in the sunlight, full of majestic flight. For Jack, waking up was more like a dead carp gassing to the top of a scummy pond.

It was late afternoon, judging from the light, when he surfaced out of his murky dreams. He lay on the couch for a few minutes and listened to the air conditioner from the bedroom while he tried to clear his head. The house creaked as the roof swelled in the sun.

Jack sat up, yawned, stretched, and looked outside. A car had pulled in front of the apartment and parked against the curb. He didn't have to think hard to figure out where it came from. A blue Reliant with an extra antenna on the trunk: They could have stuck a yellow sign on the rear window that said, COPS WEARING CHEAP SUITS ON BOARD.

Jack pulled on his shoes, walked downstairs, and

went outside. As he approached the car the driver's door opened and a large man rolled himself off the front seat. "Hey there, Jack," he said, raising a thick hand. The voice was deep and friendly, as if they were meeting in the parking lot before church. "Good to see you."

Someone else got out on the passenger's side. Jack smiled at them, waved, and kept walking to the newspaper box on the corner. He put in his quarter and took out the last paper, a display copy in the rack door. The front page had already turned yellow.

Jack turned to go back and saw the two men waiting for him, side by side next to the car, four hands in four pockets. The big one Jack knew from way back. Meshack Blanchard had worked in the Crimes Against Persons section of the Dallas police for years, one of the first blacks up there. He chewed bubble gum and acted happy most of the time, a good detective whose game was to lull you with his rube act, then pounce. Blanchard was wearing brown Hush Puppies, black slacks, a yellow shirt, a burgundy tie, and a brown sports jacket that shimmered in the sun.

Jack had not seen Blanchard's partner before. He was thin, draped in light gray pinstripes. His brown hair looked permed, about ten years out of fashion, right on cop schedule. His face was round with a weak chin and he had small, dark eyes.

"Gentlemen," Jack said when he reached them. "What do you know, Meshack."

The smaller one said, "Sees the law and keeps on going."

Jack shook Blanchard's hand. "Been a while," Jack said. "Who's your poodle?"

"We thought maybe you weren't coming back,

Jackie." Blanchard held the handshake. "My partner, Barton Eskew, he says, 'That boy's gonna keep on walking.' I told Barton that's just your way of showing us your complete lack of respect."

Jack and Blanchard laughed. Barton Eskew lit a cigarette. Jack said, "So they have you working Saturdays now, Meshack."

"Someone has to clean up the garbage from Friday night."

"What kind of sanitation problem we got today?"

Blanchard sponged his head with a handkerchief and blew a bubble. It popped and he said, "We just stopped by to chat, Jack. A few questions. Only take a minute, Jack. Just some loose ends we're tying up."

"About what?" Jack said.

Barton Eskew looked at the apartment. "It's hot out here," he said. "Let's move inside."

"And talk about what?" Jack said.

"Well, Jack." Blanchard sounded as if he were about to make a sad announcement. "It's a homicide." He blotted some more with the handkerchief. "There was a man got stuffed down a hotel commode, and we come to find out you rented the room next door."

"Who?" Jack said, wondering if it was Buddy George, Jr. who got dunked. He had a feeling he was about to get hit from the blind side.

Blanchard said, "Jack, we keep standing out in this sun I'm gonna melt down to nothing but a pile of warts."

Jack didn't think he could stall them anymore. He led them up the steps, wondering what he would find at the top. He would bet money, if he had any, that his houseguest had some kind of connection to the man in the toilet. Which would make Meshack and Barton want to stay for a while.

Jack saw himself going downtown for the evening, spending time in tiny overlit rooms where he would be expected to answer questions. He wouldn't know the answers, but they wouldn't believe that, so they would threaten to hose him with charges unless he talked. He could imagine Barton trying to tell him he would do time for drilling a hole in the hotel's door. Jack had said such things himself, back when he had steady government employment.

He opened the door at the top of the stairs and looked in but did not see Sharronda. Blanchard went straight to the couch. Barton strolled in and took his time, inspecting Jack's photographs that had been tacked to the wall, and then stopping at the bookshelf to scan the titles. Jack said, "You looking for some Hardy Boys?"

"Tell me, Jack," Blanchard said as he settled into the cushions. "What you been up to since you left the DA?"

"A little this, a little that. You know, paying the rent, that's about it. Photography, mostly."

Blanchard took out a pen and a small notebook. Barton moved on to the kitchen, where he studied the papers tacked to a cork board. That was fine with Jack—let him make a case out of old dry-cleaning tickets.

"Sit tight, I'll be right back," Jack said to Blanchard. "Then you can violate my civil rights." Blanchard chuckled. As Jack ducked into the bedroom he heard Barton say, "Some kind of asshole, Meshack."

The bed was empty. The bathroom door was closed. Jack opened it, switched on the light, and switched it off again. He guessed Sharronda had left when he was asleep.

Jack went back into the living room and sat in the lawn chair. "Now, what can I do for you?" he said.

Blanchard opened the notebook to a blank page. "The American Executive Inn on Stemmons," he said. "You were there when?"

"Last night."

"Until?"

"Last night." He could feel Barton Eskew standing behind him.

"Give me some times," Blanchard said.

"I checked in late afternoon, maybe about six. I was gone by nine or so." Blanchard wrote something. Jack said, "Meshack, what are we talking about here?"

The meaty hand fished a Polaroid print from the same jacket pocket that had held the notebook. "You see this fellow?" Blanchard gave him the picture.

It was a morgue photo of someone on a stainless-steel slab, a man with a thin, youngish face that looked to have been run over by a tank tread. Even with the damage Jack could tell the picture wasn't of Buddy George, Jr.

"Don't know him," Jack said. "He got, what, stuck in the toilet? Jesus."

"He was bobbing for apples," Barton said.

Blanchard took the picture back. "That's how the maid found him. In the room next door to yours."

"Found him when?" Jack said.

Barton Eskew, still behind Jack, said, "Did I hear right? You checked in late afternoon and you're gone by ten? Is that what you said?"

Jack didn't turn around. "You got yourself a sharp one, Meshack."

Blanchard checked his notes. "Now you were in the room from somewheres around six until nine. You hear anything coming from next door? See anybody going in or out?"

Jack took off his shoes and relaxed in the chair. In a few seconds he would begin lying to the police and he figured he might as well be comfortable while doing it. "Not a thing," he said. "Meshack, you have an ID on the deceased? Maybe I've heard of him."

Blanchard shook his head. "One of his names might be Delbert, that's all. He had a tattoo said that. And he had a cast on one arm."

"A dead man named Delbert with tattoos and a broken arm. I'm drawing a blank on that one."

"You live in a place like this," Barton Eskew said from behind him, "I can see why you'd want to sleep in a motel. Why'd you get a room and only stay for three hours?"

"I was waiting. Then I got tired of waiting."

Barton came around to Jack's side and lit a cigarette with a disposable. He was wearing rubber-soled shoes that didn't make any noise on the floor. "You're going to make us ask, right?" The cigarette bobbed in his mouth. "Okay, I'm asking. Waiting for who?"

Jack turned toward him. "Whom. Waiting for whom."

Barton bent down near Jack, bringing the smell of too much English Leather. With his round chinless face and dark little eyes he looked to Jack like a gerbil aspiring to rathood. "Waiting," Barton said, "for what?"

"A woman," Jack said with a shrug in his voice.

"Who was?" Barton said.

"Who was pretty good looking."

Barton's voice grew tighter. "What was her name?"

"Diane. I don't know her last name."

"Oh, that's rich," Barton said. Blanchard glanced up from his notebook with a look that said things were getting interesting. "Meshack, he doesn't know her last name," Barton said.

"Look, there's no big mystery here." Jack sat up and forced a little laugh. "This was a pickup, plain and simple. Friday afternoon I'm having a drink in the hotel bar. I'd been in the neighborhood, I'm having a cocktail, and I meet a lady who's in town on business. I buy her a couple of drinks."

Barton straightened up and walked behind Jack again.

"The lady and I hit it off," Jack said. "We hit it off well enough that I go to the front desk and rent a room. We can't go to hers because she's traveling with somebody else. I come back to the bar with the key, everything's cool, and she says I'll meet you in the room in five minutes. She said she had to get something first."

Jack faked a yawn and stretched. "So," he said, "I do what the lady says. I wait. And I wait, and I wait, and I wait. Three hours later I'm still waiting."

Blanchard looked at him. "That's either a bunch of bullshit," Blanchard said, "or the saddest story I ever heard."

Jack raised his right hand. "Stack of Bibles, Meshack. Eighty-nine dollars for a room and nothing to love but my fist."

"And you're telling us," Barton said, "you can't give us a name."

Jack half-turned toward him. "Diane from Tulsa,

that's all I know. Said she sold computers. A big-haired blonde, about twenty-six, I'd say, wearing a tight blue dress." He shrugged again. "She got cold feet, I guess. It happens."

Barton said, "I find it very interesting that a woman was involved."

And now, Jack thought, the Barton Eskew Show.

Barton moved in front of Jack and looked down on him. "It interested the heck out of me, there's a woman in this. Because I checked up on you, buddy. I made some calls."

"Congratulations."

"I did some checking and guess what I found?"

"Your ass," Jack said, "but it took both hands."

For an instant Barton caught it like a rubber dart between the eyes. Jack wished there was someone around he could slap a high-five with.

"Funny," Barton said when he recovered. "Hilari-ous." He dropped his cigarette butt to the floor and put his heel to it.

Jack watched him do it and said, "Meshack, your man must think he's pumping an interior decorator here. What you gonna do next, Barton, say you don't like my drapes?"

Barton leaned toward him and lowered his voice. "I found out there's a jacket on you at the DA's office. From when you had a job."

Jack watched him talk, the little bastard so excited about his big scoop he might wet his pants.

"Jack Flippo," Barton said. "Hot shit assistant dis-trict attorney. Supposed to prosecute some dirtbag coke dealer, but he's in the sack with the dealer's old lady. Am I right? Not once but multiple times. So the dealer gets to take a walk. Tell me that's not the way it was." Barton gave what Jack figured was his favorite smirk.

"That's the best you got?" Jack said. "That's your best shot?"

"All I know is you humped your way to the dumper."

"Which is where I met you."

"Was it just pussy?" Barton said. "Or was she giving you coke, too?"

Jack came out of his chair, going for Barton. The next thing he knew Blanchard was between them. Meshack moved fast for a big man. "Sit down, Jack," he barked. "Right now. Before you do something grievous. And Barton, you take a break."

"He wouldna done a thing," Barton said, stepping away but screwing his eyes to Jack. "Would you, big man?"

Jack couldn't believe he had let Barton rattle him. In the courtroom he had taken people like that apart all the time, barely breaking a sweat. He was way out of shape.

Blanchard said, "Barton, don't you need to take a leak?"

"No."

"Yes you do. It's all right if Barton uses your rest room, Jack?" Jack nodded. "There you go," Blanchard said. "Now we're all friends again."

Barton sighed and shook his head as he walked to the bathroom. When Jack heard the door shut he said, "What's with that one?"

"He's a fresh face, Jack. Gets a little overexcited."

"I mean, all this stuff about what happened with me and Johnny Hector, that's old news."

"I know it is."

"What am I supposed to do, hear it all again from some busher? Then what—I get so broken up I confess to stuffing a guy in the toilet?"

"He gets a few cases under his belt, he'll settle down."

"I hope so, Meshack. For your sake."

"He'll do all right."

"Well, while he's in there looking for clues in the medicine cabinet, I'll tell you straight. I don't know who deceased your man with the tattoos. I didn't see him, I didn't hear him, and I sure as hell didn't kill him. You can go to the bank with that."

"We just thought you might of seen or heard something."

"Only thing I saw was a roach, Meshack. Eighty-nine dollars a night and they give you roaches."

"And you left when?" Blanchard asked again.

"Nine o'clock Friday night I was gone."

"You checked out?"

"I left the key on the dresser," Jack said. "So if you're thinking can you go to the front desk and see what time I left, no, you can't."

"Come on, Jack."

"I know. Just doing your job."

"That's right," Blanchard said.

Barton came back in the room and stood beside Blanchard with his arms folded, glaring at Jack.

Jack said, "I wish I could help you more, Meshack."

"Me, too." Blanchard rose from the couch and handed Jack a City of Dallas business card. "Call me you hear anything," he said. "I wrote my home phone on there, too. You ready, Barton?"

"You get an ID on your dead man, let me know," Jack said. "I'll put out some feelers."

"Appreciate it," Blanchard said as he led Barton down the steps.

Jack watched their backs and waited for them to shut the front door. His shirt was drenched under the arms and along the back. He pulled it off and walked into the bathroom on legs that seemed a little unsteady, which he supposed happens any time the police drop by to ask you if you killed somebody.

He let the water in the sink run until it turned cold. Then he splashed it on his face, his chest, and his stomach.

Jack wasn't sure what he should do next. What had been a simple job had turned confusing, and then messy. Even if he wanted to walk away from it now, he couldn't. The dead man and the visit from the police had raised the stakes too much.

He figured he had two choices: He could call Meshack Blanchard back, tell him the truth, and let the cops sort it all out. Or he could root around in it himself for a while. He liked the second option. For one thing, it gave him a reason to run down the phony Mrs. George.

Jack gazed into the mirror and wondered where to start. Maybe with some personal hygiene: He hadn't shaved and his hair was matted on one side from the couch. He started to pull a comb through the tangles when he saw something move behind him in the mirror.

Jack spun around and watched as a hand pulled the dark green plastic shower curtain slowly aside.

"Are they gone yet?" Sharronda whispered from the bathtub.

★

Jack made coffee and some toast. Sharronda sat on the couch, Jack on the lawn chair. The swelling on her forehead had melted into a bruise. Jack could see something roiling inside her, but he didn't think it was grief.

"I hate him," she said. "You're supposed to be sorry when people die? I'm not sorry about Delbert."

Jack got up to pull the old paper shades against the afternoon sun, and the dust swimming in the light disappeared. "Let's go back to the beginning here," he said as he sat down. "Way back. That's the only way I'm going to understand this."

She said her name was Sharronda Simms and she was eighteen. She came from Corpus Christi. Almost all her life had been spent in a shingled house with an oyster-shell driveway and a mulberry tree in the front yard. The house was down the street from a refinery. You could always hear the refinery, she said, and always smell it from her house. "People say they get used to the smell and the noise. Not me."

Her mother, she said, waited tables at a diner near the port. She guessed her father still drove a truck. He hadn't come around since she was nine or ten.

"My mama's black and my daddy's white," Sharronda said. "You think that's easy?"

Sharronda left high school at sixteen, went to the cosmetologists' academy, read the want ads in the *Corpus Christi Caller-Times*, and found work at a beauty parlor. She needed money to raise the baby she was expecting.

The baby's name was LaNita, and Sharronda's sister kept her when Sharronda worked. Sharronda, her baby, her sister, her sister's husband, and her mother lived together in the house near the refinery.

"Where's the baby's father?" Jack asked.

"I don't want nothing to do with him," she said.

In April Sharronda met Delbert. "I was in my mama's restaurant one afternoon," she said. "I hate that place, I don't even know why I was there. I had brought my mama something and I was having a Coke before I left. And then here comes Delbert."

She shook her head and wiped at her eyes with the heel of her hand. "I made such a big mistake. I mean, everything I do, it's messed up. I could tell you but you wouldn't believe it, how one person could mess everything up in their life."

"You'd be surprised," Jack said.

"I didn't even know him but he just starts talking to me. Delbert had such a line of BS." Sharronda took a deep breath and crossed one leg under her. Jack drank his coffee. She looked at the toast and said, "You got any peanut butter?"

Jack found it for her and watched her spread it on

the toast and lick the knife. When she finished one piece, Jack said, "So you and Delbert got together."

"He was there working construction at the port. We didn't go out every night but we went out a lot. We had some fun."

"The three of you?" Jack said.

"The who?"

"You, Delbert, and the baby? That's who had fun?"

"My sister kept LaNita."

"You and Delbert had fun, then."

"He was only going to be there for, you know, a little while. After that he was coming back to Dallas. I thought he'd leave Corpus and that would be all. You know, back to the same old life, work and baby."

Jack nodded. Sharronda said, "You think it's bad, right? That my sister kept LaNita and I went out having fun with Delbert."

"Me?"

"The way you're looking at me."

"I don't think anything about it."

"It wasn't like I never was with LaNita. I was with her a lot."

"I'm sure you were," Jack said, on his way to the kitchen for another cup of coffee. When he returned Sharronda was eating more toast.

"The day before Delbert's supposed to leave," she said after swallowing, "he asks me do I want to come to Dallas with him. I'm like, What? He goes, Come to Dallas with me, you can live in my house. He told me when I found a job LaNita could come up, too."

Jack had heard of young girls being lured to Hollywood or New York, but not Dallas.

"I just wanted to get out of there, okay? Delbert

said he had this nice house and I could make good money up here." She played with the ends of her hair and then dropped it. "See, you don't know what it's like to feel trapped somewhere."

"All right, you move here with Delbert. This is what—May?" She nodded. "I'm going to go out on a limb here," Jack said, "and guess that life with Delbert wasn't that great."

"All he did was get high."

"High on what?"

"You name it. If it got Delbert off, he liked it. All the time in Corpus he only drank beer, nothing else. But in Dallas it's him and his friends getting high every night. He wasn't working, neither. Delbert needed money, he'd take mine. He stole all my pay so he could get high."

"So you were working."

"At the Salon d'Elaine. I bring my tips and pay home, Delbert'd slap me and take it."

"Why didn't you leave him?"

"To where? With what? The man stole all my money."

Jack let that hang in the air for a while. Then he said, "Did you kill Delbert?"

She snapped her eyes on him and then dropped her stare after a few seconds. Jack sipped his coffee in the silence while she picked at the couch. Finally she said, "No, but I would say thank you to whoever did."

"And who was that?"

"Probably some drug dealer, I don't know. He followed me, maybe some drug dealer followed him. How I'm supposed to know? You keep asking me questions like I'm supposed to have all the answers.

It's like everybody I meet wants something from me."

He watched her pull her fingers through her hair. "You want what you want," she said. "That old crazy man last night wants me to pull down my pants. The lady that set all this up makes me go in a room with that crazy man but then she doesn't pay me all the money."

Jack had learned never to let them see you react. Confessions, slanders, bombshells—years in court had taught him to keep his face blank as a wall even if he was screaming on the inside. "What does that mean, she doesn't pay you all the money?" he asked with his lawyer voice.

"She didn't pay me last night like she said she would. Then she calls me this morning, says go back to the hotel for the money. That's what Delbert was after."

"What lady?" Jack said.

"Five hundred dollars I was supposed to get. I don't know what happened at the hotel this morning. I hit my head. When I wake up, somebody's having a fight in the bathroom. I'm running fast as I could out of that place."

"What lady?" Jack said.

"When I did her nails the first time we got to talking. I told her about my situation with Delbert and all. She seemed real nice. The second time, that's when she told me about all this money I could make 'cause I'm so pretty. That's what she kept saying, I was so pretty and she had this arrangement."

Jack had to get up and walk around to keep himself calm. "Give me her name," he said. "Everything you know about her."

"She didn't tell me who she was."

"What did she look like?"

"She's old like you. But she had nice clothes and nice rings, and she took good care of her hands and nails. She had nice, thick hair, real long and—"

"Red," they said together.

"How'd you know?" she asked Jack.

"Lucky guess," Jack said. "Now, this woman just says go into the room with this man, mess around with him, I'll pay you five hundred dollars."

"Hey, I'm not a prostitute."

"I know you're not."

"You make it sound like I'm a hooker or something."

"That's not what I meant. I'm just trying to keep the details straight."

"You want to know why I needed that money?" She stood and walked from the couch to the bedroom. "You want to know why? I'll show you."

Jack saw her going through her purse. "That's okay. Really."

She put the purse down and came toward him. "Here," she said and handed him a snapshot. It was a picture of a baby on a bed. "That's LaNita," she said.

"Look, I understand." He gave the picture back. "You don't have to explain."

"I left LaNita with my sister in Corpus, okay? For a little while, only until I got settled here. That was all." She stared at the picture but kept talking. "Then I get a letter from my sister? And she's in some place in California? I'm like, what in the world. Her and her husband and LaNita, something about he got a job there, so they just move and take my baby with them."

"I'm sorry."

"Just moved and didn't tell me anything." She was looking at him again. "That's why I needed five hundred dollars. To go get my baby. So don't talk to me like I'm some kind of whore."

"If you could remember who the lady is," Jack said, "there's a chance I could go to her and get your money for you."

Sharronda slumped back on the couch. "Yeah, right. More promises."

"My point is," Jack said, "you'd do us both a favor if you would try and remember who this woman is."

"I already told you she didn't say her name."

"Well, is there anything you can recall—monograms, her first name on some jewelry, what people called her?"

"No, not really."

"How about her car? Did you see it?"

"Sure, I sat in it."

"Good. What kind?"

"I don't know much about cars. It was big and new, that's about all I remember. And it still had that new car smell on the inside, I remember that." She smiled. "I love that smell. Mm-hmm, leather seats, too."

"A woman in her mid-thirties with a new car," Jack said. "I'll need a little bit more than that."

"Oh, and she had this weird license plate," Sharronda said. "It said uptoo. You know, U-P-T-O-O, I think that's what it was. Like she got it special. What kind of license plate is that? . . . Hey, who you calling?"

22

★

The three of them were in Buddy George, Jr.'s study. Meshack Blanchard told Buddy that he and Barton Eskew were investigating a homicide. He wondered if Buddy could tell him when he had been in Room 333 at the American Executive.

"A homicide, my Lord," Buddy said. "You're saying somebody got killed?"

"That's what homicide means," Barton Eskew said.

"We're looking for someone who might have seen something unusual," Meshack said. "When exactly were you in your room?"

Meshack had his notebook ready, waiting for an answer, wondering how long it was going to take. The man's wife had answered the door when Meshack rang the bell to the George house. She was pleasant enough to them, even if she looked puzzled to find two detectives asking to come in.

Buddy himself seemed to freeze for ten seconds when they introduced themselves in the living room.

Then he pointed his wife toward the kitchen, saying, "I bet these boys are hungry. Go make 'em a pie."

Now Buddy was sitting on the edge of a wing chair in the study, and couldn't keep his hands still. They were small hands, Meshack noted, not bruised or scraped at all, with manicured nails. On his left wrist was a Rolex watch. On the right was a gold bracelet.

"You boys want a drink?" Buddy said.

They shook their heads. "Do you remember," Meshack asked him again, "exactly when you were in your room?"

"My room?"

"Yes, sir," Meshack said.

"I never did go in that room."

"Number three-thirty-three," Barton said. "It was registered to you."

Buddy shifted on the chair and scratched the back of his head. "I'd have to check on that. See, my memory for numbers, well . . ."

"We checked with the hotel," Meshack said. "It was registered to you."

"In fact," said Barton, "they told us that's the room you always get."

Buddy smiled briefly and rubbed his cheek, where Meshack noticed a tiny scratch. "Well, if that's what they said, that must be it. They're fine folks, so I'll trust 'em on that."

"But you're telling us," Meshack said, "that you never went into your own room Friday night."

"Oh, that's not unusual."

"Really," Barton said.

Buddy tried another smile. "See, every time I have a Wayupper at the American—you ever been to a

Wayupper, boys? Do you a world of good. You might think it's just for professional people, but it's not. We get 'em from every walk of life."

Meshack said, "And every time you have one at the American . . . "

"They comp me the room," Buddy said. "Like I said, they're good folks. And sometimes when I really get going, talking to the good people at the Wayupper, I'll need a place to unwind afterwards."

Meshack looked at the framed photographs and certificates that covered two walls. He wondered how one man could find time to shake hands so much.

"I imagine you two feel the same way after a tough day on the job," Buddy said. "A man needs to put his feet up, he needs to relax. Even the plow horse gets some time in the barn, you know."

Barton said, "But last Friday you didn't need to unwind in your room."

"You got it, my friend. Came straight home Friday night. Did my unwinding right where you see me right now, sure did."

"And this morning?" Meshack said. "What about this morning?"

"That's an easy one." Buddy grinned. "I'm at my office every Saturday morning. Me and my staff, nose to the grindstone. When you got your own binness, it don't run itself. Believe that."

"Getting back to the motel," Barton said. "What about the young woman?"

Buddy blinked hard five or six times. "What do you mean?"

"We have a witness that saw a young woman leaving your room Friday night."

Buddy's voice got louder. "Did your witness see me?"

"Sir, that's not what I'm asking," Barton said.

"Then what? Let's lay it out on the table."

"Did you take a young woman," Barton said, "to your room Friday night?"

Buddy stood, moved behind his chair, and opened a cabinet. There was a bottle of Jack Daniel's and some glasses. "I don't understand something about this," Buddy said. He filled up a glass halfway and sat down. "You come into my home, you ask me questions, and I tell you the truth. Then you accuse me of lying."

"No, sir, that's not what we're doing," Meshack said, meeting Buddy's eyes.

"You come into my home," Buddy said, "the one I share with my wife of twenty-six years, my angel, and you come in here to ask me a question like that? You want to know if Buddy George Junior laid on some hot sheets, is that it? You say you're solving a homicide, but then you want to know if Buddy George Junior sailed his wing-wang in the wrong boat."

"No, sir, we don't," Meshack said, watching Buddy take a big swallow of whiskey. "We're just trying to establish some facts."

"Well, I'll establish this for you. I don't know a damn thing about what you're talking about."

"All right," Meshack said.

"And I think you owe me an apology."

Meshack looked at Barton. "I apologize," Barton said in a flat voice.

"Apology accepted." Buddy nodded. "I understand you got a job to do." He finished off the glass.

Meshack decided to speed things up, get this done while the man was still sober. He showed him the photograph of the dead Delbert. "You recognize this individual?"

Buddy put on his glasses. "Good golly, what happened here?"

"That's the victim of the homicide," Barton said.

"Poor fellow . . . No, I don't know him . . . My gosh."

"Mr. George," Meshack said.

"Everybody calls me Buddy."

"Buddy. Is there anybody else who might have had access to your room?"

"Nobody I know of."

"The reason we keep asking about this is, that's where the dead man was found. In room three-thirty-three."

The empty whiskey glass fell from Buddy's hands onto the carpet. He slumped back in the chair, then shook his head slowly. "A housekeeper found him in there late this morning, beaten to death," Meshack said. "White male, mid-twenties. His name might be Delbert."

"Delbert," Buddy repeated.

"That mean anything to you?" Barton asked.

"Boys, this shakes me up, I don't mind telling you that. When did this happen?"

"He hadn't been dead long," Barton said.

"Poor, poor soul," Buddy said and got up to fix himself another drink. "Poor son of a buck. And this gal somebody saw in the room—did she have something to do with it?"

"We're working on several leads," Meshack said.

"Boys, this is scary," Buddy said when he'd filled a fresh glass. "I mean, how . . . what do you think happened here?"

"Hard to say right now," Meshack told him. "It could've been anybody in there. A hotel room key's not the hardest thing to get."

"I'll never go in that room again," Buddy said. "I'll tell you that. Never again, nuh-uh."

"You know, sometimes hookers will work out of empty rooms," Meshack said. "They'll get a master key from the maid and roam the place. Room burglars do the same thing. As I said, we're working several leads, but I can't really discuss them. You have any ideas, we'd be happy to hear them."

Buddy sat down and sighted Meshack over the top of his glass. "Let me ask you boys this. And I don't want you to sugarcoat your answer. I want you to lay it on the line, no bull. About this gal you say was in the room."

Meshack waited. "My question is," Buddy said, "with her on the loose, am I in any personal danger?"

23

★

"What was that all about?" Buddy's wife said when the two detectives had left. "What did they want?" Buddy didn't answer. He went straight to the bedroom for his wallet and his keys. As he walked back through the house toward the garage she asked him, "Where are you going?" He told her he would be back later.

Buddy started the Cadillac, but he couldn't find the remote control for the garage. He blew the horn until his wife opened the door from the kitchen. "Let me out!" he yelled. She leaned around the corner into the garage, pushed a button on the wall, and the overhead door lurched up.

Buddy backed out so fast the tires sang against the concrete. He roared down the alley and pulled into the street without looking, figuring he'd let the other sons of bitches watch out. At the end of the block he ran a stop sign and drove south on Preston.

Two times burglars had broken into his house in

the last five years. The second time they wrecked the place—tossing every drawer, turning over the furniture. They even took a shit on the kitchen floor. The police didn't come close to catching them. Couldn't recover the first piece of stolen merchandise, didn't have a clue in the world. Now here's Buddy trying to handle some personal business on the quiet and the next day detectives are knocking on his door.

It made the anger come crawling up his throat. Buddy snatched the phone and punched Paula's number.

He got her answering machine. She wasn't in right now but please leave a message and have a nice day. Buddy started shouting before the beep. "Goddamnit, I got the police on my butt! Somebody died and now it's raining shit times ten! You hear me, Paula? I want this wrapped up now! You hear me? Now!"

A few minutes later he swung into his parking lot. His space was the first one near the door, marked by the yellow concrete prism stencilled with his name. He was trying to keep himself from throwing up.

Buddy unlocked the door to the three-story mirrored box and crossed the lobby in a hurry, boots slapping on the tile floor. He pressed a button, a bell rang, and the elevator opened right away. Buddy, feeling weak, stepped into a compartment of dark paneling and indirect lighting, and rose silently into the building—his building, Motivational Park Centre.

While the rest of Dallas couldn't give away commercial space, his was full of tenants. On the first floor there was a savings and loan taken over by the feds. The second floor was leased to a data-processing operation. The top floor was filled completely with the offices, the world headquarters, of Motivational Enterprises, Inc.

When the elevator opened at three, Buddy walked past a sculpture, mounted on a column of Lucite, of an arrow pointing up a series of steps. He turned on the lights at a switch near a plaque proclaiming, THE FINEST PEOPLE IN THE WORLD WORK HERE! A few feet down another one said, YOU CAN MAKE THE DIFFERENCE!

And, WINNERS NEVER QUIT! And, NOTHING BEATS ENTHUSIASM! Each sold for $24.95.

As Buddy unlocked his office door he was breathing hard, and his forehead had started to bead cold sweat.

The door had his name in gold letters above the words President and Founder. He shut it behind him and moved unsteadily across the ocean-blue carpet. He'd once heard his assistant, the one he had before Paula, joking to a secretary about the color. Saying, he likes to walk on it and pretend he's Jesus on water. Buddy had fired her on the spot.

Now he reached his big leather desk chair and grabbed it as if it were a life raft. This was a chair that rolled like a dream, like butter melting on hot bread, over the carpet protector. It belonged behind the mahogany desk and in front of the window that gave him a terrific view of the Big D skyline.

Buddy collapsed in it. He had a tightness in his chest and was not getting enough air. The room seemed hot and still. He was afraid he was having a heart attack. He pulled the phone close in case he had to call an ambulance.

The sun had set, leaving nothing but an orange glow on the horizon. The downtown lights had come on in the dusk, and traffic moved below him. Buddy tried to take deep breaths and steady his shaky hands on the smoothness of the desk's leather and mahogany. Telling himself to calm down, to seize the momentum, to stop the strong winds from swamping the canoe.

What they didn't understand, these punks who were trying to back him to the wall, they didn't understand work. They didn't understand effort. If they walked in right how he'd ask them where they were when he was running his business from his garage. When he was putting in twenty-hour days and working every Baptist church supper. When he was selling videos from the trunk of his old car and filling out the mailing labels by hand.

You get the big office, Buddy knew, you get the nice clothes, and everybody wants a piece of you. They're all after something for nothing, looking for the free ride. Buddy sat in his big chair and imagined himself giving advice to these shakedown artists. Telling them, Listen here: A man who has climbed from the bottom to the top will do absolutely anything to keep from falling back down.

After ten minutes or so most of the tightness had left his chest. He was still sweating some and fighting the shakes, but he no longer feared he was about to die. Time to do what he had to do.

From a drawer he pulled a bottle of Jack Daniel's and a coffee cup, and put them on the desk. From the drawer below that Buddy took a metal strongbox and set it on his knees. He found the key he needed on his ring, opened the box, and removed stacks of bills by the handful.

Most of them were tens and twenties, with an odd

five or fifty among them. He counted them all twice, and wrote "$22,550" on a sheet of memo paper. The paper said "More Good News From Buddy George Jr." across the top.

Next Buddy crossed the blue carpet and opened the door to a closet. He parted two hanging Western shirts and twisted the dial on a wall safe. Using one hand to steady the other, he whispered the combination as he turned the dial. The handle clicked and yielded when Buddy pulled on it, and the thick door swung open noiselessly. Inside the bills were neatly piled, bound with red rubber bands in packets of $1,000 each.

Buddy ferried them from the closet to the desk. When that was done, he counted everything he had. The lockbox and the safe together came to $130,000 and change.

The money was spread across his desk, with the smell of it seeming to fill up the room. He drank half a cupful of whiskey and gazed on the bills, running his fingers over them and riffling the stacks.

For years he had been stuffing cash from the Wayuppers into his pockets, and this was the result. He had taken about $100 each time, maybe a little more, but not enough to make a problem in the books. It was tax-free profit, yet that wasn't really the point.

Unless you grew up poor, Buddy always told himself, you could never know what it was like to need money and not be able to touch it. Every now and then he had to take his own money out and put his hands on it, rub it, feel the way it felt, know it was there.

In West Texas he had known farmers who would, Sunday evenings after church, go out and walk their fields. They would pace slowly up and down their rows of cotton, walking in the gathering dark, just to feel their own land beneath their own feet. It was the same thing.

24

★

Paula stepped from the shower onto a soft rug and reached through the steam for a towel. She dried herself and dropped the towel to the floor. Her hand squeaked against the mirror as she rubbed a circle clear of condensation. She combed her wet hair with long, firm strokes.

The whole time she was thinking about what she would do if she had to run away from Dallas that night or the next day, what she would leave and what she would take, where she would go, how she would cover herself.

She slipped on a white silk robe and went to the kitchen, where she poured herself a straight gin on the rocks. The red light on her answering machine was blinking. It could be Teddy saying he had found Sharronda. It could be Teddy announcing he had killed somebody else by mistake.

Three swallows of gin and she pushed the button and closed her eyes as the tape rewound. After the machine beeped she heard Buddy shouting about the police and a rain of shit and how he wanted some-thing done now.

Paula rewound the tape and played it once more, listening to the absolute fear. She played it again and imagined the way his face had looked all twisted in panic. What surprised her was how suddenly clear and calm it left her. Paula listened to Buddy and thought: I've got him.

She turned off the lights and sat in the dark of the kitchen, thinking. In about half an hour the phone rang, and she was ready.

"Hello," she said. There was no answer. "Hello?"

"Paula, we got a problem." It was Buddy, his voice like a dead battery. "This mess has taken a bad turn." She had never heard him like this, with nothing to sell. She had never heard him pause after only two sentences. "Are you there, Paula?" he said.

"I'm here."

"Because things have been double-dipped in shit."

"What is it?"

"One minute you're feasting at the big buffet, then you turn around and it's coffee grounds and chicken bones. You know what I mean?"

Paula was thinking of when she first met Buddy, when she was his motel room entertainment for a few weeks. After Buddy would order her to strip and lie on the bed, and after he had finished giving him-self the business, he would primp before the mirror. She remembered the way he would stand there naked, flexing his arms and chest, saying, "Not bad, you think?" And, "Looking good, I do believe." He did have a decent body for his age. But what always got her was the way his testicles sagged while he stood there posing. It made her think of two bowling balls in a plastic garbage bag.

That was the way she envisioned him now: naked by the phone, sad voice and saggy balls.

"You know what I mean?" he asked again.

"Yes, Buddy."

"Things can change fast. You spend years building a binness, growing up a reputation, and some asshole takes it in a minute."

She wondered how many drinks he had had. Buddy wasn't a drunk, but when he grew tense he could put away too much. "What happened?" she said. "Tell me, Buddy."

"Paula, when an eagle dies the buzzards eat."

"If you don't tell me what the problem is, I can't help you. Can I."

"Didn't you get my message?" He seemed hurt that she didn't already know. "I called and left a message. Didn't you get it?"

"I haven't checked my machine yet."

Buddy sighed long and slow. "Today, Paula, the police came to my house. Two detectives, asking me questions. In *my house*."

"The police?" Paula said.

"Listen very carefully, Paula. Someone was killed in my room at the American. They found a man in the bathroom, all beat up and deadern a rock. I saw a picture . . . "

"What? You can't be—who?"

"They don't know. Paula, this whole thing is out of control."

"Oh, God . . . Do the police suspect you? Since they came to your house . . . "

"You think they had something on me, I'd be sitting here talking to you? Hell, no. They'd haul my butt down to a jail cell. You'd have big headlines, TV news, everything. Buddy George Junior arrested for murder."

"Who do they think did it, then?"

"They said they got some leads, that's all I know."

"Then we have to move fast," Paula said. She loved the way her bare feet felt on the cool tile floor. The contractor had been ready to put down linoleum, but at the last minute Paula had sprung for the Mexican tile, and it made all the difference, worth every penny. "We can't waste any time," she said.

"You're goddamn right we can't." Anger was putting some life back into his voice.

Paula had the diamond in her center and the combinations whirling in her head. "You see what they're doing, don't you?" she asked him. "I'm talking about these blackmailers. They're saying, 'Let's turn up the heat and see if Buddy George Junior boils over.' They're the ones who put the body there, Buddy. Can't you see that? They're raising the stakes."

"They want to play with the big dogs now, don't they, Paula? They kill a man and send the police my way."

"Exactly, Buddy."

"But who would they kill? That's what I don't get."

She hadn't been ready for that one and had to scramble. "Well, Buddy, you can imagine what they did, can't you? I mean . . . well, think about it. They probably got some homeless person, or a drug addict, somebody that nobody will miss. And they killed him to scare you. Can't you see that?"

"Cold-blooded, Paula."

"You know what they're going to do next, Buddy. They're going to demand more money."

"Bet the ranch they will," Buddy said.

"They'll probably threaten to frame you on this murder. That's what I'm guessing."

"Me too, Paula. Me too."

"See, Buddy, they realized their little tape and pictures scheme wasn't working. They didn't count on you being so strong. Now they're trying to trap you some other way. We've got to stop them."

"You know what the wolf does when his foot's caught in a trap? He gnaws it off, Paula. You know what Buddy George Junior does, his foot's caught? He chops it off. Then Buddy George Junior gets the son of a bitch that set the trap and makes him sorry he was born."

They were both quiet for a moment. One more leap to make, Paula thought, the biggest one.

"Buddy," she said, "I have some good news for you."

"I'm dying for good news, Paula."

"We know who they are."

"You do? *You do?*"

"Teddy and I have been working on this. We know the two people involved—the man who took the pictures and the girl."

"Yeah? Goddamn, now you're talking, Paula."

"We know who they are. We know where they live. I've got Teddy watching their house, and as soon as they show up we'll know right where they are."

"We'll have 'em by the short hairs."

"They've got to be taken care of, Buddy."

"Goddamn right."

"They can't be allowed to bleed you dry."

"I want 'em handled," Buddy said. "I want 'em gone."

"So do I. And I can get it done. Let me handle this, Buddy. It's best for you not to be involved. We've got Teddy. Let's use him."

"Teddy? We're talking about the big fellow with the clothes? I don't know, Paula."

It flies or dies right here, Paula thought. "It's the absolute best way," she said.

"Can we trust this boy? Where did he come from? He's just someone showed up in our office one day trying to steal money."

"That's the beauty of it, Buddy. He's nobody. He's a mercenary. He has no connection to us whatsoever. We give him a job to do, he does it, we pay him, it's done."

"Will he do it?"

"For the right money he will. I've talked to him about it. He wants fifty thousand dollars, Buddy. That's a lot of money, I know. But your problems will be over."

There was a long silence on the other end. Finally Buddy said, "Desperation makes a man do desperate things, Paula. I never thought I'd find myself capable of something like this."

"They forced you to do it, Buddy."

"Never in my wildest nightmares."

"They made you. You didn't go after them. They came after you. They set out to destroy you, Buddy."

"If this fails, Paula . . . " He stopped. "If this fails we're all caught. You know that. It'll be the end of the highway for all of us."

"It won't fail," she said. "You've got to trust me, Buddy. After all we've been through, you've got to trust me now."

*　　*　　*

When she finished with Buddy, Paula fixed herself another drink. She felt as if she had fallen down a dark shaft and landed in a bed with silk sheets.

The first thing she thought about doing was nothing at all. Just go into Buddy's office the next day and say, Everything's taken care of, that'll be fifty thousand, please. Tell him, these people will never bother you again. Let his imagination do all the work.

There was no reason to mess with the man who had taken the photographs. She tried to remember his name—Jack something. He was obviously out of the flow at this point, a minor character Buddy's mind had inflated into a player. She never expected to see him again.

Sharronda could be a problem. If she had any sense she would have left town by now. But there was no guarantee of that. She could resurface with her own tale to peddle, or if she were scared enough she could run to the police. Sharronda knew who Buddy was, and she was a link to the dead man.

There was only one safe thing to do, Paula decided. Sharronda had to go.

★

Once Jack had the woman's license plate, tracking her was easy. He phoned Bill Willacy, an investigator at the DA's office, still a friend. Bill Willacy said he would make some calls from his home and get back. Fifteen minutes later he did. Texas UPTOO, Bill Willacy said, was registered to a 1991 Lincoln Town Car owned by Paula Fontaine, of 1309 Fishburn in Dallas. He ran Delbert's record, too: a public intoxication conviction, two arrests for possession of a controlled substance and an aggravated assault.

You're a prince, Jack said. He would have called the public library next, but it was Saturday night. So he phoned the city desk at the *Morning News* instead, talked sweetly, and persuaded a clerk to look up Paula Fontaine in the criss-cross directory for him. The clerk put him on hold for a minute and came back with the information that Miss Fontaine was listed as an executive vice president of Motivational Enterprises, Inc.

Jack set the phone down and looked at Sharronda. She was in the kitchen making more toast. "I have an idea," Jack said.

"Don't go outside," Jack told her before he left. "Don't answer the door, don't answer the phone. If it rings, let it ring. The machine'll get it."

"Okay," Sharronda said, not sounding sure. "How long I have to stay in this house?"

"Whoever took care of Delbert is probably looking for you, that's my guess."

"Okay."

"Not to mention the cops might come back. They put you together with Delbert, this whole thing burns to the ground. Us, too."

"But you think you can get my money?"

"I have this funny feeling."

She stretched out on the couch. "I'll wait right here. When you come back you can put the money next to me and we can count it."

"Good, clean fun," Jack said.

He walked downtairs and into the hot night. The Buick fired up right away, and he backed into an empty street. Jack drove west, making a list of the things he didn't know.

He didn't know who had killed Delbert, or why. Someone like Delbert, it could have been anybody. He didn't know why Paula Fontaine had framed Buddy George, Jr., though money would be the odds-on favorite. He didn't know how much of what Sharronda had told him was trustworthy, but figured he would soon find out.

He started to tell himself he didn't know why he

was getting involved, but he knew that wasn't true. First, there was the matter of the police breathing on him. If nothing else, he might stumble on something that could point them some way other than his. Second, there was this Paula Fontaine.

His brother, Jeff, could have doped it all out in a few minutes, could have made it look easy. Jefferson Flippo, the smartest criminal defense lawyer you'd ever need. The name was legend among the sleaze of Dallas: You had enough money, Jeff Flippo could almost always find a way to get you off.

He was fifteen years older than Jack and had had his own firm for a dozen years by the time Jack got out of law school. They had never been that close, given the age difference, but when Jack passed the bar Jeff offered him a job. Jack thought about it for a couple of weeks and then said yes.

It was scutwork for the most part. Jack put in long hours doing research for Jeff and the other two partners, taking papers to the courthouse, proofreading, keeping a leash on some clients, tracking court dates. Three months into the job, as Jack was about to go home around ten, Jeff called him into his office.

Jeff wore Italian suits and drove a Jag. He got his hair cut at a salon and didn't smile so much as bare his teeth. He lived in Bent Tree with a leather-pants blonde who used to be a Cowboys cheerleader. You'd look at him and never guess his father had been a welder.

"So," Jeff said, "how's the job?"

"Great so far," Jack answered.

"Good. Everybody treating you okay?"

"Everybody's been nice."

"I see you've been putting in the hours."

"I don't mind. It's what I expected."

Jeff seemed to think this over for a few seconds. Then he said, "By my count there are two attractive, single women working here. That's Tobie the paralegal and Lisa the receptionist. Have I left anybody out?"

"Don't think so."

"Good. Now of those two, how many have you hit on?"

"Um," Jack said, "just Tobie."

Jeff nodded. "Tobie. That's nice. The two of you went out, did you?"

"Yes."

"Had a nice time?"

Tobie, it was not hard for Jack to recall, liked to scream when she had an orgasm. "I think so."

"Well, I should have told you when you came to work here." Jeff leaned back in his chair and put one foot, inside one expensive shoe, on the corner of his desk. "We have a rule in this firm. Don't hump the help."

Jack laughed. "Don't hump the help. You have a cite on that?"

Jeff showed him the teeth. "Tobie's always looked like a nice way to spend the evening to me. But I don't want lovers' spats screwing up the office. Practicing law's hard enough without having to sort that crap out."

Jack kept smiling. "You're telling me it's my job or Tobie."

"I'm telling you what our rules are."

He looked around Jeff's office, taking in the view of the bank buildings and the freeways. Jack hadn't been in it since the day he accepted the job. It was five times the size of the windowless cubicle he had been given. "Okay. No more Tobie."

"Good." Jeff pulled his foot off the desk. "Now that we've got that settled, let's celebrate your three-month anniversary with the firm." He took a small plastic bag from a drawer and poured some white powder from it onto his leather desktop.

Jack leaned forward and stared. "What are you doing, Jeff?"

"Just got this from a client yesterday." Jeff formed the powder into four white lines, then licked his finger. "Richard Francis, securities fraud. You worked his file yet?" He got a bill from his wallet, rolled it and offered it to Jack. "Help yourself."

"No, thanks."

"Supposed to be good. Slick Ricky never did me wrong yet."

Jack said, "Jesus Christ, Jeff. You won't let people in the office date but coke's okay?"

"Hey, I'm not passing it out to the secretaries. I thought you might want a blow."

"Not for me."

Jeff made a face. "Jack the Boy Scout. When did this happen?"

"It has nothing to do with that, Jeff. I just don't like the stuff."

"To each his own. Have to say, I figured you for the type." Jeff put the bill to the powder and inhaled two lines.

"What type is that?"

Jeff shook his head, looked at the ceiling, and said, "Memo to Ricky Francis. Outstanding shit."

Jack said, "What do you mean, I'm the type?"

Jeff sniffed a few times, cleared his throat, and

wiped his eyes. "Remember I'd come and watch you play basketball when you were in high school?"

"Sure."

"Not every time, but a few times."

"Uh-huh."

"After Dad died."

"I remember, Jeff."

"I'd sit with Mom in the stands and watch our boy, Wildcat forward Jackie Flippo."

"Number fifteen."

"Two things I noticed about you on the court." Jeff made the other two lines disappear. "Very nice blow."

Jack said, "You think that's enough coke?"

"Two things I noticed," Jeff said, talking faster. "One, you spent too much time looking at the cheerleaders." Jack thought about Roberta Linn and how it felt on Friday nights, putting his hands up that little red and gray pleated skirt. "The second thing," Jeff said, "the only time you were any good was when your team was losing."

Jack laughed. "Right."

"No, I mean it, Jack. You'd be out on the floor when you guys had the lead, and you looked like the dumbest player I ever saw. I'd tell Mom, goddamn Jackie's sleepwalking out there. But then your team'd fall behind, and you were a different man. Like somebody'd flipped a switch, Jack. You'd throw elbows if you had to. You'd go to the hole, you'd grab boards. You *loved* putting the fake on other players, I could tell that. But you only played hard when you were behind."

"I liked the challenge." Jack shrugged.

"You liked the rush, you mean. You liked being on the edge with nothing left to do but fight."

"Maybe so."

"All in all, not a bad thing for an attorney. I mean somebody doing trial work, not some jerk in tax law. You go hand to hand in the courtroom, you have to know how to get up off the mat and scrap like hell."

Jeff turned to the stereo on the shelf behind him and put in a Warren Zevon tape. "Of course, you dig yourself too much of a hole to begin with, you got a problem. Can't be too stupid about it. You have to know when to start your kick."

"I'll remember that," Jack said.

"Free advice from someone who's learned the hard way . . . Anyway, that's why I figured you for someone might do a little coke."

"Sorry."

"I would say I admire your virtue," Jeff said. "But I'm sure you have compensating vices."

They talked for a few more minutes. As Jack left, Jeff was lining up more cocaine on his desktop, bouncing to the music and saying, "Thank you, Slick Ricky."

Jack worked at his brother's firm another six or seven weeks. He never had another long talk with Jeff. One of the partners, unable to raise Jeff on the phone late one night, went to his office. He knocked, got no answer, and let himself in. Jeff lay on the floor, rolled-up bill still in his hand. Coronary arrest, the medical examiner ruled, attributable to cocaine.

After the funeral the partners told Jack he was welcome to stay on, but he said no, he couldn't stand to be around the place. Couldn't take having to walk by Jeff's old office every day and think about what happened.

The District Attorney's office made him an offer and

Jack accepted. Soon he married Kathy, a pretty girl who taught school, and they bought a three-bedroom brick ranch-style on a cul-de-sac in Farmers Branch. It had a fireplace in the living room, an all-electric kitchen with a self-cleaning oven, and a walk-in closet in the master bedroom. The master bath had two sinks. Kathy put little sweet-smelling soaps, shaped like shells and roses, in a basket between them.

Jack kept a lawn mower and a Weed Eater in the two-car garage. He owned half a dozen department-store suits, and Kathy told him which tie to wear every morning so the colors matched. No children yet, but they had talked about it. It wouldn't be hard, looking at them, to imagine a couple of kids soon. Easy to see them all in a minivan, leaving church on a Sunday noon for lunch at Wyatt's Cafeteria.

In the meantime Kathy and Jack made friends, young couples like themselves. They got together most weekends, had a great time, you would think, from all the conversation and laughter.

The men especially: standing around the hamburgers on the grill, drinking beer, talking sports and jobs and yard work, laughing loud. But Jack felt it, and he thought the others did, too. They never said it outright, but you could see it in their eyes and sometimes hear it in what they didn't say. It was hard to know what to do when you wanted steadiness in your life, needed an anchor, and at the same time you were bored to death by it. You were a young man at a backyard barbecue, and all that adventure was out there somewhere, passing you by.

Jack found the Rangers game on the Buick's radio. They were losing. He crossed North Central on Knox

Street, rumbled over the railroad tracks, and then ascended into Highland Park. The mansions glided by left and right until he reached Turtle Creek.

Here was some of the most beautiful parkland in the city, with woods, cliffs, water, meadows, and flowers. What it didn't have were playgrounds and ballfields. You had a picnic, you broke the law. Same thing if you fished or swam. That way, the people in the projects wouldn't pile into their heaps and drive over for the afternoon.

Past the creek there were more mansions until Jack rolled across Oak Lawn, back in the land of people who made car payments. A left turn and a right and he found himself gazing at Paula Fontaine's house. It was a white bungalow with a big live oak in the front yard. On one side was a frame house with a stove abandoned on the front porch. The other neighbor was a half-finished townhouse ringed by a chainlink fence. The bank probably owned it now. This was one of those neighborhoods that people had talked about fixing in the eighties, which meant out with the old poor and in with the young affluent. Like a lot of other things in Dallas, that plan had run out of gas.

Jack parked on the street, crossed the yard, and climbed three steps to the bungalow's concrete porch. The light over the front door was off, but there was a glow through the shades from inside. A warm breeze stirred some bamboo wind chimes hanging a few feet away and Jack thought he smelled wisteria. He knocked three times.

The tiny spot of yellow that was the front door peephole darkened, and in a moment the porch light came on. Jack looked at the door's little glass bubble, and at the eye behind it staring out at him, and smiled.

The bolt clicked, she opened the door. "Miss Fontaine," Jack said, holding the smile. "Remember me? Jack Flippo."

She looked past him, toward the car, and then at him. Her face told him nothing. Finally she said, "I remember. Best keyhole man in the business." She wore a white silk robe and, as far as Jack could tell, nothing else. There was a drink in her hand, something clear with a twist. Jack breathed in and smelled the gin.

"It's a beautiful evening," he said, "and I was in the neighborhood . . . "

"Yes?" she said and sipped her drink.

"It's about Sharronda Simms," Jack said.

"Come in," she told him.

The living room had a bleached cow skull and Indian paintings on the walls, and some Navajo rugs and a cactus in a clay pot on the wood floor. The shelves and coffee table held a dozen or so polished rocks. Jack sat in the middle of a white couch. The woman dropped smoothly into an armchair. She crossed her legs and the robe rode up her thigh. "About Sharronda Simms," she said. "You were saying."

"Our mutual acquaintance."

"But you didn't bring her with you."

"She's resting."

"She sent you?"

Jack could make out faint freckles on Paula Fontaine's chest tumbling down into her robe. "Sharronda's my client," he said.

"You're working for her now?" The woman laughed once.

Jack cleared his throat. "Can we establish something first? A few facts, like your name. It is Paula Fontaine? As opposed to, say, Mrs. Buddy George?"

"Mm-hmm. So where is Sharronda?"

"Resting," Jack said. "Now, you are employed by George's company?"

"That's right." The woman sipped from her glass. Jack watched her throat when she swallowed. She said, "I'm Buddy's second in command. And you? When you're not making tapes in hotel rooms?"

"I'm an attorney," Jack said. "On leave from the profession."

"So I heard."

A man said something like that to you, Jack thought, he was pissing on you. Then it was up to you to piss back. With women, it could mean two or three or seven different things, depending on which way you turned it to the light.

Paula said, "What is it Sharronda wants, exactly?"

"Her money."

"I'll pay her, I'm ready to pay."

"That's why I'm here. One reason, anyway."

"I'll pay her," Paula said, "but I need to see her. Otherwise, how do I know it's going to Sharronda?"

Jack managed to take his eyes from her, like pulling a magnet off iron, and looked around the room, searching for the trace of another man. He saw no pictures of a happy couple on the shelves with the rocks, and no size-eleven shoes by the door. At the end of the hall the bathroom door was open and the light on. He stared hard, trying to see if only one toothbrush hung over the sink.

"Don't you think so?" she said.

"What?"

"I think I should pay Sharronda in person."

Jack studied the shadows of her robe until he realized she was watching him watch her. "You know," he said, "there are easier ways to steal money."

"Excuse me?"

"Why didn't you just take your friend Buddy's wallet? Or tap his petty cash fund? You're there in the office, aren't you? It can't be that hard."

She shifted in her chair. "You don't know what you're talking about."

"Maybe not. But I'll tell you, I've met a lot of people who got caught chasing someone else's money." He waited while she turned the glass upright and got the last swallow. "When I was with the DA, I prosecuted one guy who worked for the school district. On the side, his part-time job, he was robbing convenience stores all over town. The last one he hits he's still wearing his employee ID on his pocket, and he can't figure out why the cops are waiting for him when he gets home. A lot of them were like that, just stupid."

The woman blinked once, slowly. "But," Jack said, "every now and then you run across someone too smart about it. You can trip when you make things too complicated, you know. It's like you want some chicken noodle soup, so you design a nuclear can opener."

A clock in the back of the house chimed ten times. "My favorite time of night," Jack said. "And that drink looks good."

★

Teddy had showered, shaved, brushed his teeth, flossed, gargled, rolled on some deodorant, moussed his hair, clipped his nails, sprinkled on cologne, and trimmed his nose hairs. It improved his mood a little, but not much. His butt still hurt from the tetanus shot and his finger still ached from slamming into the hotel faucet. Plus the cleaners had not been sure they could remove Delbert's blood from his shirt. A $150 piece of clothing ruined by the dogman—Teddy would've had to kill him if he hadn't killed him already.

Just after nine Teddy got a call from Mark Jolly, who lived in the same North Dallas apartment complex, Timberpark Hill, which was nowhere near timber, park, or a hill. Mark Jolly liked to hang out at the Timberpark health club and pool. "Hey, man, get your ass down here," he said when Teddy answered. "There's about ten bitches poolside." Teddy told Mark Jolly he had to work. It fouled his mood even more.

Teddy caught the last few minutes of an install-

ment of "The Hitchhiker" while he slipped on his
shoes. It had been one of his favorite shows when
you could watch it on HBO. You could always count
on a couple of skin shots every episode. Now another
cable outfit was showing the reruns but cutting out
all the naked parts. Sometimes it seemed to Teddy
that standards were dropping everywhere. Like with
"The Newlywed Game," which used to have Bob
Eubanks as host. The greatest MC in the world, as far
as Teddy was concerned. Then they came out with
"The New Newlywed Game," but no Bob Eubanks.
Instead you got some Puerto Rican clown Teddy
wanted to stomp on the basis of his hair alone.

Within a half hour he was on the road, going east
on Northwest Highway and then south on LBJ. He
was headed toward Pleasant Grove because that's
where the redhead had told him to go. He was five or
six miles out when he pounded the dash and yelled,
"Fuck!" The piece of paper he needed, the one with
directions to the house he was supposed to stake out,
was back in his apartment. Teddy started to get off
LBJ and turn around when he remembered he had
put Delbert's wallet in his glove box. So something
good had come from flushing the dogman after all.

Teddy exited on Military Parkway and pulled into
a convenience store with a potholed parking lot.
Inside he chose a pack of spearmint gum and a roll of
Certs, putting them on the counter in front of the
clerk. She was a scrawny thing with bad teeth and
dirty hair, but Teddy saw that she wore a wedding
band. He was sure it had to be a fake because no man
would touch a nightmare like that.

Teddy looked at Delbert's driver's license and said,
"Where's Burnell Street?"

"Um," she said, twisting her face and turning her eyes toward the ceiling.

After a few seconds Teddy made the sound of a buzzer. "Time's up," he said. He scooped up the gum and the mints, put them in his coat pocket, and walked out without paying.

A half mile down the road, at another small grocery, Teddy found an old man sitting on a stool behind the counter, watching the ball game on a small TV.

"Yo, where's Burnell Street?" Teddy asked him.

"Burnell Street. Burnell Street," he said. "That's a good question. I'll have to study that one. Burnell Street."

"We're wasting time here." Teddy was thinking, At least in New York they tell you to get fucked right away, but down here they kill you with the slow stupids. "You know where it is? Yes or no?"

The man waved a hand toward a rack of kung fu videos. "I believe it's right down Military about two mile. Keep her going the way you was if you was going east, and turn left at the Piggly Wiggly. I believe that's it. You can't miss it."

"Now I need a phone book," Teddy said.

"You want the yellow or the white pages?"

"White."

"I believe all we got is the yellow."

"Gimme the white," Teddy said.

"I'll have to check, see if we got the white." The old man climbed off his stool and rummaged under the counter. Teddy put a keychain, some Tictacs, another pack of gum, and a set of Batman trading cards in his coat pocket. "We got the white residential but not the white commercial," the man said from below the counter.

Even though his hand still ached, Teddy nabbed a pair of sunglasses from a rotary display and a pack of Velamints. "I'll take the white residential," he said.

The man stood up and placed the directory on the counter. "Don't know what happened to them white commercial pages," he said.

Teddy looked at Delbert's license again and flipped through the book. "Where's your phone?" he said.

"Outside. Cost you a quarter."

He found the page he wanted and tore it from the directory. As he walked out the old man told him, "Come see us again, now."

Teddy wiped the pay phone down with a moist towelette and called the number for Delbert Beauchamp, 2229 Burnell. Twenty rings and he got no answer.

The street he wanted was just past the Piggly Wiggly, right where the old man said it would be.

★

Paula came across the floor toward him, her feet bare on the bleached wood, and handed Jack a full, cold glass. He thanked her as she floated into her chair with a whisper of silk. She had fixed a fresh one for herself, too. She took a sip and licked her lips sleepily.

This was his second drink. Gin always made him feel as if his head were being ventilated, like a convertible racing with the top down on a cool night. "What was I talking about?" he said.

"Your former job," she answered. Midway through Jack's first drink they had stopped interrogating each other long enough to try something that approached conversation. Paula had told him she had worked for Buddy George for about a year. She was the equivalent of his chief of staff, she said, which meant fifteen-hour days.

Jack had a lot of questions about that but he laid them aside while he told her about working at the district attorney's office. He even explained why he left—the whole story, his affair with Marla Kendrick, everything.

"I do impulsive things sometimes," Jack said. "It can be a problem."

"Me too," she said. "I left my husband one night and never went back." They both drank their gin. He waited for her to say more about it, but she didn't.

"I like your house," Jack finally said. "The way you've decorated it, very nice."

She seemed pleased. "You like Santa Fe style?"

"Sure. Though I've never been to Santa Fe," Jack said. "I spent the night in Alamogordo once. That's about as close as I've come. I went to question a witness the locals had arrested."

He couldn't stop looking at the way the hem of her robe was, after she crossed her legs, inching up her thigh.

"I remember the strangest thing happened that night," he said. "I couldn't sleep, which is nothing new, so I got up and drove around town for a while. Eventually, I stopped at this tavern, I forget the name, a joint. Had a country-western jukebox and a lot of antlers above the bar, I remember that."

He and Paula were about six feet apart. "I've been in those places," she said.

"I was standing at the bar," Jack said, "having a drink or two, and I notice the girl two stools down from me crying. Not sobbing, just a few quiet tears dropping onto the cocktail napkin. I mean, you got George Jones on the jukebox and a pretty girl crying all alone in a bar in Alamogordo, New Mexico. We're talking real life here."

"I know what you mean," she said. He noticed for the first time that her toenails were polished red.

"So we strike up a conversation. She's only twenty-three but she's had this rough, rough life. A couple of bad marriages, money problems, dead-end job with a bad boss. I kind of touched her on the shoulder and told her everything'll be okay."

Paula nodded.

"Then," Jack said, "she asks me if I have a car. I say, yeah, I have a car. She says, let's go talk in the car, it's too loud in here. The next thing we're in the front seat of my rental, kissing each other. Then she begins to cry again. I brush her hair aside with my finger and she pulls both my hands to her face. She bends over, her head's almost in my lap and she's just sobbing away. One of her hands is rubbing my thigh, though, and I'm beginning to wonder where this will all end."

"I think I know."

"Now this is the strange part," Jack said. "She sits straight up all of a sudden and says, I can't do this, I can't do this to you, I can't. I say, Do what? She says, I can't pull you into my life. So she wipes her eyes, opens the door, and she's gone, that's it. Just gone without another word, the party's over."

Jack shrugged and grinned.

Paula smiled faintly. "She stole your watch."

"What?"

"Or your wallet. Your watch or your wallet, one or the other, right? When she had her head in your lap she stole them."

"She didn't steal anything. She just left."

Paula sipped from her drink, then tossed her hair. "So why did you tell me that?"

"We were talking about New Mexico, that's all. It was just a story about New Mexico."

They studied each other for a few moments. "You

mentioned Sharronda," Paula said. "I was wondering how you two met. Since you seem to like stories, I'd love to hear that one."

"I think I told you we were old friends."

"I think you did."

"The truth is, I only met her last night when your pal Buddy knocked her around."

"So you're the one."

"I guess so."

"You're the hero."

"How do you think it looks to the police, he kills her while I listen in from the next room? I think it looks like heavy grief for me."

She uncrossed her legs. "Buddy wouldn't have killed her."

"How do we know this?"

"He would have stopped after a while. He always does."

Jack stored that one away. "So this is kind of a hobby of his."

"You don't understand."

"You could explain." Jack smiled. "You talk and I'll watch."

There was a half minute or so of silence while she wiped the sweat from her glass with two fingers making slow downward strokes. "I would not want to interrupt," she said when she finished, "the fascinating account you just started."

Jack took a deep breath and let it out. "There's not much to tell," he said.

"I'll take what I can get. For example, where she is."

"She's around. We're in touch. It's sort of an agent-client relationship."

"You're working for her."

"No. I'm doing some work for her, I guess you could say. Look, she doesn't mean anything to me. I'm doing this because—well, for one thing, she's had a pretty tough time of it, trying to get her kid back and all that, so I thought she could use some help."

"Kid?" Paula said, eyebrows up.

Jack gave her the version of Sharronda's story as he knew it. Paula said, "And you believed that?"

"What did she tell you, then?"

"She told me something different."

Her eyes seemed to take him and pull him in. They were light gray streaked with yellow. The color reminded Jack of a spring dawn, and of arsenic.

He told her, "You know, I thought you really were Buddy George's wife. This morning I went to his house looking for you. Rang the doorbell, hoping you would open up."

"I wasn't there," Paula said.

"Which I was sad to learn."

"But now you've found me." She leaned forward to scratch her ankle. Jack got the whole show down the loose front of her robe.

"Yes, I have," he managed to say. "I've found you."

"All that seems a lot of work," she said, "just to help out some girl who may or may not have lost her kid in California."

"There was more to it."

"What would that be?"

"As I said"—he paused and finished his drink—"I've found you."

The gray and yellow eyes drifted over him, taking their time. Then she rattled the ice in her glass. "Let's have another," she said and stood without a lot of trouble.

Jack got up and followed her into the kitchen, watching the way she moved under the silk. He felt like one of those characters in a black-and-white Western who gets tangled in the reins and dragged by a runaway horse.

The kitchen was uncluttered and clean, with black countertops and a stainless-steel sink. Not the type of place, Jack thought, where you find granny baking bread. "You said you left your husband," he said. "Are you married now?"

She sliced a lime with a paring knife. "Not anymore."

"Me either."

"I gathered that." She put more ice in the glasses and poured in the gin. "I'm out of tonic," she said.

"Better than being out of gin."

When she handed him his glass she stayed close. "I'd like to talk to Sharronda," she said. "I'd like to settle things with her."

"We could work that out." Jack was near enough to her now that he could smell the perfume again.

"We could reach an arrangement," she said.

"I'd like that. An arrangement."

She moved half a step closer to him.

"Where do you put it?" Jack said, setting his drink on the counter. "The perfume. On your wrist or your neck?" He touched the robe at her collarbone.

"And other places," she said.

He moved his finger up the side of her neck and to the bottom of her ear. She closed her eyes. With his other hand Jack pulled gently on the sash tied at her waist. It came free and the robe fell open.

Bo Harrison, the Ace of Places, had been right. Some jobs did have excellent benefits.

★

The house was dark, the door unlocked. So easy to get in that it started a song going in Teddy's head. *Walk right in, sit right down, baby let your something, something* . . . The hell was the rest? Now he would go crazy all night, trying to remember the other words.

The living room was cool and smelled of cigarette smoke. The TV was on. Next to the television Teddy saw a pretty good-looking stereo. He made a note to nose out the electronics when he finished searching the house. It looked like it might be decent equipment—not top of the line, but nothing to be ashamed of.

Teddy stepped into the hallway and let his eyes adjust to the dark. Then he checked the two bedrooms, the bathroom, and the kitchen. When he found no one he pulled down all the shades and turned on a few lights. It wasn't much of a place—the carpet could use a good shampoo—but what did he expect from the dogman?

He flipped the channels on the TV and stopped at a rerun of "McCloud." It killed him the way they had this hayseed marshal busting chops in New York. Take a real piece of country shit in a cowboy hat, drop him somewhere in Brooklyn, he wouldn't last ten minutes. He'd be on the phone screaming for mercy before the first commercial, begging the chief, get me outta here.

All that, Jesus, and Dennis Weaver, too. Teddy changed channels, not believing the dogman didn't have cable, and settled on "Entertainment Tonight." The refrigerator had some beer so Teddy popped one. Then he unplugged the stereo components and stacked them by the front door. He neglected the tapes, though: it was all metalhead stuff, not worth taking. He also left a stack of comic books.

The first bedroom had a dresser and a closet full of old lady clothes and not much else. In the second bedroom he found a couple of bucks in change, which he slipped into his pocket, and a camera, which he put next to the stereo. A clock radio was too old to be worth the trouble. There was a jewelry box with some earrings and necklaces, but most of it cheap. Teddy took only the few pieces of gold.

The dresser drawers held underwear, T-shirts, jeans, bras, belts, some odd junk, stockings, and socks. All he nabbed were two pairs of black lace bikini panties, for souvenirs.

The closet had some hanging clothes, shoes on the floor and a few shoeboxes. The girl's threads looked all right, but some taste the dogman had—T-shirts and old jeans, old jeans and T-shirts. Teddy had to dress like that, he'd never leave the house.

With his foot he flipped the top off one of the shoeboxes. Inside were old shoes. Same with the second box. But in the third box he found something almost as good as new Italian loafers his size. He found a gun.

Teddy had never been much of a gun person. He liked to use his strength and, if something extra were needed, a baseball bat. He used to tell his friends guns were for niggers.

But he'd come close to changing his mind lately. For one thing, he had a car now and was forced to share the road with the stupid Texans. A gun would be a nice addition to his Mark VII, the way they drove here.

And when he picked up the gun—it must have been a .38—he was surprised at how much he liked the way it felt in his hand. Even his sore hand: it just seemed as if it belonged there. He held it next to his ear, barrel toward the ceiling, and checked himself in the mirror. Made Magnum PI look like a pussy. He dropped the gun into the side pocket of his jacket, looking in the mirror to make sure the load wasn't stretching the fabric.

Teddy carried the stereo tuner and cassette player to his car and then the speakers. He put it all in the trunk and turned to go back for the TV. He heard a door open and saw an old woman in shorts come out of the next house. "Where is he?" she shouted. "You tell me right now!" Teddy watched her motor across the yard toward him and wondered was it Ugly Day and somebody forgot to tell him. "Where is he?" she shouted again. She waved a spatula in one hand.

The woman braked about ten feet from him. Her T-shirt said, FOR GOD SO LOVED THE WORLD . . . Teddy shut the trunk of his car. "Where'd he go?" she wanted to know.

Teddy said, "Who you talking about, lady?"

"That little criminal that lives there." She pointed to the dogman's house with her spatula. "The one that stole my car this morning."

"He stole your car?" This was news. Teddy had checked the dogman's pockets and didn't see any keys. He could go back to the hotel now and maybe find it still in the lot. Easy money. "What kind of car? What color?"

"I've had the po-lice out here once. You don't tell me where he is, I'll call 'em again."

"He went swimming," Teddy said. The bit about the police made him decide to leave. He opened the door to the Mark VII and got in. "What kind of car you missing, anyway?"

"Swimmin'?" the woman bellowed. "Swimmin' where? I'm callin' the law."

Teddy started the Mark VII, then powered down the window and asked the woman, "How much money you think that car of yours would bring, you had to sell it?"

Barton Eskew drove into the parking lot of the American Executive Inn and Conference Center and thought about what Meshack Blanchard had told him an hour ago. Meshack on the phone saying, Get a life, Barton. Asking him, don't you have better things to do on your time off?

Barton told Meshack he had a feeling, he had a hunch. What he didn't say was an old man like Meshack could afford to take things slow and easy, but Barton Eskew was hungry. Saturday night and Meshack had the in-laws over, cooking weenies in the backyard. I duck out now, Meshack said, the old lady will kill me. Fifty-what years old and afraid of his wife. Hey, Barton said, I'll handle it. Don't worry, he told Meshack. Anything turns up, I'll let you know.

He parked his car in a fire zone near the lobby entrance of the American, found the assistant manager at the front desk, and showed his badge. The assistant manager looked nervous in his official hotel blazer and his plastic name tag pinned to his pocket.

The tag said his name was Robert. Robert folded his hands on the counter in front of him the way they must teach at assistant manager school.

Barton said he'd like to see—pausing, checking the name on a piece of paper—Nella Billman. Assistant manager Robert said Nella was in the laundry but he would call her. If he wanted Barton could use the manager's office.

"I'll just drop in on her," Barton said. "Which way's the laundry?"

Robert told him and said, "She's not in any trouble?"

"Just a few follow-up questions," Barton said.

"Because I know you guys talked to her already."

"I'm checking a few things," Barton said. "That's all. Now the laundry is where again?"

"Follow that hallway to the end, take a right, and it's the first door past the ice machine." Robert directed with both hands and then folded them back on the counter. "I told her already today, 'Nella, where the police are concerned, just tell the truth.'"

"Good advice," Barton said.

As Barton turned away Robert said, "I told her, 'Nella, you have to cooperate even if you don't like the police.'"

Barton stopped, did a slow pirouette, stepped back toward Robert and leaned an elbow on the front desk. "Now why would she not like the police?" he asked.

"I thought she might have told you. About her son."

"What about her son?"

"Well, he's in jail for killing a man in a bar fight, as I understand it."

"And?"

"And Nella believes he's innocent. She tells anyone who'll listen the police got the wrong man. I even
caught her talking to a guest about it. Let me assure
you, that is not tolerated."

"What's his name?"

"Whose?" the assistant manager said. Barton
waited for him to figure out the question. "The son's?
Oh, I have no idea."

Barton found her in the laundry room stuffing
dirty towels into a washing machine. "How's it going,
Nella?" he said from the doorway. She looked up but
never stopped with the towels. "I'm Detective Eskew.
Let's talk for a minute."

Nella didn't answer. She was in her sixties, with a
tired face and iron-gray hair going thin at the part.
Barton looked at her and saw one of those weary,
heavy old women he could never believe had been
young.

"How about right here?" He motioned toward a
table in the middle of the room. Nella sighed and sat
in one folding chair. Barton took the other. "Just a
few questions," he said.

"I done told everthing I know," Nella said. He
could barely hear her over the churning washers.

"I know, and we appreciate it," Barton said. She
looked at him for a second and then the sad eyes fell
away. "But sometimes," Barton said, "you remember
things better if you've had a while to think about
them."

"I already said what I seen."

"Do me a favor and say it again. What was it you
witnessed?"

Nella reached into the pocket of her light green

smock and found a hotel mint. "Friday night I was turnin' down beds in the rooms and I come acrost two men yellin'. That's all." She unwrapped the candy and slipped it into her mouth.

"What time?"

"Friday night."

"What time Friday night?"

"I don't know."

"And this was room three-thirty-three."

"Thereabouts."

"Two men yelling," Barton said. "Yelling what?"

She shook her head and looked at the floor. Barton lit a cigarette, blew out the smoke, and said, "This boy of yours, what's he in for?"

Nella stiffened, then slumped and stared at the washers. "They say he kilt somebody."

"What's he up on, murder? Or manslaughter?" She nodded. "How much time?"

"Fifteen years," Nella said.

"Fifteen years from when?"

"He didn't do it," Nella said, talking louder. "I know he didn't."

Barton sniffed and flicked some ashes on the linoleum. "Right now nobody gives a rat if he did or he didn't, Nella. Boy's in the Texas Department of Corrections now, that's what matters." Nella seemed to be watching the suds slosh around in the machine portholes. Barton pulled a couple of times on his cigarette. He said, "I could make some calls for your boy."

Nella turned her face toward him, showed him the sad eyes again. Barton said, "You help me out on this, I could make some calls."

"What kind of calls?"

"Hey, *calls*. To people that matter. The warden, for

one. Let the warden know he should lighten up on . . . what's the boy's name?"

"William Billman."

"Tell the warden to take it easy on Willie Billman, ask him to go generous with the privileges, whatever. I could call the judge, maybe, see about him taking a fresh look at the case."

"You could do that?"

"I could do a lot of things."

Nella took another chocolate mint from the pocket of her smock. "What do I got to do?"

Barton dropped the cigarette and put it out with his shoe. "For starters, this yelling business. Who's yelling at who?"

"All I seen is a man comes out of three-three-four and starts bangin' on three-three-three. He's shoutin', 'Turn loose a that girl.' "

"Uh-huh."

"Then I guess the door opens 'cause this gal run out. Nothin' but underwear on and got her clothes in her hands. She run next door to three-three-four."

"The man banging on the door," Barton said. "What's he look like?"

"Just a man, that's all. He was a good piece away. Blond hair, I remember that." She lifted one round shoulder.

Barton reached into the breast pocket of his Sears jacket and came out with an envelope. He opened it and withdrew a wallet-sized black-and-white photo. DIST. ATTY'S. OFFICE DALLAS COUNTY had been rubber stamped on the back, above a strip of white label on which had been typed, FLIPPO, JACKSON A. Barton put it on the table face-up and said, "Is this the man?"

Nella looked at it and said, "I don't know."

"You're not saying it isn't."

"Well . . . " She leaned in and studied the picture.

"So it could be."

Nella slowly nodded her head yes. Barton picked up the photograph and put it back in the envelope. "The girl runs out. Then what?"

"Somebody inside the room she come from starts yellin' he should take the whore."

"Take the whore."

"Mm-hmm."

"What did the man outside do?"

"Shot the bird?"

"In other words," Barton said, "made a threatening gesture."

"Shot him the bird, big as life."

"And then?"

"The girl run in his room, and he went right in behind her."

"What did the man in the other room—three-thirty-three—what did he do?"

"He stuck his head out the door and he yelled, 'You pimp.'"

"He called the man a pimp?" Barton said.

"That's right." Nella slipped another mint in her mouth.

Barton took a second photograph from the envelope. "The man saying, 'You pimp,' what did he look like?"

"He had brown hair," Nella said.

Barton placed the second photo on the table in front of her. This was Delbert's Polaroid from the morgue. Just head and shoulders against a stainless-steel slab, eyes closed and face battered and swollen. "Is this the man?"

Nella bent over the photo. She breathed through her mouth and Barton could smell the chocolate. "I only seen the back of his head," she said.

"Yeah, well, this is the front of the head. What I'm asking you is, could this have been the man you saw?"

"That's awful hard to say." She studied the picture.

"Keep trying," Barton said. "By the way, what unit's your boy in down there?"

"He's in Eastham."

"Eastham, Eastham. I think I know the warden there. I'm pretty sure I do."

They sat in the noise of the washing machines. Finally Nella said, "That man stickin' his head out the door . . ."

"I'm listening."

"He might of turned around once. I might of seen his face a little, a good bit."

Barton celebrated by lighting another cigarette. "When he turned around, what did you see?"

Nella pointed one finger at the picture on the table, not quite touching it. Her hand trembled slightly over the photograph for a few seconds. Then she rested it in her lap.

Barton smiled. "You've been some kind of big help, Nella." She nodded. "Now. You saw this man"—he tapped the dead man's photograph with his thumbnail—"stick his head out the door and address the man who had threatened him. Who you've already identified."

"Uh-huh," Nella said.

"What happened then?"

"Well—I left," Nella said. She looked at Barton. "Didn't I?"

*   *   *

"It's the snout," Meshack said on the phone. "It's the tail, maybe. But it ain't the whole hog."

Barton couldn't believe it. He wanted to slam down the pay phone. Better yet, pull his piece and fill it with bullet holes, right there in the hallway outside the men's room at the Kettle. He said, "You're shitting me. Right, Meshack? You gotta be."

Meshack sighed. "Look, Barton, you did some nice work. I'll mention it to the sergeant, get you an attaboy. But no way we—"

"Were you listening? Did we have a bad connection or something? I got an eyewitness, Meshack, that puts Flippo with the victim."

"I heard you the first time, Barton."

"And not just with him, but making threats. Verbal threats. I mean, what do you want?" Thinking, I'm busting my ass while Meshack's done nothing harder than spread mustard the last two hours.

"I want something that'll stick," Meshack said. "That's what I want."

"This'll stick."

"Don't believe so."

"The guy's good for it, Meshack. I take one look at him, I know that. All this crap about waiting for a woman, that crap he fed us, now I got a witness says it's all bullshit."

"Let me tell you what, Barton. Say we arrest him. You think the DA'll take that charge? Old Jackie might of fallen from favor over there, but he's still one of their exes. And what are they gonna charge him with? Shootin' the finger at somebody?"

"At somebody who got killed," Barton said.

"Yeah, the next day. All that blood was fresh when

the housekeeper found our boy, Barton. Remember that? No chance he'd been dead overnight, no chance in the world."

Barton shook his head, stared at the ceiling. "Man . . . " was all he could say.

"Look, it's something," Meshack said. "I mean, you did good work. It's something, but it ain't everything. It's a piece, that's all. My advice, Barton, is get something else to go with it."

30

★

Paula said, "Are you one of those who falls asleep right after?" She lay on her side, facing Jack, running one finger from his hip to his knee.

Jack was flat on his back, still breathing hard. The blinds were open and an alley light threw broken stripes of faint green across both of them. "No," he said. "But I do get hungry."

"Me too. Let's go see what I've got." She slipped from the bed and lifted her robe off the floor. "I'll meet you in the kitchen."

Jack used the toilet, then found his pants in the near-dark of the bedroom. When he wandered down the hall Paula already had coffee brewing. The clock on the coffee maker said it was 3:15. He was starting to feel as if he had flown east across seven or eight time zones.

Paula cracked some eggs in a bowl. "How about an omelette?"

"Sounds great."

She saw him looking at the coffee. "I thought we could talk a while," she said.

"Talk and watch the sun come up, you and me," Jack said. "You know, less than twenty-four hours ago I'm sitting in a diner out by Big Town at sunrise, been up all night, I'm trying to figure out how I can get myself in this very spot."

Paula smiled. "Sometimes things work out after all." She opened the refrigerator, crouched, and peered in. "All I have are onions and tomatoes."

"That's my favorite, onions and tomatoes."

"See what I mean? Things work out."

Jack took a chair at the bleached pine table and watched her chop the onion. He was there in his long pants and no shirt, like a construction worker just home on a hot night, waiting for the missus to get supper, except a construction worker would have better biceps. "I'll be right back," he said. He went to the bedroom and retrieved his shirt.

By the time he returned Paula was frying the eggs. The smell of olive oil and onions filled the kitchen. The coffee had finished, so he poured both of them a cup. Jack took his seat at the table again and asked her, "So why did you do it? Frame up Buddy George, I mean."

Paula seemed to be thinking it over while she watched the eggs. "You probably believe it was only money," she said.

"Not necessarily."

"There is money involved, but it wasn't only money."

"You mean you and Buddy had something going." She slid her glance on and off him. "I don't mean to be crass," Jack said, "but in these sorts of things if it's not money, it's sex. Most of the time, anyway."

Paula scowled at the frying pan. "This is not really an omelette. It's just scrambled eggs."

"Even better," Jack said.

She put the food on two white bone plates and brought them to the table. Jack watched her walk and thought about the way she had moved under him. "My husband hated it that I couldn't cook," she said.

Paula sat across from him and drank her coffee. Jack was about to ask her again, but she started it herself. "As far as Buddy goes . . ." She pushed the eggs around her plate with her fork but didn't eat anything. "I can tell by the way you talk about him that you don't think much of him."

Jack swallowed and said, "His habits with women seem a little strange."

Paula set her fork on the edge of her plate. "Now you're going to ask me if he did the same thing to me."

"I might not."

"He didn't."

"Okay."

"I'll tell you exactly what Buddy and I did together."

Jack wasn't sure he wanted to hear about Buddy George, Jr. being where he had just been. "Look, you don't have to—"

"I want to." She reached and laid her hand on his. "I want you to know because you and I need to trust each other."

That was a word Jack hadn't heard in a while,

trust. Paula took her hand back with a little rake of her fingers across his. "I want you to understand me," she said, "and why I did what I did."

Jack sipped his coffee and let her talk. "I met Buddy a little over a year ago," she said. "I was living in Pascagoula, Mississippi."

"I don't know Pascagoula, Mississippi," Jack said.

"Count yourself lucky. We moved there from New Orleans when my husband bought three pizza restaurants. We had one in Pascagoula, one in Ocean Springs, and one in Biloxi. Some life, right?"

"I'm guessing your answer is no."

"Every cent we had he put into those three pizza restaurants. Our house barely had furniture. We drove used cars, and vacations—no chance." She picked up her plate and scraped the eggs uneaten into the garbage. "Look, I had three years in college before I got married. I lived in New Orleans most of my adult life. I'm supposed to be happy when I'm figuring withholding for busboys in Pascagoula?"

Paula came back to her chair, shaking her head as she sat down. "I remember one day," she said, "I was back in the office—if you could call that an office, this closet with crates of napkins stacked in it. I'm sitting there and Albert, my husband, comes running in just having a shit fit. Totally out of control. I ask, what's the problem? Albert says, did you order Bac*O bits? I'm going, what? He says, Bac*O bits, we're out of Bac*O bits at the salad bar, did you order any? He goes crazy about how he told me to special-order them that morning and did I call the distributor? I thought he was going to hit me, I swear to God."

Jack the prosecutor would have asked, And did your husband strike you, Miss Fontaine? Jack the private citizen watched the way she pulled her fingers gently through her hair.

"Then one time my husband told me he was taking the night off. Which he never did. I mean, Christmas Eve, you could buy pizza in south Mississippi. But Albert tells me, you've got to hear this man. And he takes me to the Broadwater Beach in Biloxi."

"Oh, no."

"To see Buddy George Junior."

"I don't believe this."

"Whose message that night was, 'You Can Do Better.' I still remember. He was right."

Jack got the coffee pot and refilled their cups.

"The next night," she said, "Buddy moved his show to Mobile. I told my husband I was going to visit my mother in Baton Rouge, but I went to Mobile instead. After Mobile it was Panama City, Florida. I introduced myself to Buddy there and we had dinner after the show. He hired me on the spot."

Jack thought about Sharronda's story of how Delbert plucked her out of a South Texas dead end. Now here was Buddy saving a woman from a life of Mississippi pizzas. He wondered if when Paula met Sharronda, they saw the refugee in each other.

"I was the best thing that ever happened to him," Paula said. "I turned his life around. When Buddy met me it was the luckiest day of his life."

Jack thought he heard thunder outside. He asked Paula, "Would Buddy say that now, that it was his lucky day, meeting you?"

"Why wouldn't he? You know what I did for Buddy's business? In one year I doubled his revenue. Doubled." She held up two fingers. "Buddy was taking his show all over the country, one-night stands, a hundred and fifty dates a year. I told him he had a good concept but he was throwing away time and money on travel. I'm the one who got Buddy to start doing television."

"The thanks of a grateful nation."

"I told him, stay home, build a base here, let the TV sell your tapes. I turned everything around for him."

"When did it go sour?"

"Sour's the wrong word."

Jack sipped his coffee and looked at her nipples against the robe.

"I helped him build his business," she said, "and he'd try to throw it away with women in hotel rooms."

"As I said, strange habits."

"He's a brilliant man at what he does, he really is. He just has . . . Look, I don't think Buddy touched any of them. He was scared to. He simply asked them to do certain things, and he did certain things . . . "

"I heard the tape," Jack said.

"Sometimes, for whatever reason, some of them would make him angry. He'd give them a black eye or a loose tooth or maybe just rip a dress. In those cases, a lot of them wanted him to pay for the damage."

"If that's all they wanted, you're lucky."

She placed her hand back on his. "I tried to tell Buddy that. I told him if he kept it up, one of those girls would sue, or go to the police, or try to black-mail him. You know they would, and then what? I told him he was going to bring down the whole com-pany, everything we'd built." She shook her head. "He wouldn't listen. So I had to show him what could happen."

"All this just to teach Buddy a lesson? Man."

Paula stood and poured her coffee in the sink. "I thought about it for a long time. At first I was just going to put a tape recorder under the bed. You know, embarrass him with it, let him hear what he sounds like. But I wasn't sure that would be enough."

"Probably not."

"Then I was getting my nails done one day and I met Sharronda. She was pretty, she needed money, she wanted to leave town. All those. I started working up something I could do with her."

Jack raised his coffee cup toward her. "You fooled us all."

"And when I had a plan in place, I went looking for some people who could pull it off for me. I wanted someone who could make it look, you know, professional. But who wouldn't ask a lot of questions."

"At your service," Jack said. "How'd you find us?"

She smiled. "I came upon your friend Mr. Roper in the newspaper advertisements."

"In the TV listings? Jesus." Jack saw it on Sundays: *Have you had an accident and don't know where to turn? Do you seek justice? Is your marriage in trouble? Divorces. Wills. Occupational claims. Confidential investigations. Hal Roper, Attorney-at-Law.* It usually ran next to an ad for Ms. Desiree, who offered psychic treatment for love and weight loss. "I guess it pays to advertise," Jack said. "Hal will be happy to hear this."

"I thought if I presented myself as Buddy's wife that Mr. Roper would be persuaded to take the case. If I, you know, made it look like a divorce."

"That's probably what did it," Jack said. "That and the cash."

Paula carried his empty plate to the sink. Jack rose and stretched. There was more thunder outside.

"Don't you see, this was my big chance, what I had with Buddy's company. I've never had an opportunity like this. I didn't want to see it all lost because of something stupid Buddy did with a woman."

Jack turned toward the window behind him. Rain was hitting the glass.

"If he ever found out what I did, he'd think I had betrayed him," she said. "He would. I'm sure he would. But it's not like that."

Jack raised the blinds on the window. The rain grew heavier against it. "There are different types of betrayal," he said.

"What are you talking about?"

Jack reached to open the window latch. "Say you're married, you run off with somebody else. You didn't really set out to betray your husband or your wife, but you do. That's one kind."

"You're talking about me?"

"I'm talking about a lot of people." He pushed hard and opened the window enough that he could slip his fingers under the bottom wooden sash. "The other kind is when you're out to teach a lesson. Or get revenge, maybe. It's a different deal. For one thing, it's premeditated."

Jack tugged, but the window would not budge. "As for getting revenge, there's only one way to get revenge."

"Tell me," she said.

"You do your deal and then you look the person right in the eye and say, 'I fucked you bad.' They have to know it was you. You want to really bury them, they have to know they've been had, and they have to know it was you."

Jack put more muscle into it. The window gave way with a groan of wood and opened. Cool, wet air billowed into the house. "First rain in I don't know how long," Jack said. He smelled it and listened to it and watch it blow into the screen.

Then he closed his eyes. He could feel Paula coming from behind him. He leaned against the windowsill and waited.

31

★

Teddy couldn't understand why it was so hard to find a pawnshop open on Sunday morning. Like the pawnbrokers all went to church or something. He had cruised for one for an hour or so, looking for a place to unload the dogman's stereo. He finally saw one on Singleton Boulevard in West Dallas. A black dude with a mouth full of gold gave him $200 for the equipment, all in tens.

Around noon Teddy tried calling the dogman's house to see if the girlfriend had shown up. Again he got no answer, so he phoned the redhead. Her answering machine picked up. After the beep Teddy said, "Hey, you think I'm hanging at that house all day and all night, you're outta your freaking mind." He started to hang up but added, "This is Teddy Deuce, by the way."

Now Teddy couldn't decide whether to be in a good or a bad mood. He drove north on Stemmons, enjoying the light traffic, but his hand still hurt, and he was bored. Still, he had two bills in his pocket from the pawnshop, plus the gun in the glove box. And if the girl he was chasing ever showed up it would mean a major payday.

What he thought he might do with the money was cut a demo video, just Teddy talking to somebody on a couch, then drop it by Channel 8. Tell them about his idea for the Teddy Deuce Show. Go by in person so they could see what kind of talent they were dealing with.

Teddy saw himself talking to the station manager. Asking him, What happens when a Donahue or a Geraldo or a Sally Jessy has a guest full of shit? They have to stand there and talk anyway. But on the Teddy Deuce Show, if some guy's being an asshole, Teddy grabs him and throws him off the set. Maybe you could have a studio audience that yells, Toss him! Toss him! And each show would end with a brief workout segment, like "Teddy Deuce's Bicep Tips."

For right now, Teddy didn't know which would be more satisfying, getting his own show or telling Hal he was quitting. Hal—little man with a cheap rug always screaming at Teddy, Do this, do that. What kind of life was that? Plus the money was shit. Teddy hated to admit it, but there was something to the B-B-Q beans story. You had to be your own boss.

He was at the Northwest Highway exit when he decided to dump Hal on the spot. No reason to wait, Teddy told himself. He'd gone freelance for the weekend and look how great he'd done, so why not make it permanent?

He could call his new operation Teddy Deuce Investigations. Action taken, scores settled. A few good cases and the town would lap him up like milk.

The thing to do now, Teddy figured, was drive to Hal's and deliver the news. Plus pick up his last week's pay in cash, and maybe something extra. Call it a performance bonus, equal to whatever amount Hal had around the house.

32

★

Jack awoke in the sunlit white room, naked in the bed and alone. The clock radio said 9:35. He heard water running in the bathroom.

In a minute or two the water stopped and the bathroom door opened. Paula came out, floating toward the bed. She was smiling, and her hair in daylight in the white room, against her bare pale shoulders, was like the blast of a horn. Jack watched her the whole way. There was nothing quite like the sight of a woman with no clothes on making a course straight for you.

"Turn over," she said, and he rolled onto his stomach. She kissed the back of his knees, his thighs, and the small of his back. Jack wondered if the mention of a corpse would ruin the mood.

He said it anyway. "The police came to see me about that body."

That put a brake to the lips. He waited for her to say something. "What are you talking about?" she finally asked.

Jack turned over so he could see her. "The dead body in the hotel room. Sharronda's boyfriend. The police came around asking questions."

Paula shook her head but couldn't speak.

Jack said, "Sharronda told me she talked to you yesterday about getting her money and you told her to go back to the room at the American."

"She's lying again." Paula left the bed and got her robe from a hook behind the door. Then she folded her arms, leaned against the dresser, and burned her eyes into him from across the room. "I can't believe you come here, you talk to me, we make love twice, and then you say, 'Oh, by the way, somebody got killed.'"

Jack felt stupid lying there with no clothes on. He covered himself with a sheet. "It's a hard thing to drop casually into a conversation."

"You didn't have any trouble just now."

"All right, my timing's bad. But it's done. So let's talk about this."

"Talk about what? I don't know anything about this. You're telling me Sharronda's boyfriend got killed, and I'm completely in the dark."

Jack held up his hands, palms out. "I'll tell you what I know."

"That would be nice."

He gave her the story as he had been able to put it together from Sharronda and the police. She never took her eyes from him as he talked. "And that's what I have," he said when he was through. "The truth as best I can determine."

Paula turned toward the dresser. She stood before the mirror and pulled a brush through her hair with long, slow strokes. After a minute she said, "Everything she told you about me, it's all a lie."

Jack waited while she brushed some more. "You want to know what really happened?" she said.

With Jack thinking, You can never know that. He had all those years of listening to people swear in court to tell the truth and then hearing them testify as if facts were like food, cooked to their wishes and seasoned the way they wanted, and if it didn't taste good they could throw it away. "Of course I want to know what really happened," he said. "That's why I brought it up."

"I called Sharronda at her house yesterday morning," she said. "I owed her money from the night before and I was calling to arrange payment." Paula set the brush on the dresser top and looked at him in the mirror while she talked. "I thought she sounded very frightened. She talked so quietly I could barely hear her. I would say, 'What? Please speak up,' and she'd whisper, 'I can't, I can't talk, Delbert will hear.' "

The room was so bright with sun it was hurting Jack's eyes. The early morning rainstorm had long ago moved on. He lay in the bed and watched Paula, and felt again as if he were strapped into something that couldn't be stopped. Nothing to do now but ride the rocket.

Paula turned and faced him, arms folded again. "I told her, 'All right, then go somewhere where I can call you.' I wasn't going to give her my number here, right? So I told her to think of a place where I could call her, or meet her, and we could talk freely. She said she had a key to the room at the American. I don't know how—she must have taken Buddy's."

A girl's running for her life, Jack thought, and she stops to steal a key. Then she volunteers to go back to a place where a man attacked her the night before.

Where, for all she knows, he might still be. In court Jack would have been all over this one with sharp teeth. "That makes sense," he said.

"I waited half an hour," Paula said, "and then called the room. Nobody answered. I tried again and got nothing. All in all I probably called ten times over the course of an hour. Nobody answered at all."

Jack swung his feet to the floor, keeping the sheet over him. "It's hard to pick up the phone, say hello, if you've drowned in the toilet."

She dropped her arms to her side. "In that room? Oh, no . . . "

"That's what the police say. They don't know it's Sharronda's boyfriend. They don't know who it is, period. But from the description, it's definitely him."

"What about Sharronda?"

"Just a bump on the head."

"What does she say happened? Does she know who—"

"All she's sure of is Delbert followed her there, she hit her head, she ran out."

"So she doesn't know anything."

"No," Jack said. "But she knows enough to do us all in."

Paula's eyes shifted left and right and then back on him. Both hands gripped the edge of the dresser. "What does that mean, do us all in?"

"Look." Jack stood up and wrapped the sheet around him like a toga. A Roman orator wearing the Ralph Lauren bedroom collection. "I'll just . . . Well, first, let me ask this. Was that room registered to Buddy?"

"To the company, to Motivational Enterprises.

The Executive cuts us a deal on it as part of the ball-room rental. Buddy always insists on having a room. Guess why."

"Then if the police haven't questioned Buddy yet, they will soon. That should get him plenty excited."

She moved over and sat at the foot of the bed. "Will they arrest him?"

"It depends on what he says. I doubt it. But you'd better hope he doesn't start talking about the black-mail. He can't be that stupid, can he? If he does that, and mentions that you know all about it, your house is the detectives' next stop. They get serious enough about it, they'll pull your phone records and find ten calls to the motel Saturday morning. They'll also find your call to Sharronda's house, where the dead man happened to reside. They make the right moves, things could fall apart real fast."

Paula rubbed her eyes and then her temples. It was the first time Jack had seen her look tired, and it added a few years to her. "I can't believe this is happening," she said.

"Just hope Buddy keeps his mouth shut." Jack stepped toward her. "He doesn't start blabbing, this could work out well for you and me and Sharronda, too."

She stopped rubbing her temples and said, "How, exactly?"

"Look at how it probably happened. Sharronda says when she went to the motel Saturday morning, Delbert followed her. For whatever reason, he tailed her there. Maybe he knew something was up."

"Or maybe Sharronda is lying," Paula said. "She might have brought him with her because they were planning to rob me. Your imagination doesn't have to run wild for you to think about her doing something like that."

"It's possible." Jack shrugged. "The important thing is Delbert goes to the American Executive Inn and meets his maker. It doesn't really matter who did it. It doesn't. Whoever he was, he did the world a favor. Listen, Delbert was the dirtbag poster boy. I've seen hundreds of lowlifes and Delbert was right there. He deserved what he got."

She looked him over. Jack stood in the middle of the room and felt the coolness from the air conditioning vent on his shoulders. He could hear the distant sound of a lawn mower, and could imagine how it was outside—the heat already building, the sky a cloudless deadly blue. "You have some kind of plan?" Paula said. "Or are you just talking?"

"First, forget about who killed Delbert. The important thing is he's dead by violent means. That is our hammer. And there's one person who can make a connection between Delbert and Buddy George Junior."

"Sharronda."

"Thank you. Now, she can't make Buddy good for the homicide," Jack said. "But she talks to the police, she can throw Buddy's name into the mix in a big way. She also causes you and me enormous problems. None of us is a virgin here."

"Does Sharronda want to go to the police?"

"I don't think so. But it may not be long before they find her. Especially if they make an ID on Delbert. So imagine that they track her down, and she tells them everything she knows. Then imagine the TV stations pick that up—Buddy George Junior linked to a murdered druggie and his cute half-black girlfriend in a motel room. They do that, Buddy's going to have a hard time selling any more speeches at twenty-five dollars a head."

Jack let her digest it all, gave her the five seconds or so it took him to settle back onto the bed. Then he said, "How much do you think Buddy would pay to have Sharronda gone?"

Paula turned to face him. "Gone?"

"Out of town. She'll leave Dallas and never come back. I would think that's worth a lot to him now."

The way she studied him reminded Jack of an appraiser taking in a building. She seemed to be adding numbers or drawing charts in her head. Then her look softened, and she bent and kissed him on the neck.

"You think like me," Paula said. "I don't know whether to be afraid or in love."

★

Teddy drove northwest out of Dallas on I-35, doing about eighty-five when the Sunday afternoon traffic would let him. At Lake Lewisville the bridge ran low over the water and Teddy gassed the car to ninety. The Mark VII felt like a big bird skimming the surface of the lake. He turned up the radio and it was as if he had the soundtrack to his own movie.

The second exit past the bridge was his, and then left. He crossed under the highway and drove past five miles of empty fields and a few dumpy houses. Why Hal wanted to live way out in nowhere was beyond him. Bad enough to be in a place like Dallas, but then to make some kind of Hooterville scene . . .

Teddy had been to Hal's house once before, a week after he arrived in town. Hal had invited him out. Come to a big party, Hal had said. Teddy gets there and finds a bunch of old drunks talking about golf. Old drunks and their cow wives, wearing poly.

Teddy's at the party maybe ten minutes, enough time to put away a couple of beers, when one of the cows plays a Lionel Ritchie tape. They're acting like this is hot music and a few of them try to dance. Teddy grabs a six-pack from Hal's kitchen and heads for his car. Hal stops him at the door, says, Where are you going? He asks Hal, Man, what is this place? Soul Train for old white feebs?

Now Teddy drove into the sunset on a bumpy two-lane. At the Kwik-N-E-Z Mart, standing there like the last outpost of civilization, he took a right on a road that was even narrower and bumpier. Five miles down the asphalt made a T, and Teddy couldn't remember if he should go left or right. He turned left, and decided that the trip was taking so long he'd have to hit Hal for a $300 personal inconvenience sur-charge. He drove another five minutes and raised the fee to $500.

Finally, in the middle of nothing, he saw the mail-box that said H. ROPER. Teddy hit his brakes and steered the Mark onto the unpaved road that ran from the mailbox. Gravel sprayed against the car's under-side, drowning out an ad for zit cream on the radio, as Teddy cut through a thicket of scrub oaks and brush. After about fifty yards of this the Mark broke into a clearing half the size of a football field. Across it, nuzzling the shore of a small lake, was Hal's house.

Hal's Oldsmobile was parked in front, and Teddy pulled up behind it. Then he took a garden hose that he found coiled in a flower bed and began to rinse a coat of dust from the Mark. He had finished about half of it, admiring the way the water beaded on the wax job, when the front door of the house opened and Hal came out. "The hell you been?" Hal said.

Hal wore a Ban-Lon pullover and some plaid shorts, showing legs that were skinny and white with a map of blue veins. Teddy said, "You could use a tan-ning bed."

"The hell you been, Teddy?" Hal said again.

Teddy turned back to washing the dust. "Taking care of business, Hal. T-C-B, that's what. T-N-T, T-C-B." He liked the sound of that and decided to make it his new slogan.

Hal kept barking. "I've been calling. I've been waiting. I expected to see you yesterday afternoon the latest. I wait in my office all day, you don't show. I call your place, no answer. I'm asking myself, Is Teddy screwing me or has he just screwed up?"

The water ran over the trunk lid. "Hey, maybe I tryda call."

"And maybe I'm Perry Mason," Hal said, "and maybe you're Paul Drake. I doubt it."

Teddy gave that one some brain time. Thinking, That Della Street always looked like a pretty nice punch, even in black and white. Hal said, "So what did you find out?"

Teddy finished washing the car, rinsed his hands, and tossed the hose into the grass. "What," Hal said. "Come on, let's hear it."

"Three things, Hal. The first is, I don't work for you no more. I'm going free agent. So I don't work for you no more."

Hal laughed. "That's a good one."

"The second is, you owe me a week's back pay. Plus a bonus 'cause I been so good for you. So pay me and I can get the fuck outta here."

"What's the third thing?"

"The what?"

"The third thing. You said there were three things."

Teddy counted them up. He was going free agent, Hal owed him a week's pay, and he deserved a bonus. That was three, wasn't it? The little bastard was trying to mess with his head. "Pay me," he told Hal.

"For what? I send you out on a job, you come back with zilch. I'll pay you what that's worth. Get lost."

Hal turned and walked toward the house. Teddy followed and was only two feet behind him as Hal opened the front door. When Hal tried to shut the door, Teddy blocked it with his foot. Hal looked back, made a funny face, and said, "What's this?"

Teddy barreled through him and into the house. "Jesus, Hal, you're soft as a pillow." He strolled into the living room. "You really need to work out. Get yourself a Jane Fonda tape, man, or a Raquel. You could drop some pounds and watch bitches in leotards the same time."

"Get out," Hal said.

Teddy checked out the VCR on top of the twenty-seven-inch Sony. Both looked pretty new. He saw himself making another stop at the pawnshop on Singleton Boulevard. With the black dude behind the counter smiling gold and saying, My man! as Teddy walked through the door with the merchandise. Two fences in one day and you're old friends.

"Right now," Hal said. "Out."

There was a golf match on the TV. Teddy sat in a black reclining chair, put his feet up, and flipped channels with the remote. "Hal? This a La-Z-Boy or a BarcaLounger?"

"I mean it, Teddy."

"It's comfy, whatever it is. I'll relax here while you pull the cash together. You get HBO?"

"Screw you."

Teddy looked at Hal and wondered what would happen if he took that toupee and dropped it into a hot frying pan. "I'll make it easy for you, Hal. Fifteen hundred bucks and I'm out the door. That seems fair."

"You've lost the little bit of mind you had."

"And if you're short a hundred or so, I'll take the balance in electronics. It's an inconvenience, but that's the kind of guy I am. Easy to please, you know it?"

Hal made a step toward the phone in the kitchen. "I'm calling the sheriff," he said.

"Sure you are, Hal. And as soon as you're done wit that, Teddy Deuce calls the IRS. Huh? Huh?" He got up from the chair and cut off Hal's path to the kitchen. "You think they wouldn't like talking to me about your operation? I'll have 'em creaming inna jockeys, the things I seen around your office."

Hal looked up at him and shook his head. "IRS, CIA, AFL-CIO—call them all, my friend. A couple of minutes talking to you, Teddy, they'll see a jerk who can't make change for a ten."

Teddy stepped toward Hal and thumped him in the chest with two fingers. Two fingers and the old man sagged and wheezed as if a hammer hit him. "The thing that really gets me, Hal? The one thing? The way you always treat me like some kind of dumb fuck. You and that faggot Jack Flippo."

He thumped Hal again and said, "You think a guy's got a good build and good looks, a guy knows how to wear a suit of clothes, that he don't know how to use his brain."

Teddy put his thumb against Hal's throat and backed him against the wall. He liked the way Hal made a croaking noise and bugged his eyes out, so he pressed harder.

The phone rang. After the third ring Teddy pulled his hand from Hal's neck and grinned. "Better get that, it might be the phone." Hal slumped against the wall, coughing hard but keeping his scared, blood-shot eyes on Teddy.

Six rings. "Jesus, answer it," Teddy said. "Keep yourself busy while I figure out what I'm gonna do wit you."

It made Teddy feel pretty good knowing he could ace someone with just his thumb. He had been about to do it, too, if the phone hadn't broken his concentration. But that was okay, because he needed some time to work out his plans. Somebody who didn't have his business sense might have put Hal away right then, got everything he wanted from the house, and called it a day. But Teddy was thinking long-range. Teddy was considering the future.

He turned his back on Hal and walked to the sliding-glass door at the rear of the living room. Hal's golf bag leaned against a corner. The view out the back was of a sloping brown lawn leading to a half-dried-up lake that, when it was full, was maybe seventy-five yards across.

Teddy heard Hal pick up the phone and rasp, "Yeah?"

Except for where the lawn met the shore, the lake was surrounded by the same scrub woods that separated Hal's house from the road. He remembered that Hal once told him he owned all the land around the lake.

Hal on the phone said, "Yeah . . . yeah . . . *what?*"

A guy in business as long as Hal, Teddy figured, a

guy who could buy a whole lake, could be a good source of cash.

Hal said, "So why call me? This is outrageous." He was getting his voice back. "This stinks . . . No, *you* listen."

There was a sign Teddy had seen in Buddy George's office, one that kept running through his head. The whole hallway had been lined with shiny plaques talking about eagles and leaders and teams and other weirdness, but one of them had stuck with Teddy. It said PLAN TODAY AND BE RICH TOMORROW! Which seemed to make a lot of sense, you thought about it.

"You keep asking the same question," Hal said to the phone. "Maybe I answer, maybe I don't. First you tell me what's going on."

Teddy looked out at the lake, saying to himself, Plan today, plan today. Wondering if he could apply that to his situation with Hal: He nails Hal this one time, gets everything in the house—it's a pretty good haul. But it would be like hitting the tellers in a bank and forgetting the safe, or like taking Hal's pocket change but passing up his wallet.

"I thought we had an arrangement," he heard Hal say. "Attorney and client, that was our arrangement. But you—"

Maybe the thing to do, Teddy decided, was to scare Hal a little and keep him scared. Do some damage today, get paid, threaten some damage the next week, get paid again. And so on, giving Teddy a ready-made cash flow while he was getting his video productions going. Plan today, rich tomorrow.

Hal, with the phone still to his ear, backed up as Teddy walked toward the kitchen. "He's here, all right?" Hal said. "Yeah. Okay? You happy?" Teddy's plan was to jerk the phone from the wall—disconnect Hal from the world as a first step.

He was a few feet away when Hal said, "All right, I said all right," and put the receiver on the kitchen counter. "It's the redheaded broad," Hal said, backing away some more. "The fake Mrs. George. She says she's been calling all over, searching for you."

★

Hard to believe, but Jack's apartment looked even worse than usual. It was late afternoon when he walked into the baking, airless stairwell and made the effort to the second floor. He opened the upstairs door and found Sharronda on the couch. She was shuffling a deck of cards, and didn't look up.

The door to the living room closet, which had a cracked full-length mirror nailed to the inside, was open. Piles of junk lay around it as if there had been a small explosion. Boxes, books, papers, clothes, shoes, suitcases, tools, an old radio, a blender, two commemorative plates from Graceland, and a painting of a matador on black velvet were scattered on the floor. Lying across the painting was a baseball bat—a Henry Aaron Louisville Slugger, Jack's from Little League days. "What the hell happened here?" Jack said.

"Nothing happened," Sharronda said. "How come you're gone so long?" She had yet to pull her eyes from her cards.

"I said I'd be back."

"People say lot of things."

Jack walked over, set the bat aside, and picked up the matador painting. A friend had brought it to him from Laredo as a joke, and it had hung in his office when he had one. A little white-trash trailer-park mockery, before he knew he'd be living in a place like this. "What are you doing with my stuff?" he asked Sharronda.

"What stuff?" She began to deal the cards to herself, placing them on the couch cushion next to her.

"*This* stuff." Jack waved a hand over the boxes. "My stuff." He saw a shoebox that held family pictures from his old life. Jack had sealed it with six or seven layers of packing tape, tight as a crypt. "My private stuff."

"Trying to find some cards," she said. "What else I'm supposed to do, cooped up in this place?"

Jack looked at the black and white TV. The horizontal hold had broken loose, making Yogi Bear roll endlessly into the top of the set. "Plus all day and all night I'm starving to death," Sharronda said. "I look in your Frigidaire, and you got like two things in there. And both of them moldy. Finally I spy way back in the cupboard and find this dusty old can of tuna fish. Man, the way you live." She shook her head as she laid the cards down.

"I'll order some Chinese for us," Jack said, and walked to the phone. "What do you like?"

"I don't like Chinese food."

He sighed. "What do you want, then?"

"What I want? I want out of here, Dad. You get my money? I'm not hearing the first thing about my money. All this complaining about your closet and shit, let's talk what's real."

"Maybe," Jack said.

"Maybe what?"

"Maybe you'll get your money. I should know sometime tonight. I'll get a phone call and we'll know, both of us."

"So what you're talking about is you don't have it."

"I'm saying we'll know tonight."

"Yeah, right." She folded her arms and stared at the ceiling. "More promises."

"You know," Jack said, "you are really beginning to get on my nerves."

"What about me, man? I'm stuck here, nothing to do, nothing to eat. You give me all these lines about how you might get my money, I'm supposed to smile and wait for some phone call. You're like, Just wait here, Sharronda, I'll handle everything. Now you say nothing's handled yet, we gotta wait by the phone."

Jack told himself there was nothing to gain by arguing with her. One more night and she would be on her way. He could last that long. "All right, what kind of pizza you want?" he asked her.

While they waited for the delivery man Jack adjusted the TV and changed his clothes. When the doorbell rang he looked out the window and saw the Domino's car parked out front. "Dinner is served," he said.

He walked downstairs, opened the door, and took the pizza from a young man in a red shirt. "That's fourteen ninety-five," the pizza man told him. Jack checked his wallet and said, "Wait here." He walked back upstairs. Sharronda was still on the couch. "You got five bucks?" Jack asked her.

Just after ten, as Jack and Sharronda watched the news, the phone rang. Jack answered.

"I have some good news," Paula said.

"I knew you would."

"I talked to Buddy. It's all set."

Jack looked across the room at Sharronda. She was paying him no attention. "Set how?" he said.

"You were right," Paula said. "The police did come to see him, and it scared him bad. And that means he's drinking. That's the only time he drinks, when he's scared."

"What did he say?"

Paula laughed, and Jack liked the sound of it. "He went for it all, no hesitation whatsoever. I told him I found out the dead man was Sharronda's boyfriend, and he went totally out of control. Babbling about how he's ruined if she tells the police, how he'll never work again. I thought he was going to break down and weep."

"That would be something to see."

"I told him Sharronda's scared too, and that all she wants is enough money to get her out of Dallas and give her a fresh start somewhere else. Jack, I'll cut right to it. He said he'd pay twenty-five thousand dollars."

Jack put his hand to his forehead. "You're kidding."

"Cash. Just bring her to Buddy's office tomorrow morning at ten."

"He's going to give her twenty-five thousand?"

"Which we both know is too much. Don't we, Jack? We both know she'd get lost for a lot less than that, right?"

"She gets a thousand," Jack said, "she'll think she's hit the jackpot."

"Exactly," Paula said. "So you know what we do? We give her five thousand of it. Then you and I split the twenty thousand that's left."

Jack thought about what $10,000 would mean to him right now. "Are you there?" Paula said to him after a moment. "Is there a problem?"

"No," he said, and watched Sharronda stare at the TV. "There's no problem."

"You're thinking you shouldn't take the money, aren't you? You're having reservations all of a sudden."

"No, I'm not," he said.

"Ask yourself, where would little Sharronda be without you and me? We give her five thousand dollars, that's five thousand more than she had yesterday. All she wanted was to have money and the chance to leave. And that's what she's getting."

He was trying to find a down side, and couldn't.

"It's perfect." Paula talked as if she knew what he was thinking. "It's perfect all the way around. Sharronda gets what she needs. Buddy gets what he deserves. You and I don't have to worry about the police and we pay ourselves a bonus besides."

"I like it. It sounds good."

"We could celebrate together," she said. "We could spend some time with each other."

Jack checked his watch. "You said ten o'clock tomorrow?"

"He doesn't want to do it while it's still dark. He's afraid of the dark. A grown man."

"Maybe he can't put his hands on the money until the banks open."

"He's got it," she said. "He's got it right now, ratholed in his office. He told me that the other day, I almost fell out of my chair. All this time he's been stuffing cash."

"Maybe you and I should get together tonight," Jack said. "I could come over."

Paula laughed again. "Get some rest, Jack. Rest yourself up for me. Then you and Sharronda come to his office in the morning."

"Wouldn't miss it," Jack said.

"After that you and I will have lots of time for each other."

"Wouldn't miss that, either," Jack said.

He told Sharronda she would get her money, but didn't say how much. She was not happy about having to wait until the next day. "I can't believe another night in here," she said. "What's the holdup?"

"Some things take time."

"What I'm supposed to do now? You got the answer to that?"

"Wait. The same as me."

"Man." She tossed her head to show her disgust, got up from the couch, and stalked toward the bedroom. "Everything around here goes slow motion."

She went into the bathroom, and Jack heard the shower. Ten minutes later he could see her from the couch as she walked from the bathroom with a towel wrapped around her. She stood in the bedroom, her profile to him, and pulled off the towel. She had on nothing underneath.

He knew she knew he was watching, but he didn't stop. She bent at the waist, her back parallel to the floor, and dried her hair.

Jack wondered how far she was going to take it. He got his answer a few seconds later when she straightened, whirled to face him, and demanded, "What *you* looking at?" Then she slammed the bedroom door.

Not only was the free entertainment portion of

the evening over, but she had cut him off from the air conditioner.

He opened the windows, hoping for a breeze, but didn't feel any. Soon it would be too hot in the room even to consider putting all the boxes and keepsakes back in the closet, which he had planned to do before bed. Jack killed the lights and the TV, stripped to his underwear, and lay on the couch.

He closed his eyes and and felt a strange thought come over him. For the first time in a long time, he was looking forward to the morning.

35

★

At 1:00 A.M. Jack was curled on his couch, his head nestled on a pillow, the room dark and his eyes wide open. He lay sweating in his underwear, listening to the house creak and the kitchen faucet drip.

A car with the radio blaring went by, a mockingbird sang, dogs barked. A few blocks away someone blew a horn twice. The heat wasn't too bad if he didn't move.

He was thinking of Paula Fontaine. He thought of swimming at night in swift, unknown waters. He thought of snake handlers in hillbilly churches. He thought of the difference between weakness and desire. An old song lyric floated through his head, *They say it'll kill me, but they don't say when.*

As he rolled to his side Jack heard what sounded like the slight squeal of brakes from the street. There was no engine noise, and no sound of car doors opening or closing. He listened for another minute or so, heard nothing else, and got up for a drink of water. Three or four steps from the couch, navigating by memory with the lights off, he stepped on his Louisville Slugger, Henry Aaron model.

Jack knew what it was as soon as his foot touched it, but he couldn't stop. The bat rolled on the wooden floor. It was as if something had jerked his feet forward and up for the perfect stuntman's pratfall. For an instant he felt suspended in the blackness. That was the thing about falling at night. You never knew how far down you were going.

He hit the floor on his left hip and elbow, and then the side of his face. There was blunt pain and a low-grade flash in his head like heat lightning. He lay on the floor for a good five minutes, waiting for his senses to clear. His elbow throbbed and his face ached with the slightest touch, but he could tell nothing was broken. He must not have disturbed Sharronda, or else she didn't care enough to come look. The bedroom door stayed closed.

Jack was about to pick himself up when he heard a noise downstairs. He raised his head and listened. It was not loud, but it was steady and sharp. Five more seconds and he knew what it was. Someone was prying the sheet metal off the hole in his front door.

Jack crabbed around on the floor groping for the bat. He found a shoe, a newspaper, a sock, and the matador painting. The noise kept coming from downstairs.

He stood and moved toward the kitchen, routing himself around the lawn chair. In the kitchen he felt his way to the drawer where he thought he had a knife. He remembered the full carving set he had owned when he was married, but his wife got that in the divorce. Jack slid the drawer open and ran his hand inside it. All he could find were two spoons, a plastic fork, and a pair of needle-nose pliers. He took the pliers.

Jack crept to the bottom of the stairs. Whoever was on the other side had pulled off the outer metal panel and was now working on the one nailed to the inside of the door at knee level. Jack positioned himself at the corner where the side wall met the doorframe and tightened his grip on the pliers. Telling himself, I'm in good shape if it's a robot breaking in.

A small, dirty fan-shaped window above the door let in feeble light from a streetlamp. Jack watched as a corner of the sheet metal gave way and peeled back stiffly, pushed by two fingers. Next a full hand poked through and worked the top of the panel free. The nails came out of the door as if they had been hammered in cake. In seconds the panel was on the floor, next to Jack's feet.

He could hear hard breathing on the other side. Then someone began to crawl through the hole.

First came the right arm, with a large watch on the wrist, and the head and shoulders next. Jack stared down at the person and thought, It's like watching a thug hatch.

He could see the back of the man's head—dark hair and thick neck with a gold chain shining weakly in the near-light. Jack knew without a doubt that it was Teddy.

Teddy N. Tunstra II, breaking into his house. Squirming and grunting to squeeze through an opening big enough for a basset hound. He was probably doing what he hated most—breaking a sweat. Jack considered shouting, "Hey!" and giving Teddy a scare. He thought about sitting on Teddy's shoulders and saying, "Giddyup." Then Teddy pulled his left hand through the opening. Teddy had brought a gun.

It was a small revolver, a .32 or a .38. Jack had seen them in court plenty of times for homicide cases. He had heard pathologists take the stand and use clinical language that made murders sound like science projects. They usually brought their charts, which showed an outline of a human form with dotted lines for the bullet's path, going from entry to exit, making you think of maps or mechanical drawings until you saw the actual photographs of the bloody victim full of real holes.

He lifted his foot and stomped his heel onto Teddy's left wrist—hard enough, he hoped, to break it. Teddy cried out and jerked his face toward Jack.

Jack reached down and attached the pliers to Teddy's nose. He squeezed and felt the flesh give. It was the classic Moe Howard technique. Teddy yelped the way a dog does.

With his free hand Teddy tried to break the grip on his nose. He had let go of the gun when Jack's foot got him, so Jack knelt and grabbed it and pushed the barrel against Teddy's ear. Then he freed Teddy from the grip of the pliers.

Teddy put his forehead to the floor and his hands to his face. "Jesus fucking Christ, that hurt. Oh, my nose. Oh, God."

Jack forced the gun harder against Teddy's ear. "You should phone before dropping by," he said.

Teddy moaned and blubbered through his hands. "Oh, God, my fucking nose." He looked up at Jack. In the dim light of the stairwell the blood trickling through his fingers was black. "You ripped it off, man," Teddy said. "You took my nose off. I'm a mess. What did you do that for? Oh, man . . . "

"Somebody breaks in with a gun, I take it seriously. I defend myself."

Teddy said, "Oh, God, oh, God," and pulled himself the rest of the way through the opening. Jack kept the gun to his ear. "You didn't hear me knocking, Jack? I was out here half an hour knocking, no shit. You dint hear me?"

"You're lying."

Teddy labored to his feet. He stood hunched over, bleeding into his cupped hands. Jack backed off but kept the gun on him. "All right, maybe it was only five minutes," Teddy said. "But I knocked, man. Hal's got a job for you and he sent me here to get you, just like always. You dint answer so I figured I'd go in and check everything's okay."

"I thought you didn't like my apartment."

"Hey, I was doing you a favor, all right? The thanks I get, you rip my nose off my face. Man, I gotta get to the hospital. This hurts like a mother."

"You were doing me a favor."

"That's right, man."

"With a gun."

"It's my gun and I carry it, okay? Usually it's in my pocket but when I'm crawling through a dog hole I take it outta my pocket 'cause I don't want it to go off. I don't wanna shoot my balls off by accident, all right? Is that a crime, man, you don't wanna shoot your balls off by accident? Does that sound square to you, Jack? Fuck, man, I thought we was friends."

Jack still had the gun aimed at Teddy's head, but he wasn't sure what to do now.

"Plus, man," Teddy said, "I think you broke my watch when you jumped on my arm. A Rolex, Jack. You know what a Rolex costs?"

"Why did you come here, Teddy?"

"I'm gonna have to bill you for the watch, Jack." Teddy slipped it off his wrist, put it to his ear, shook it, and put it to his ear again. "I think it's croaked."

"I don't believe Rolexes tick," Jack said.

"I might have to get plastic surgery, too, Jack." Teddy gingerly touched the raw part of his nose. "You really tore it up, man. God, this hurts." The watch fell to the floor, and Teddy knelt to retrieve it. "I'm a mess, Jack."

Jack decided the best thing to do would be to keep the gun and tell Teddy to get the hell out. If Teddy made a scene, refused to go, Jack could threaten to call the police and have him arrested for breaking and entering. That should do it.

"I tell you what," Jack said. "I'll let you—"

Teddy leaped out of his crouch and into Jack, pinning him against the wall. His shoulder crushed Jack's chest as he wrapped both his hands around Jack's hand on the gun. Jack reached with his left hand over Teddy's head and tried to bury a finger in each eye as if he had a two-holed bowling ball.

Teddy screamed and jammed an elbow hard into Jack's solar plexus. It was like a blowout at eighty-five. The next thing Jack knew he was on his knees trying to find his breath. He could feel the cold gun barrel against the back of his neck.

"Move and I kill you," Teddy said. "But then I'm gonna kill you anyway, so what the fuck."

The door at the top of the stairs opened. Sharronda's voice said, "What is it?"

"Now who could that be?" Teddy said. "Who's our mystery guest?"

"Is everything okay?" she said.

"He's fine, baby. He'll be right up. Turna lights on for us." Teddy poked the back of Jack's head with the gun. "Tell her to turna lights on."

"Do it, Sharronda," Jack said.

After a few seconds the lights came on upstairs. "Let's go party," Teddy said. Jack climbed the steps with Teddy behind him muttering, "Fucked me up bad, Jack. My nose, oh, man . . . "

In his final months with the DA's office Jack had taken three homicide cases to jury trial. One victim was a night clerk at a motel in Oak Cliff, shot in the mouth during a $58 robbery. One was a prostitute, beaten to death in a Texaco rest room when the john discovered she was really a he. Number three was a potato chip delivery man, shot outside a West Dallas store by a kid who was dumb enough to try to escape in a bright red van with a smiling Mister Krisp potato head painted on the side.

For each case Jack had begun his final summation to the jury the same way. The dead, he said, don't forget the dead. Remember the ones in the ground now who can't speak for themselves. And then Jack had tried to make the jury see a human being like themselves, someone whose death demanded justice. That was easy enough with the clerk and the potato chip route man. They were hard workers with families and dreams, snuffed for a few bucks. But as a general rule in Dallas County, Texas, it was hard to give a jury the weeps over a cross-dressing hooker.

You hoped for some kind of redeeming factor. Maybe the hooker was supporting a retarded brother at home, something like that.

Jack climbed the steps with the gun to his head, the panic blowing through his mind like a big truck down a narrow alley, but for a second or two he saw an underpaid prosecutor trying to make something of him before a jury. Jack had no job, no family, no great works or service to mankind. He hadn't been in the military. Twenty years had passed since he had last attended church. What could be said? *Ladies and gentlemen of the jury, don't forget the dead, a sad case who got shot one night in his underwear.*

"Why are you doing this, Teddy?" Jack said. "What do you want?"

Teddy prodded him hard in the head with the gun barrel. "I want you to keep moving."

Jack paused at the top landing, thinking he could spin around fast now and give Teddy a hard kick. Send him tumbling down the stairs. Put him in a heap of broken bones at the bottom. You saw it all the time in the movies. Teddy must have seen the same shows. Before Jack could do anything Teddy shoved him through the doorway.

Sharronda stood in the middle of the room, feet together, hugging herself. She was wearing one of Jack's old T-shirts.

"Hey, baby," Teddy said. "Good to see you." He moved to the windows and drew the shades, keeping the gun pointed at Jack. Teddy's fingers left smudges of blood on the white shades as they came down like eyes closing.

"Who are you working for?" Jack said. "You have to be working for someone. Who is it?" Sharronda backed away until a wall stopped her. She kept moving her feet as if to push the wall.

"The highest bidder," Teddy said. "And it's a nice piece a change." There was blood down the front of his shirt. He touched the air around the red pulp of his chewed-up nose. "Man, this hurts."

"We can work something out," Jack said. "We can do business."

"Wit you? Some pathetic goob in droopy drawers? The fuck you got I want, Jack?"

"I know stuff you don't." Jack heard himself talking as fast as he could. "We can work this thing together, Teddy. I can help get you a better deal."

Teddy nodded. "We're friends, you and me, Jack? So I'll do you a favor. I'll do it quick and easy, one shot."

"What's your deal? What's your cut on this? I can help you do better. Think about it."

"Now you start running around the room, tryna get away like a rat, I might have to wing you a couple times first." Teddy smiled. "I mean, I'm gonna get you anyway, so what's the use wasting your energy? Am I right?"

Jack's thoughts flashed on a victim he had questioned once while doing a pretrial workup. The man had been robbed, taking a bullet in the side. He was a water-well driller from Venus, Texas, a man in his fifties who had come to Dallas and found work at an all-night doughnut shop, which was where he had been shot. Jack, sitting at his desk and writing on a yellow legal pad, had said, "Can I ask you something? Just out of curiosity, how did it feel?"

"To get shot?" the man said. He leaned over and spit tobacco juice in Jack's metal trash can. "Well, bub, it don't feel too damn good."

Now Teddy said, "Since we're friends and all." He had the gun barrel on a line with Jack's throat. "Get over there."

When Teddy motioned with his head toward the wall he caught a glimpse of himself in the cracked mirror of the open closet door. "Holy Christ," he said. His free hand went slowly to his face like something lifted by a balloon. "My nose, my face, man, look at me. How could you do this to me?"

Teddy had nailed his stare to the mirror. The only chance, Jack thought, for a leap at the gun. Then he saw Sharronda, on Teddy's blind side, bend forward and wrap her fingers around the Louisville Slugger, Henry Aaron model. "Just look at this," Teddy said to the mirror, his fingers gently on his cheek. "You ruint my face."

Sharronda raised the bat, stepped forward, and swung. At the same time Teddy shouted, "Fuck!" and whirled toward her.

The bat was a blur until the end of it caught Teddy square in the crotch. He went down like a big puppet whose strings had been cut.

Jack kicked the gun from Teddy's hand. Teddy lay in a fetal ball on the floor making loud, guttural moans. As Jack bent to pick up the gun Sharronda swung the bat again, connecting with one of Teddy's kneecaps. He screamed and tried to roll away from her.

She was about to hit him once more when Jack yelled, "Hey!" She stopped at the top of her swing and looked at him. "Don't break my bat," Jack said.

36

★

"Come on, man!" Teddy bayed from the bathroom like a sad man lost in the fog. "You hear me, Jack? Talk to me!"

In the living room Sharronda said to Jack, "What's this you wanted to make some kind of deal with him?" She sat on the edge of the couch, the baseball bat beside her. Jack thought about her swing—quick and compact, the stroke of a scrappy hitter who goes to all fields. She said, "What I'm supposed to do when you go with him? I thought you and me had it together. Then you talk like that with him, about working something out."

"Jack!" Teddy called. "Come on, man, let's talk this out! Jack! I think I'm gonna pass out here, Jack!"

"All I wanted," Jack told her, "was for him to put that gun down. I wasn't selling you out. I was trying to save our lives." He had slipped on some pants and was leaning against the kitchen doorframe. The gun lay on top of the TV. "You understand that, don't you? I had to do something."

Sharronda said, "*You* do something? That's pretty funny." She looked at the bat and rolled it across a cushion with her fingertips. "Everybody'd be dead now, waiting for you to do something."

"Okay, I admit it. You're the one who took him down, all right? I admit it. Happy?"

"You saving our lives. I'm like laughing at that."

With Jack thinking, I'm letting myself be mocked by a teenager. "You said that already."

"So what you going to do now, man with the big plans?"

"I'm going into the bathroom and I'm going to talk to Teddy. See if I can get this all figured out."

Sharronda stood. "I'll listen at the door."

"Sit down," Jack said. "This is for me only."

"No way, Dad. Let you handle this now?"

"Sit down," Jack said again. He took a step toward her. Sharronda tensed and tightened her grip on the bat. Jack was out of swinging range but close enough to her that he didn't think Teddy could hear through the bathroom door. "Let me tell you something, little girl. You're the bait here. You understand that? I'm just in the way. You're the one they're after."

She glared at him. Jack said, "I don't know who. I don't really know why. I do have some ideas."

"Yeah, right."

Teddy bayed, "Jack! I'm dying in here!"

Jack pointed over his shoulder with his thumb. "That's the dude with the answers right there. But he's not going to give them to you."

"He might."

"For what? He wants his money. The only way he gets it is to produce you. Can't you see that? So I'm going to walk in there right now and make him think I'm ready to deal."

They stared at each other until Sharronda broke away. "This sucks," she said.

"You don't like it, you can walk. Right now, go ahead. Hit the door if you want."

"Maybe I will."

"Just remember, whoever hired Teddy can hire somebody else."

She dropped slowly back to the couch and shook her head. "I don't know why I believe anything you say."

Because, Jack thought, you have no other choice. He took the gun from the top of the TV and left Sharronda watching a show about UFOs.

Jack found Teddy where he had left him, on his knees in the bathroom, his face a few inches from the floor. The blood still dripped from his nose, fresh red on the gray hexagonal tiles. Jack's bicycle lock, a U-shaped piece of black pipe with a bar across the top, secured Teddy's neck to the chromed gooseneck below the sink.

"Teddy Deuce," Jack said as he stepped over him and sat on the edge of the tub. "How's it hanging, my friend?"

"I'm dying here. Unlock this before I pass out."

"I have some questions."

"Hey, I'll answer 'em all. Just get this collar off me."

"In due time," Jack said.

"I don't say word one till you unlock this."

"Fine." Jack stood and walked out.

"No, man, wait," Teddy called after him. "Have a fucking heart, huh? Jack!"

Sharronda looked up from the TV as Jack crossed the living room but said nothing. Jack went to the kitchen, filled an empty jelly jar with tap water, and drank it. He took his time while Teddy moaned.

After a couple of minutes he stepped over Teddy and sat on the edge of the tub again. He held the gun with both hands. "Want to give it another try?" Jack said.

"Like I got a choice." Teddy had his fingers under his chin and around the lock bar, keeping the pressure off his windpipe. "Jack, no shit, I think I'm puking up blood from my nuts."

"Why are you here?"

"Jack, it was nothing against you, man. I just wanted the colored bitch, that's all. She shouldna run away."

"Run away from what?"

"You got the gun, man. How about this lock off my neck?"

"Run away from what?"

"I can't talk, this bar's so tight."

Jack stepped over to him, placed one foot on the back of his head, and pressed. Teddy gagged and squirmed. When Jack removed his foot and sat back on the tub, he said, "Run away from what?"

Teddy coughed and spit some more blood. "The motel, all right?"

"That was you? You're the one who killed Delbert?"

"What do you know, the lights come on for Jackie. How about a break now, let me sit up straight."

"Why'd you do it?"

"Cause he was an asshole got in the way."

"What were you doing in the motel?"

"The fuck you think I was doing?"

"I'm asking you."

"You got some reason, Jack, for asking me stupid questions? 'Cause you can't be that dumb."

Jack listened to the water dripping from the shower head. Finally he said, "Teddy, you're not any closer to getting that lock off your neck."

Teddy coughed again and spit red bubbles. "Can she hear us?"

"You talking about Sharronda? She's watching TV."

"This bitch is worth big money."

"Whose money?"

"Hey, who do you think? Think about some pictures, think about a tape, and take a wild guess."

"You saying Buddy George?"

"Hey, Jack got another one. Now take this thing off and let's talk business."

Teddy's face was red, and veins stood out yellow on his neck. His nose looked as if an animal had chewed on it. "What kind of business?" Jack said.

"I swear to God, Jack, she's worth fifty thousand. You and me, we could split that. And, hey, maybe boost the price before we deliver. Make him go sixty or seventy, all for you and me."

"Ten minutes ago you were going to kill me and now you want to be friends."

"It was nothing personal, Jack. You know that. I love you like a brother, man. Tell you the truth, I'm glad you nailed me. Now we can be partners."

"The same way you were partners with Buddy George."

Teddy blew a blood mist from his nose. "Why you blaming me, Jack? It wasn't my idea. I was just doing a job, man. You wanna blame someone, try the red-head."

Jack said, "What?"

"You know, the one told Hal she was the Gomer's wife. The true fact is, she works for him. You believe that? You shoulda seen her face when I show up in his office. I thought she was gonna shit her pants. But she seen right away she had first-class material in Teddy Deuce. She's the one came up wit the whole deal, man."

Jack was having his own problems breathing all of a sudden. The room seemed to tilt and grow smaller. "What do you mean?"

Teddy made more gagging sounds. "Jack, you gotta unlock me, I'm gonna croak from no air. Plus there's pubic hairs here on the floor."

"What do you mean she came up with the deal?" Jack said.

"I'm tryna tell you. This whole setup is hers. She got me on the phone today and laid the whole thing out."

Jack saw her face. He thought about the way she had raked her nails across his back.

"Listen, I kept begging her, Don't make me do Jack, Jack's a pal, I can't do that to Jack, no way."

Jack made himself stand. The tiles were cold against his bare feet. He could feel the blood pounding in his head.

"She told me four times," Teddy said. "Four times, you believe that? Get rid a them both, the girl and Jack Flippo. That's what she said, man. You do something to piss her off or what?"

37

★

"I can't believe you left me here with him," Sharronda said when Jack walked back into the apartment. "You don't say nothing, you just take off. I'm like, what now?"

"I had to think some things over," Jack said.

"Yeah, I know. I look out the window and see you sitting on the curb. Half hour later I look again, still there. The whole time I'm in here with that maniac. Dude's in the bathroom going crazy and banging on the pipes."

Jack went to the kitchen, found the number he wanted tacked to the corkboard, and dialed the phone. After eight or nine rings a thick voice answered with, "What time is it?"

"Wake up," Jack said. "We need to talk."

Hal Roper said, "What the hell . . . wait a minute . . . let me get . . . keep your shirt on . . . just a minute." Jack heard him fumbling for something and figured it was either his glasses or the light switch. He waited until Hal said, "All right, who's this?"

"It's Jack."

"You're in jail, right? Two, what, three o'clock in the morning you call me 'cause you're in jail."

"I'm coming over, Hal. I want to talk to you."

Hal had a coughing fit, then said, "Forget it. I got nothing to say to you, Benedict Arnold."

"I'll be there in half an hour," Jack said.

"The hell's that screaming and wailing in the background?"

"It's nothing."

"Sounds like you're in the state hospital."

"Half an hour," Jack said, and hung up.

Sharronda lay on the couch in the flickering blue light of the TV. "Let's go," Jack said.

"Go where?"

"I'll tell you in the car. Put your shoes on."

"Go where?"

Teddy made a kind of howling noise and banged the lock bar against the sink's drainpipe.

"You want to come with me," Jack said, "or stay here with him?"

Sharronda glanced toward the bathroom. "I have to pee."

"We'll stop at a gas station. Come on." Jack took the gun from the kitchen, where he had left it while he used the phone. He slid it into the front of his jeans, with the grip hanging over the waistband, the way your men of action did it in the movies. Jack discovered there was nothing in the world quite like having the barrel of a loaded gun resting against your cock. He slowly pulled the gun out, got a seersucker blazer from his closet, and put it on. The gun felt better against his chest. And there was a bonus: Jack found three crumpled dollar bills in one of the coat's pockets. "Let's go," he said.

Jack checked his watch as they walked outside— nearly 2:00 A.M. He unlocked the Buick and got in. Sharronda hesitated, then opened her door and slid into the passenger seat. "Where are you taking me?" she asked.

"To a friend's," Jack said as he started the car. "To someone else's house. You can wait there while I set things up. That's all I can tell you right now."

"I'm just supposed to go with you, not ask any questions. Just follow you like everything's cool."

Jack didn't answer, looking straight ahead into the dark and listening to the engine hum. He could feel Sharronda's eyes on him while she tried to decide if she believed him or not. Finally she said, "Man," and turned sharply away. He switched on the headlights and backed out.

Five minutes later he stopped at a Mobil mini-mart on Greenville Avenue, parking near the street, next to a garden of plastic shrubs planted in some orange gravel. While Sharronda used the rest room, Jack got some coffee for himself. It came in a plastic foam cup and had been fresh five or six hours before. Jack sat in the car, forcing muddy sips and waiting for Sharronda. He took a pen and a pad that he had bought with the coffee and wrote, *#1, leave Dallas. Do not come back. Do not contact anyone here.*

Jack looked up from the pad and saw Sharronda coming out of the rest room. While she gave the key back to the cashier he wrote, *#2, establish new ID ASAP. Never use your old name again.*

He put the pad and pen in the back seat as Shar-ronda got into the car. "What's that?" she said.

"Nothing you want to know about," Jack answered. He tossed the coffee out the window, started the car, checked the side mirror, and shifted into drive. As he began to pull away he glanced at the mirror again. "Jesus." Jack hit the brakes so hard Sharronda nearly bounced her face off the dash.

"What's *wrong* with you, man? What kind of driv-ing's that?"

Jack kept his eyes on the mirror. "I don't believe this," he said.

"Believe what?"

He could see a car, parked in an empty lot half a block away. Its lights were off, but someone was behind the wheel.

"Hey, believe what?" Sharronda said.

"This is not good."

"I'm like real tired of you not telling me nothing."

"I think someone's following us," Jack said.

Sharronda twisted and looked back. "Who? I don't see a thing."

"This side of the street, beneath the Mexican restaurant sign. See it?"

"Where?"

"You'd think they'd get some better cars," Jack said. "Those old Reliants, you might as well put a light on top."

"That car? That's the one?"

"This screws things up in a big way."

Sharronda kept asking questions, wanting to know who it was and why he was there and what was going to happen. Jack tuned her out and stared at the mirror. He was trying to stay calm while he broke into an itchy sweat, trying to think while the voice inside screamed that it was all over now.

Finally he turned to Sharronda and said, "Stay here till I get back. Don't move, you hear me?" He started to open his door, then turned back to Sharronda and held out his hand. "Let me borrow ten dollars."

Inside the minimart Jack found what he wanted on a shelf next to some duct tape and a couple of packages of thumb tacks—a tube of Amazing Miracle Glue. DRIES IN SECONDS! the label said. Even had the Good Housekeeping Seal of Approval. Jack could see himself sending them a letter: Dear Good Housekeeping, I'm writing you from jail, which means the damn glue you approved didn't work.

Back in the car he told Sharronda, "Listen to me."

"Here we go again."

"I mean it," he said. "Listen to me."

"I'm here, right? You see plugs in my ears? No, you don't, so what else you want?"

"Two things you'll have to do when we get out of the car."

"Who said anything about getting out of the car?"

"Two things." Jack turned from the mirror, looked at Sharronda, and softened his voice. "The first is, act like you're my girlfriend. Like you're crazy about me, like you're so hot for me you can't stand it."

"In your dreams, Dad."

Jack put the tube of glue in her hand. "That's the easy part."

They walked to the pay phones outside the minimart together, their arms around each other, and Sharronda nuzzled his neck. She stayed close to him while he pretended to make a call. Then he hung up the phone and told Sharronda, "Here we go."

Jack faced the car beneath the Mexican restaurant sign and waved his right arm above his head. "Hey, Barton!" he called. Sharronda joined in, both of them waving and calling, "Hey, Barton!" like a couple on a desert island trying to flag down a rescue ship.

After about thirty seconds of this the car door opened. The driver stepped out and Jack could see that it really was Barton Eskew. Barton locked his door and walked fast toward them.

"You see what he did?" Jack said. "He locked the car."

"My eyes work," Sharronda answered.

"He's headed our way," Jack told Sharronda, "Smile, laugh. You're having the time of your life."

When Barton was twenty feet away Jack greeted him with, "Hey, it's my old friend." Barton was wearing the same suit as the day before. He kept coming, and coming some more, bearing down on them with the same rabid gerbil face Jack remembered.

He finally stopped near enough to them that Jack could smell the English Leather.

Barton said, "You think that's funny, asshole?"

"Call me a lowbrow," Jack said, "but dumb cops crack me up."

Barton moved so close that even in the bad light Jack could count the blackheads on his nose. "I oughtta hammer you right now."

"Sharronda," Jack said, "you know what it means when somebody says ought to? It means wants to but can't." Sharronda giggled and licked Jack's ear. It gave Jack a shiver.

Barton watched with disgust, then came back in

Jack's face. "That's endangering a police officer's life. I'm on surveillance, you call me out like that, that's compromising the investigation and the officer's safety."

Jack looked at him. "Right."

"You don't have no idea who I was watching—"

"I see your grammar still has its problems."

"—and you don't know what you're screwing up, you start yelling my name." Barton brought his right hand up, his index finger almost touching Jack's chin. Jack wasn't surprised to see that Barton bit his nails to the nub. "You keep pulling this cute shit," Barton said, "you'll have police blood on your hands someday."

Jack rubbed the corner of his mouth and said, "How long you had this problem, Barton, of separating truth from fiction?"

Barton, never taking his eyes from Jack, backed off half a step, lit a cigarette, blew out the match, and dropped it on top of Jack's shoe. Jack shook it off. Then Barton looked at Sharronda and said, "Who's this?"

Jack pulled her tight. "She's my entertainment. Aren't you, Sharronda?"

Sharronda nodded, kissed him on the side of the neck, and laid her left hand on Jack's crotch. Say this for the girl, she put everything into the role.

Barton said, "You are some pathetic piece of work, buddy."

Jack leaned toward him. "The hell you want, Barton? You just want to follow me around? Fine. I don't care. Follow all you want, waste some city money."

"I might."

"Go right ahead."

"Or I might just take you downtown right now. Save us all a lot of time and trouble."

Jack stroked Sharronda's hair. He said, "Sharronda, I think Barton's been watching those old movies where the cop says, 'I oughtta run you in' when he doesn't know what else to do. What do you think?"

"I think so," she said.

"Me, too," Jack said. "Is that true, Barton?" Instead of answering Barton smiled, or something like it. The corners of his mouth turned up into his round little cheeks, but his eyes weren't part of the package. They stayed shiny and cold, making Jack uneasy. Jack was thinking, The rodent has spied some cheese.

He opened his wallet and gave Sharronda two dollars. "I'm hungry, babe. Go in the store and get me something good, like a Dr Pepper and some beef jerky." Sharronda took the money and left. Jack looked at Barton and said, "You think you've got something on me, don't you?"

Barton gave an imitation laugh and said, "Want to tell me the real story? Instead of that bullshit you laid on me and Detective Blanchard yesterday?"

Jack stared at his feet and sighed, buying time. A man coming out of the minimart passed between Jack and the phones, which was what Jack had been waiting for. He glanced at the man, then said to Barton, "It's too crowded here. Let's go over to my car and talk."

Barton stayed half a step behind Jack as they crossed the parking lot, his rubber soles making no noise on the pavement. Jack worried that Teddy's gun created so much bulge in his coat that Barton would notice. Barton sees that, he thought, and the evening takes another bad turn.

Thinking about the gun made Jack flash on all the

things that could go wrong with what he was doing, how if one wheel locks up the whole train derails. For a second or two he had to fight the urge to drop everything and run, just sprint into the dark and don't look back. He was so close to doing it his legs twitched.

When they reached his car Jack leaned against the trunk and rested one shoe on the rear bumper, which he thought might appear casual. Barton stood three or four feet away, his arms folded across his chest, looking pleased with himself.

Jack started talking. "You know, Barton, I've been around." He slid his hands in his back pockets. "It takes more to scare me than your huffing and blowing."

Barton said, "That a fact." He flicked his cigarette butt to the pavement in front of Jack.

Glancing over Barton's shoulder, Jack saw Sharronda come out of the minimart and run toward Barton's car. He looked quickly away to the bad paint on the trunk of the Buick. "So don't get the idea," Jack said, "that I'm about to tell you something just because you showed up and barked awhile. What's that joke? You know, about the rooster that took credit for the sunrise."

"You have some kind of point in all this?"

Jack looked up and away, giving himself the half second it took to see Sharronda kneeling beside Barton's car. "Yeah. Yeah, I do. But let me ask you first, why are you following me?"

"Never said I was."

"Did you see me sitting out in front of my house? I was out there a long time tonight, sitting on the curb. I wasn't paying much attention, I guess, 'cause I didn't notice you staking me out."

Barton sniffed and said, "What difference does it make?"

With Jack thinking, because I want to know if you were there when Teddy was breaking in, I want to know what you saw, what you know. "No difference," he said. Sharronda was up and moving around Barton's car. "Just wondering."

"You said you wanted to tell me something."

"I said I wanted to talk."

"Same thing."

Jack nodded once. "Maybe so." He saw Sharronda kneeling at the other side of car, then locked stares with Barton. "About the guy killed in the motel." Barton waited. Jack said, "Some things have happened since you and Meshack came by. I think I may have some information for you on that."

"Imagine my surprise."

Now Sharronda was up and running away from Barton's car. Jack tried to remember if the Amazing Miracle Glue was supposed to dry in minutes or seconds. "I've come into some information," he said.

"You said that. Like what?" Barton burrowed into him with the eyes.

"And I'm happy to share this information with you." Jack saw Sharronda go back into the minimart. "But not here in the middle of a parking lot."

"Then let's go downtown," Barton said.

"Fine. Because I want this to be tape-recorded, and I want a lieutenant or a sergeant there."

He showed the smile again. "I got no problem with that."

"You can dredge somebody up this time of night?"

"Shouldn't be hard," Barton said.

"'Cause I don't want to go down there and then

have to spend a lot of time just waiting around for somebody to show up."

"We'll call ahead and make some reservations."

"I don't know." Jack scratched the back of his neck. "Maybe tomorrow would be better."

"Tonight," Barton said and ran his tongue across his front teeth. "Right now."

Sharronda came out of the store carrying a can. Jack gestured with his chin toward her and Barton turned around. "The girl can take my car, go on her way. She's got nothing to do with this."

Barton watched her walk up to Jack and hand him a Dr Pepper. "No more beef jerky," she said. "They sold out."

"She's got no idea in the world about any of this," Jack said to Barton.

Barton studied her and seemed about to ask her something. Jack thought of Buddy George, Jr. up on stage, bathed in the spotlight, chanting to his paying customers, *Close the sale, close the sale, close the sale!* He asked Barton, "So are we doing this deal or not?" When Barton pulled his eyes off Sharronda and came back to him, Jack said, "I'm ready to talk. You want it or not?"

Barton looked at Sharronda again, then back at Jack and said, "All right. Let's go."

"Give me a second to talk to her," Jack said. "I'll be right with you. You bring the ride up, I'll be ready to go."

Barton walked backward for five or six steps, then wheeled and made straight for his car. "Get in," Jack told Sharronda.

When Barton was almost to the Reliant, Jack slid in next to Sharronda and started the Buick. At the sound of it, Barton whirled and looked. Jack stuck his hand out the window and gave a quick wave as he pulled from the lot. He got one more glimpse, a shaky one in the rearview mirror as he roared away, of Barton crouched in front of the Reliant's door, trying to put his key into the lock.

After taking a quick left, running a red light, and then making a right turn, Jack and Sharronda were on North Central Expressway doing sixty and blending into the traffic. "What's he gonna do when those doors don't open because of all that sticky mess?" Sharronda asked.

"Probably break the window," Jack said, and had to laugh. "I hope the department takes it out of the little bastard's pay."

38

★

They moved up North Central, passing trucks and dodging a few weaving drunks. Merle Haggard did a song on the radio.

"His eyes scared me more than anything," Sharronda said.

"He what?" For a moment Jack thought she was talking about Merle Haggard.

"He had that gun when he came into your house, but his eyes scared me more than the gun. I can't really say why."

Jack was grateful not to have her yammering at him for once. "You're talking about Teddy? Don't worry about him. You'll never have to mess with him again. Because he's history. He's out of your life."

"Good."

"So's Barton Eskew, for that matter. You did a good job back there."

"Yeah," she said and smiled. "I did, didn't I."

They went west on LBJ, and no one said anything for about six miles. The radio played a song about a guy escaping to a tropical island. It sounded good to Jack.

As they turned onto I-35 north Sharronda said, "Delbert would get this look when he couldn't get high, it was like a dog that was growling and about to bite you. But this other dude, this Teddy, his eyes, I don't know . . . Made me think of busted-out windows in a vacant house."

Jack lowered his left arm on the steering wheel and felt the gun in his pocket. "Yeah, well, you took care of him. One swing from you and he dropped like a sack of peas."

"Somebody had to."

She was starting again. Jack turned up the radio so he wouldn't have to listen. "This music sucks," she shouted.

In ten minutes they passed the Dallas County line and in another ten left the suburbs behind. Jack made his exit just past the lake, took a left, and pointed the Buick down a dark two-lane doing about sixty-five. He lowered the radio volume and told Sharronda, "We'll be there soon."

After a while she said, "Be where?"

"Remember I told you about Hal Roper, the lawyer? He lives way the hell out here in the country."

"Who?"

"We talked about him a little bit when we were eating our pizza. I was telling you how I made my living, remember?"

"I know you were talking some shit but I wasn't listening."

Jack turned the radio back up. After two turns and six or seven miles he saw a white mailbox with an orange newspaper tube and three round red reflectors. Just past the mailbox the unpaved driveway met the road.

"Pay attention to this," Jack said as he made the turn.

"To what?"

"Just watch."

The car bounced and lurched over the driveway through a thicket. Tree branches brushed against the side windows. "You know where you're going?" Sharronda said. Then the car broke into a clearing. Hal's low, long brick house stood across it.

Jack remembered his afternoons out here, riding Hal's lawn mower back and forth across the expanse of grass and weeds, waiting for his life to pull together. And now, he thought, it just might happen. A few hours ago he was almost dead. Now, with a little luck and the right moves, it's Easy Street, smooth sailing, the gravy train. What was it Buddy George had said in the book Jack bought? The only hole you can't crawl out of is the one in the cemetery.

He parked the Buick in the driveway behind Hal's car. Hal's porch light came on, the front door opened, and Hal stepped out. He was wearing a red jogging suit with fuzzy blue bedroom slippers.

"What's up here?" Sharronda said. "Who's that old dude?"

Jack rolled down his window as Hal walked toward the car. Halfway there Hal said, "Is someone gonna tell me what the hell is going on?"

"Good morning, Hal," Jack called.

Hal stuck his face in the open window and said, "I'm plenty pissed, my friend." The words rode in on a smell of nicotine and morning breath. "Teddy disappears, then shows up and makes like some goddamn muscle. Talks like he's cooking a deal I got no part of. Teddy Tunstra, thinks he's gonna screw with me, you believe that?"

"Hal," Jack said, "meet Sharronda Simms. Sharronda, this is Hal."

"Then you call me up three o'clock in the morning with some big emergency. Like I owe you a favor, Jack."

Jack switched on the dome light. "Meet Sharronda Simms," he said again. "You recognize Miss Simms from her pictures?"

Hal flipped his gaze on her, then back on Jack, then back on Sharronda. When it registered he pounded the roof of the car with his fist. "I knew it. I *knew* it. You were working an angle all along. You son of a bitch. You were, weren't you. Huh?"

Jack snapped off the light. "If it makes you feel any better to think so."

"You're a goddamn pickpocket. A snake. Turn my back you put a knife right in it." Hal took a long draw on his Camel. The orange glow threw shadows on his face. He blew the smoke into the car.

"Sharronda needs a place to stay the rest of the night," Jack said.

"You mean a place to hide." Hal looked at her. "That what he means, honey, a place to hide?"

"No way I stay here," Sharronda said, staring straight ahead.

Jack said, "She needs a place to relax for a few hours. You do it, Hal, there's a thousand dollars for you."

Hal worked a laugh through the phlegm. "You have a thousand bucks, Jack? That's a good one."

"No way I stay here," Sharronda said.

"One thousand dollars, Hal. Yes or no." Jack

focused on the speedometer. You believed it, this car could go 110 miles per hour. "Yes or no, Hal."

Hal shoved his palm in front of Jack's face. "Show me the cash."

Jack pushed his hand away. "Show me the cash," Hal said again.

"As soon as I leave here I'm going to pick it up."

Hal snorted. "You don't have a grand on you? Who'd a thought it, Jack."

"Yes or no," Jack said.

Sharronda shook her head. "No way, man."

"For how long?" Hal said.

"I told you."

"The police looking for her?" Hal fixed on Sharronda. "Hey, hon, the police looking for you?"

"Ask the police," Jack said.

"Maybe I should. Give 'em a call, maybe."

"Maybe I should take the thousand dollars someplace else," Jack said.

Hal quit talking for a few seconds. Sharronda, too. Jack could hear crickets and the ticking of the car's cooling metal.

"Fifteen hundred," Hal said. Jack shook his head and reached to turn the key in the ignition. "Fifteen hundred or no deal," Hal said. Jack started the car and said, "Bye."

"All right, Christ," Hal said. "Get her in here." He turned and walked to the house. Jack watched him go, saw him waving his arms and heard him muttering.

"Forget it, Dad," Sharronda said.

Jack turned the car off. "Why don't you go in, get some sleep, maybe something to eat. Hal's a little cranky, maybe, but he won't hurt you. He'll probably fix you breakfast."

"No way."

"It's the only way." He tried to say it softly. "I'll be back in a couple of hours." He put his hand on her shoulder. She shook it off.

"Like you got it all figured out."

"Yeah," Jack said, "I think I do. Just give me a chance."

She glared at him. "Then tell me what it is."

Jack waited, then said, "You'll have to trust me."

"Oh, yeah. Every time somebody white says that to me, time for lie your ass off time." She looked away. "Just take me to my home."

Tender wasn't working. Jack was tired of tender, and it was getting late. "Sure," he said. "Just take you home, let you go back to your normal life."

"That's right."

"And Monday morning you show up at the Salon d'Elaine. Polish a few nails, all this never happened."

"Uh-huh."

Jack could see her shoulders trembling, could hear her taking shallow breaths and letting them out fast. "What about Delbert?" he said. "Pretty soon those detectives figure out who he is. That happens, you're the first person they visit."

"I don't care."

"And don't forget Teddy. He won't be in the mood to laugh about that incident with the bat."

She didn't answer. He was about to ask her, Don't you want to see your kid? What about your baby? Before the words could snake from his mouth, Sharronda opened the car door and stepped out.

She slammed the door hard, rocking the car, and crossed in front of Jack on her way to the house. Hal had left the door unlocked, and she walked in without knocking. Jack doubted her host would greet her with a hearty welcome and a tray of hors d'oeuvres, so he got out of the car and followed her in.

He found her in front of an open refrigerator. "At least this dude's got food," she said. Hal was coughing somewhere in the back of the house. Jack trailed the sound down a hallway and through a bedroom. He saw Hal leaning over a bathroom sink, hacking like a TB patient. A smoldering Camel rested on the edge of the sink in a nest of brown cigarette burns. The red jogging suit lay in a heap on the floor. The sight of Hal in his boxer shorts made Jack think of a turtle that had lost its shell.

When he stopped coughing Hal said, "I thought you left."

"Don't let her go anywhere," Jack said. "I don't think she'll try. But if she does, don't let her."

"Who, the girlie? You didn't say anything about baby-sitting."

"I don't think she'll run away. Just discourage her from taking a walk or anything."

Hal reached into the shower stall and turned on the water. "Whatever."

"She needs to be here when I get back."

Hal dropped his boxer shorts to the floor. "In other words, I have to keep her around the house to collect my grand."

"Exactly," Jack said.

The bathroom began to fill with steam. "I'll be out in a minute," Hal said. He opened a glass door that had a sandblasted mermaid on it and stepped in. "Make a pot of coffee. I'll be right out. I get out, we'll be like Siamese twins, her and me."

Jack left the bathroom and pulled the door shut.

He glanced around Hal's bedroom. A pair of slacks had been thrown over a chair. There were golf tees on the dresser, along with an ashtray and pennies in a glass, but no family pictures. The bedside table had water rings on the wood and an electric alarm clock. Jack picked up a pillow, pulled it from its case, and stuffed the case in a pocket of his jacket. It made his throat tighten when he looked at the bed, the way the mattress sagged in one narrow place from one body for so many years.

He went to the kitchen and found Hal's keys on a hook next to the telephone. There was a flashlight on top of the refrigerator, and he took that, too. Sharronda sat at a round table eating a bowl of corn flakes. "I'll be back in a couple of hours," Jack told her. She didn't look at him or answer. "Did you hear me?" he said.

"Hey, man," she said without glancing up. "You owe me fifteen dollars. Five for the pizza and ten for back at that store."

"Take a number," Jack said as he walked out of the house.

He had less than three hours until dawn. Jack started the Buick and returned across the clearing and through the woods, up the driveway to the paved road. There, he turned right and went about twenty yards to the next driveway. It was another stretch of dirt and gravel. He backed into it.

The brush was even thicker here, scraping the car on both sides, with the branches making small screaming noises against the metal. Jack worked his slow way with the Buick's backup lights. If he remembered right, the road went all the way to the lake. It had been access for fishermen and duck hunters.

When he cleared the brush at last, he hit the brakes. He was where the shoreline would be if there had been enough rain to keep the lake full. Jack turned on the interior light and took the pen and notepad from the back seat. He added to the list he had started, just to make the point again, #3, *Never come back to Dallas*. Thinking, It's going to be nothing but scorched earth for you anyway.

39

★

Jack left the Buick at the end of the dirt road. He used Hal's flashlight to find his way through the woods and brush back into Hal's yard. The only sounds as he crossed to the house were the crickets and frogs, his feet in the dry grass and himself breathing hard.

Hal's car was an Oldsmobile, four or five years old. It smelled of cigarettes. The driver's seat was so far forward that Jack could barely squeeze in. He found the right key and started the car. The radio was set on easy listening.

He turned the heater on high and kept the windows rolled up. By the time he reached Paula's street a half hour later, Jack had sweated through his shirt and his coat. His hair was matted wet, his face dripping.

Jack left the gun in the car. He parked at the curb, ran to her porch, and pounded on her door with his left hand while ringing her bell with his right. Yelling, "Paula! Paula!"

A light came on behind the blinds and the peep-hole darkened. Jack took deep breaths, ran a hand through his hair, checked the street, pounded the doorframe, and shouted her name again. He even bugged his eyes out a little bit.

The door opened and he pushed inside. Paula said, "Jack?"

He remembered the way she had walked into Hal's office two nights before. She had acted then like a ballsy room burglar striding across the lobby of a big hotel, pockets stuffed with stolen diamonds. Now she had the look of someone who had taken a blow and couldn't focus.

She began to back away from him. He stopped her with, "You've got to help me."

Paula managed to say, "Help you . . . "

"I don't know what to do," Jack said as he began to pace the room. He darted his eyes around, swabbed his face with an open hand, and talked fast. "It's Buddy George. He's gone psycho. He's gone nuts, Paula." He rubbed his head like a man with a migraine. "You hear what I'm saying? He came after me. Buddy George. Paula, he tried to have me killed."

She swallowed, blinked, and said, "Buddy did? You're saying Buddy?"

"It's unbelievable. I never dreamed—I mean, I thought we were just working a little pay-for-play, you and me. Just making a couple of bucks off him, that's all. But then he flips out. Buddy George sends a goon after me and Sharronda."

Paula held her hand to her face, the nails like five big drops of blood against her skin. She licked her lips, looked away from Jack for a second and then back at him.

"You're sure it was Buddy?" she said.

"Hell yes, I'm sure."

She shook her head slowly. "Buddy can be a ruthless bastard when he wants."

"I need a drink bad," Jack said. "You still got that gin?"

They sat at the table in the kitchen again. Paula was wearing the same white silk robe. Jack tossed down one gin, refilled the glass, and put another one away. "I can't stop shaking," he said. Paula poured him a third glassful, which he picked up but didn't drink. If he had to take one more swallow he'd throw up on his shoes.

Paula crossed her legs and folded her arms. Then she smoothed the robe against her thigh with an open hand, retied the sash, looked at him for a moment, and glanced away. She kept her hands busy. With Jack thinking, She's afraid to ask what happened.

"I don't know what I'm gonna do now," he said. "I might be in Lew Sterrett tomorrow. I'm headed for jail if I don't do something."

"I don't know what you mean."

Jack stood and walked across the kitchen, clenching his fists behind his head, moving like a man with cramps. "I was asleep, sound asleep in my own house. After you and I talked on the phone I had some dinner and then I went to sleep, right? My own house."

He came back to the table, sat down again, and took her hands in his, struck by how cold they were. "The next thing I know somebody is sticking a gun barrel up my nose."

"Oh, God."

"The guy puts a gun on me and switches on the lamp and it's Teddy Tunstra." Paula pulled her hands away. "Can you believe that?" Jack said. "You remember him?"

"Not really." She folded her arms again and looked at Jack's chest.

"Big jerk who was at Hal's office with us."

"Uh-huh."

"Teddy Tunstra in my house with his gun in my face, wiping my nose with it. And he's laughing. He says, 'Present from Buddy George. For you and the colored bitch.'" Jack paused to let it take root. "A gun up my nose and it's a present from Buddy George."

"He said that."

"And he's laughing, too. Did I tell you that? Big joke, the asshole's laughing." Jack jumped to his feet so fast he knocked his chair over. He whirled toward the sink and pounded his fist once on the countertop. After a few seconds he turned back toward her and held his arms out. "I killed him, Paula. The stupid fuck, putting a gun on me."

"You?" She searched his face. "You did?"

"He had the gun on me. I knew I was about to die, I had to do something." Jack made two fists beneath his chin. "I shot my hands up like this. Fastest I've ever moved in my life, what terror will do. I was trying to push the gun away from me. What else could I do, right?"

Jack ran some cold water and splashed it on his face. He dried himself with the tail of his shirt. "The gun went off," Jack said quietly, and turned to face her. He put a finger on his throat. "One shot, right there. He was dead before he hit the floor.

Sharronda and I dragged him into the bathtub."

He stood still as Paula got up and came to him. She put her arms around him and squeezed, her face against his chest. "Jack, Jack, Jack," she said. "I'm so glad you're here."

40

★

The two of them did it on the kitchen floor, fast and loud with the lights on. Jack never even got his pants all the way off. They stayed bunched around his ankles, which made him feel like a high school kid nailing his prom date.

This was a new experience for Jack, sex with a woman who had just sent someone to kill him. The whole time he kept his hands on hers, pinning her wrists to the floor. That helped him feel her entire body under him, pushing and giving. It also kept him from worry over taking a pair of scissors in the back.

When they were finished and he lay on top of her, still inside her, Jack thought of the last time he had seen Marla Kendrick.

It had happened after he had lost his job, after his marriage had become the playground of divorce lawyers. He had not talked to Marla since the day District Attorney Johnny Hector called him in and told him what a dumb bastard he was to sleep with the wife of a coke dealer pending trial. Which, look-

ing back, was hard to argue against. Unless you'd
seen Marla.

One gray muddy day in February he woke up
wanting to talk to her, so he called the office where
she had worked. She had quit last year, a secretary
told him. Next he drove to her old apartment. It was
vacant, and the manager said she had moved out
before Christmas. Jack phoned a friend with the DA
who ran some records and got her new address.

He drove to a peeling frame house in a tired
neighborhood a few blocks west of Love Field. The
front yard had a spindly bare mimosa tree and some
brown weeds. A bedsheet was hanging in one front
window, a towel in another. The doorbell didn't seem
to work, so Jack knocked.

Marla opened the door, looked at him for a few
seconds, and said, "I figured you'd be by sooner or
later."

She gave him a cup of instant coffee and sat on a
threadbare couch next to him. He could smell the
space heater. An old German shepherd slept on the
oval braided rug. Marla wore tight faded jeans and a
T-shirt, and she looked as good as she always had.

"Barron's working," she said. "He got a job painting cars."

"You're still married, then."

"Oh, yeah. That's a good thing that came out of all
this. Barron went straight, no more coke or nothing.
We don't have much money, I mean you can see that,
but it's a whole lot better."

The coffee table was an old telephone-cable spool.
Six or seven empty Miller cans had been left on it,
surrounding a tartan sandbag ashtray. Jack watched
Marla put a match to a Marlboro Light and blow out

the smoke like someone with nothing in the world to worry about.

"I should've called you after I got fired," Jack said. "You knew I got fired?"

She nodded. "Barron's lawyer told us."

"I should've been in touch or something. Let you know what happened."

"Hey, no problem." She smoked her cigarette and stroked the dog's belly with her foot. The shepherd scratched itself with a hind leg and Marla laughed. "Look at him, what do you think he's dreaming about?"

Jack told her he had come by to let her know that he didn't blame her for what happened. Marla said it was okay if he did. Jack said no, he was the one who had let it go forward and he was the one who should have stopped it. Marla shrugged and said it was all in the past now.

Then Jack had set his coffee cup down amid the empty beer cans and put his hand on her arm. "I need to ask one thing," he said. "I want to know if you have any idea who made the call."

"Made the what?"

"I just need to know. Not for payback, not for anything except to close it in my own mind. Do you know? I'm talking about who called Johnny Hector and told him about us. Was it Barron? If it was Barron, you can tell me. Or his lawyer, was that it? I'm not going to do anything to them, I just need to know."

Marla gave him a puzzled look. "This is you trying to be funny, right?"

"No, listen. No. I want to know who turned us in." He gripped her arm harder. "On top of everything

else I lost you, too. I want to know how that happened. I want to know who did it."

Marla pulled his fingers from her and shook her
head. "I did, Jack. I mean, who else?"

Jack, standing over Paula in the kitchen, pulled up
his pants. "I think I've got it," he said. "Get Buddy on
the phone."

"Jesus, what?" Paula rolled over and knelt on the
floor. She pulled the robe around her and tied the
sash. "Run that by me again."

"There's a way out of this."

She stood and faced him. "There always is."

"A lot has changed, but two things haven't." Jack
buttoned his shirt. "Buddy still needs things cleaned
up, and he still has the money to pay for it. At least I
assume he has the money."

"He's rolling in it," she said. "I told you, he's been
ratholing it in his office."

"He still needs it taken care of so that Sharronda
won't talk. That's still his problem. He'll pay for that,
won't he?"

She smiled. "What are you thinking?"

"I'm thinking I do it for him," Jack said, watching
her face. "For fifty thousand dollars, I do it for him.
Then you and I go away. We disappear, I'm thinking
Mexico. The Pacific Coast, maybe Manzanillo."

He waited for her to answer. "No," Paula said
finally. "No." She came close and ran a finger around
the ridge of his ear. "Let's make it a hundred thousand, not fifty. And not Mexico. Costa Rica."

41

★

Jack stood in Paula's kitchen using the phone. He let Buddy George, Jr. shout for a while about chiselers and roaches, gave him a couple of minutes to get it out of his system. Buddy sounded as if he had been drinking most of the night.

When Buddy finished Jack said, "I'm a businessman. I'm proposing a business deal."

"Oh, yeah. You bet. Lemme tell you about binnessmen and binness deals, friend. You don't know a damn thing about—"

"I know you tried to have me killed," Jack said in a level voice. "I know all about that." There was silence on the other end. Finally Buddy asked him, "What is it you want?"

"Like I said, I want to make a business deal."

"This oughtta be something."

"Here's the deal. You're going to pay me one hundred thousand dollars cash."

Buddy made a gurgling sound. "Like hell I am."

"In return, I'm going to handle Sharronda." Jack

gave him a few seconds to swallow that. "And you're going to be there while I do it. We'll all be there, so if one of us goes down someday or somewhere, we all go down. Sort of a group insurance policy in reverse."

Get your hundred grand together, Jack told him, and wait in your car in front of your office. He and Paula would be there in twenty minutes, and Buddy could follow them.

"To where?" Buddy said.

"Where Sharronda is," Jack said. "About twenty-five miles north of here. Follow us."

"I don't like this one damn bit. I don't cotton to this."

"Neither do I. But it's the box we're all in."

"And what the hell are you doing at Paula's?"

"Using the phone."

"Howda I know," Buddy said, "that you're not gonna hit me on the head, take all my damn money? Way out there in the middle of who the hell knows where."

"You don't. Just like I don't know if you're going to send somebody over to my place with a gun again."

"I don't like this one damn bit."

"We'll be there in twenty minutes," Jack said. "If you're not there in your car waiting, we keep on going and I turn Sharronda loose on the world. My guess is she'll want to talk to the police right away. And after she talks, then I start blabbing. Who loses more from that, me or you?"

"Listen up, friend. Ain't nobody in this town'd believe a damn word of it."

"Try us." Jack hung up the phone.

"Is he going to do it?" Paula asked him.

Jack ran his hand inside her robe and kissed her on the neck. "Get dressed," he said. "Then we'll drive on over and see."

He was waiting in his car in the parking lot. Jack pulled into the next space and rolled down his window. "You have the hundred thousand?"

Buddy began to shout. "Hey, lemme tell you what, you weasly son of a bitch. When Buddy George makes a decision—"

"Just nod yes or no. Do you have the money?"

Buddy gave him an angry stare, then nodded yes once.

Jack nodded, too. "Show me."

Buddy stared some more, then lifted a black briefcase next to his open window and cracked the lid an inch or two.

"It's dark out here," Jack said. Buddy turned on his car's inside light and opened the briefcase a few more inches.

"My God," Paula said to Jack. "Look at all that."

"Stay behind me," Jack told Buddy. "It's a long trip."

Jack drove to the parking lot exit. Buddy's car didn't move. Paula turned to look. "He's not coming," she said. "What do we do now? He's just sitting there. He's not coming."

"Well . . . " Jack wasn't sure what the rest of his answer would be.

"You've got the gun," she said. "Just go take the money from him right now."

Jack, watching in the mirror, saw Buddy's lights go on. "He's coming now."

"You could still take the money from him right now. He couldn't do a thing about it."

Jack turned to Paula and touched her thigh. "Let's do this the right way."

"What does that mean?"

Buddy's car coasted to a stop behind them. "Just watch," Jack said.

42

★

Buddy weaved all over the road and almost rear-ended them twice, but he managed to stay with Jack and Paula. It was just after 5:00 A.M. when Jack pulled the Olds in front of Hal's house and killed the engine. Behind him the headlights of Buddy's car shut off. Jack kept his foot on his brake and watched for a few seconds in the rearview mirror. Buddy, coated in the orange-pink from the taillights, gazed straight ahead like a wax statue. "Guy's scared out of his mind," Jack said.

Paula laughed. "Good."

"Wait here for a minute." Jack opened the door and stepped from the car. The gun pulled on the breast pocket of his jacket. He walked halfway to Buddy's car and said to him, "Stay there until I come back out."

The front door to Hal's house was unlocked. Jack found Hal in his recliner, smoking and drinking coffee. "The girlie's asleep in the back," Hal said. "Pay me."

Jack turned on a lamp. "I'm bringing two people

in here. You'll recognize them both. We're going to do some business together. You might want to step out of the room for a while, Hal."

"Hey, joker, it's my house, remember? I sit where I want. Hal Roper wants to park his tush right here and watch the whole show, he does it."

"Suit yourself, Hal. I'm just trying to spare you some complications."

"I'm gonna watch this show you're putting on, whatever it is, Jack. Front-row seat. Wouldn't miss it." Hal lifted his coffee cup as if making a toast.

"Sharronda's in your room?"

"That's what I said."

"I'll be right back."

"Wonderful. And bring my grand with you."

Jack stepped out the front door. To the east he could see the dark starting to bleed away. He waved at Paula and Buddy to come in. Paula did, but Buddy stayed in his car.

Jack walked over fast and knocked on Buddy's window. Buddy turned his key and powered the glass down a couple of inches. "What's the problem?" Jack said.

Buddy gripped the black briefcase in his lap. "Where's the girl?"

"Inside the house."

"How do I know that?"

"You could come look."

"You'd like that, wouldn't you?"

"Are you afraid of something, Buddy?"

"You want me in that house. I don't know what's in there."

"The girl is."

"I have no idea about that."

"Miss Fontaine is, too. She just walked in, you notice?"

Buddy jabbed a finger toward him. "And I notice she hasn't come back out."

Jack leaned close to the opening. "You think I've set a trap. That I'm going to lure you into the house and steal your money."

"What I know is, you walk into a dark cave, you keep your eyes peeled for the bear."

Jack reached into his coat pocket and pulled the gun out. He poked the barrel through the window opening and aimed it toward Buddy's groin. "If I wanted to steal your money like that, don't you think I could do it right here and now? I could put this gun in your mouth and say, 'Give me the cash, chump.' Couldn't I do that? I don't need the inside of a house."

Buddy tried to say something.

"But that would be armed robbery," Jack said. "Wouldn't it. And armed robbery's for punks. You and me, Buddy, we're doing a deal here. I agree to get rid of the girl. You agree to pay me a hundred thousand dollars. Is this not true?"

Jack heard him swallow. "Yes," Buddy whispered.

"All right, then. Come on in the house."

Jack put the gun back in his coat. He walked inside first with Buddy behind him. Hal from his recliner said, "Oh, this is rich. This is beautiful."

Paula was on the couch, and Jack took the seat next to her. Buddy stood just inside the door, gripping the handle of his briefcase and looking around the room warily. His hair hadn't been combed and his face beaded sweat. His Western suit badly needed a press. But his boots, Jack noticed, were shining.

"Let's do some business," Jack said.

"Hey, Jack." Hal blew a cloud of smoke. "What'd you do, get everybody in the parlor here so some schmuck can confess to a crime?"

Jack looked at Buddy. "First let's see the hundred thousand up close."

"A hundred grand?" Hal sat up straight. "A *hundred*?"

Buddy shook his head. "I ain't seen the girl yet."

"Let me ask you something." Hal pointed the lighted end of his Camel at Paula. "This your setup?"

"No girl until I see what's in the case," Jack said. "I want you to show me all of it."

"'Cause if it was yours," Hal said, "you're the most devious broad Hal Roper's seen in a long time . . . "

"It's one hundred thousand," Buddy said. "I counted it already."

". . . and I mean that as a compliment."

"Let's see it." Jack cleared a space on the coffee table by sweeping aside a pile of golf magazines.

"I mean, I'd like to know how you pull something like this off." Hal was looking at Paula, who was watching the briefcase. "How do you do that?" Hal said. "How do you take a little nickel-and-dime motel room ambush and parlay it into a suitcase full a bills? Just curious."

Buddy screwed his stare to Paula. "What's he talking about?"

"What difference does it make, Buddy?" She lifted her gaze from the briefcase to his face. "Right now, right here, it doesn't make any difference at all."

"Put it right here and count it." Jack slapped his hand against the table top.

"I knew you weren't his wife," Hal said. "From the first day you walked in my office, I knew." Hal turned to Jack. "I didn't tell you that, but I knew. This whole thing smelled."

"What's he saying?" Buddy's voice was rising. "What's he mean?"

"I just had a feeling." Hal buried his Camel in the ashtray. "You hang around long enough, you get a nose for the real. Right, Jack?"

"I'm thirsty," Paula announced. She stood and walked toward the kitchen.

"I knew the whole time," Hal said.

Buddy had the mashed, lumpy look of a ball that had lost its air, but his eyes were on Paula as she came near him. She was passing about two feet away when he reached with his free hand and grabbed her throat.

Paula tried to scream. Hal yelled, "Jesus!" Jack took the gun from his pocket and fired a shot into the ceiling. The noise froze them all as a cloud of gypsum dust floated down from the bullet hole. "Let's look at the money," Jack said.

Hal craned his neck to inspect the hole. "You son of a bitch, you owe me a new ceiling. Maybe a new roof, too, that slug went all the way through."

Paula backed away, holding her throat. "The briefcase," Jack said. "Right here." Buddy hesitated, looking for a moment as if his eyes were about to roll up into his head. "Now," Jack said.

Buddy placed the briefcase flat on the coffee table. He put a thumb on each button and flipped the latches open. He lifted the lid with uncertain hands. Jack stared at the bills inside. They seemed to give off a green glow, like numbers on a watch face.

"Christ almighty," Hal said.

"Each packet is five thousand dollars." Buddy

forced a finger across the bills. "That's twenty packets. Now where is she?"

Jack looked at his face. It was all twisted with anger and betrayal and the way you feel when you've thrown everything away. Jack had seen that face in the mirror. "Now," Buddy said. "Where's the goddamn girl?"

And she came walking out of the hallway. Not two seconds off. You could hire a director, Jack thought, you wouldn't get such timing. Sharronda stood at the edge of the living room, taking in the crowd with disbelief. "Enter the chattel," Hal said.

Sharronda saw the man who had tried to strangle her and the woman who had set her up, and then turned to Jack. The way she looked made him think of someone going under and making one last grab for any rope or hand. He didn't think anyone could ever look more frightened.

But she could, and she showed it when Jack got up, went to her side, grabbed a handful of hair, and put his gun to her head. "It's time to rock 'n' roll," he said.

"Just a goddamn minute—" Hal struggled from the recliner, his jowls shaking. "You never said a damn thing about this. This is—"

"Sit down, Hal." Jack pulled harder on her hair and a cry flew out of her. "Shut up and sit down or I'll shoot her right here in your house." Hal sank back into his chair.

Jack was breathing as if he had just run a mile. "Take five thousand out of the case." Buddy removed one packet and set it on the table. Jack looked at Paula, who was staring at the money. "You've been paid, Hal, so stay inside. Bring the briefcase, Buddy."

Jack shoved the girl out the front door, with Buddy and Paula behind them. He could still see the stars, but barely. He had maybe ten minutes. "Walk," Jack told Sharronda, and pushed her with the gun toward the woods. Strange small sounds came from her throat as the parade of four crossed the dead grass.

"Where're we going?" Buddy said. "What're we doing?" Jack didn't answer.

Just before they reached the trees and brush Jack stopped and turned. "Give me the money now. I don't kill anybody unless I have it in my hands."

"Now?" Buddy said. "Now?" Jack gripped Sharronda's hair tighter. He dragged her with him as he moved close enough to Buddy that he could smell the whiskey and body odor. The gun was against her temple. She was saying, "Please," over and over.

Jack stuck his face a few inches from Buddy's. "You want me to do it right here, right now? Blow her head off and let the blood fly all over you?"

"Oh, God." Buddy leaned over and gagged.

There was enough light now that Jack could see Paula's eyes. "Slip it under my arm," he told Buddy.

"I'll hold it for you," Paula said.

"Under my arm," Jack said. Buddy managed to stop retching long enough to give him the briefcase.

Then Jack played his last hand. Thinking, Even if it doesn't work, I still have the gun and the money. If it had to be, it was a done deal now. "We're going into the trees," he said. "That's where I'll do it. You want to watch me or not?"

Buddy went back to gagging. "Stay here with him," Jack told Paula.

"Why?" she demanded.

"Because I need you to." He said it as if he were talking to someone he loved. "All right?"

She relaxed some. "All right?" Jack said again.

"All right."

"I'll be right back," Jack said to her. He pushed Sharronda ahead and into the woods. When they were well into the brush, out of Buddy's and Paula's sight, Jack took the gun from Sharronda's head and moved his other hand from her hair to her arm. "Keep going," he said. The branches raked their faces and they nearly fell twice as vines pulled at their feet. After thirty or forty hard steps they found the road. "I'll do whatever you want," Sharronda said. "Please."

"This way," Jack said, turning her to the right. They walked down the road, toward the lake. The Buick was where he had left it. Jack opened the driver's door and said, "Get in." Sharronda sat behind the steering wheel, head down, shaking. Waiting to die. Jack leaned close to her ear. "I'm sorry."

"Please don't hurt me," Sharronda said. Her eyes were closed.

"I mean I'm sorry I had to scare you." Jack climbed into the back seat, moving fast. "I'm not going to hurt you. Turn around here and look." He opened the briefcase and dumped the money into the pillowcase he had taken from Hal's bedroom. "Turn around. Look. There's a lot of money in this bag. More than you've ever seen, Sharronda. Enough to get you to California and to make a life there with your kid."

Her eyes went back and forth from the money to Jack's face. He put two of the packets in his jacket pocket. "I'm keeping ten thousand. I'll have to pay for this car, and I might have to make bail."

Jack knotted the top of the pillowcase and set it on the back floorboard. Then he filled the briefcase with old newspapers.

"Now listen to me. Are you listening?" She nodded. "We don't have much time. All the money in the pillowcase is yours. Unless we got shortchanged, there's eighty-five thousand there."

"That much money . . . "

"Now listen to me. I'm going to get out of the car and fire the gun twice. Then I'm going to leave. In five minutes there'll be enough light for you to see where you're going without headlights. Take this road to the highway and keep on going. You understand?"

"Yes."

"There's some instructions I left for you in the glove box. Follow them."

"Okay."

Jack put two fingers to his lips, kissed them, and placed them on her cheek. She was still shaking. "I don't ever want to see you again," he said.

He got out of the car with the briefcase. At the edge of the lake bed he fired two shots toward the water. There was a feeble wind from across the lake and the smell of mud. Jack threw the gun as far as he could and listened for the splash.

He picked his way through the brush and emerged into Hal's yard carrying the briefcase like a banker home from the office. Paula and Buddy stood a few arm's lengths apart, watching him come toward them. Jack walked close to Buddy and then past him. Buddy said, "My God, is it done?"

Jack stopped and turned. "You want to see the body? It's over there in the trees and its face is gone. You want to go check if I did it right?"

Buddy shook his head and stared at the ground. He whispered, "No . . . no." He was crying.

Paula floated over and stood next to Jack. "After dark," he said, "the body goes in the lake. Her and a couple of concrete blocks." Jack thought about adding, "She'll be catfish bait," but didn't want to see Buddy with the heaves again. He said, "My advice to you, Buddy, is get the hell out of here. Go home, go to a bar, go somewhere and forget about it. The deal's done. Mission accomplished."

Buddy wiped his eyes with the back of his hand and said, "Yeah, I guess." He began to drift toward his car with the expression of someone who had awakened in a place different from where he went to sleep.

Jack and Paula walked together to the house. The birds had started. In the east wisps of low clouds were growing pink at the edges. "It's going to be a pretty sunrise," Jack said.

Paula put her arm through his. "It's going to be a beautiful day."

They went in the front door and found Hal in the kitchen. "I heard shots," he said. "I heard two shots, Jack. Don't tell me I didn't. The hell's going on?"

Jack set the briefcase on the kitchen table. "Nothing, Hal. Can I use your phone?" He opened his wallet and took out a business card.

"I heard two shots. That ain't nothing, Jack."

Paula sat in a chair at the table. "Why don't I count the money?" she said. "Let's make sure he didn't cheat us."

Jack dialed the number on the card and listened to one ring, then two. "Good idea," he told her. "Count it all." He watched Paula spring the latches.

Four rings. She opened the lid. Five rings and she stared at the old newspapers as if seeing her own death.

Then she looked at Jack. He winked. Paula clawed through the papers in search of the money.

Hello, a voice on the phone said.

Jack spoke loud enough that Paula would be sure to hear. "I'm looking for Meshack Blanchard of the Dallas Police Department."

This is Meshack, the voice said.

"Meshack, it's Jack Flippo . . . That's right. That's right. Listen, remember the dead man in the motel you asked me about? There's a guy in my apartment right now who knows the whole story."

Jack studied Paula's face. Truth was spreading across it like a stain.